Daughter of Mine

A Novel

Laura Fabiani

D1470950

iUniverse, Inc.
New York Bloomington Shanghai

Daughter of Mine

iUniverse books may be ordered through booksellers or by contacting:

iUniverse
1663 Liberty Drive
Bloomington, IN 47403
www.iuniverse.com
1-800-Authors (1-800-288-4677)

Because of the dynamic nature of the Internet, any Web addresses or links contained in this book may have changed since publication and may no longer be valid.

This is a work of fiction. All of the characters, names, incidents, organizations, and dialogue in this novel are either the products of the author's imagination or are used fictitiously.

ISBN: 978-0-595-47857-6 (pbk)
ISBN: 978-0-595-71752-1 (cloth)

Printed in the United States of America

Daughter of Mine

To Eleni,

Thanks so much
for your friendship and your
support. Happy reading!

Jane M

To my sister Katia,
for inspiring me to write again,

And to my wonderful parents, Bertilla and Domenico

"'Honor your father and your mother';
which is the first command with a promise."

Ephesians 6:2

New World Translation of the Holy Scriptures

ACKNOWLEDGEMENTS

This book was made possible through the loving support of many. Thanks to my husband, Fil, for his unwavering belief in me and his patience as I "hogged" the computer time and again. To my children, Calista and Alessio, for putting up with "a mommy who furiously scribbled into her notebook everywhere"— while cooking supper, playing at the park, or supervising bath time.

A much-needed thank you to my sister Katia, for her insightful expertise in the world of mechanical engineering, and for always encouraging me along the way. Thanks to my sister Teresa, for quietly believing in me.

Thanks to my parents, Bertilla and Domenico. Their love and understanding make it a pleasure to "honor" them. To my mother-in-law, Maria, whose stories of Naples were the initial inspiration for this story.

A special thank you to Ricardo Figoli, for rescuing me with his computer; to Marilena Paolucci, for getting my creative juices flowing through dancing in her Nia classes; and to Kathleen Girard at www.cookiephoto.ca and my photographer, Valerie Simmons, for their enlightening photo sessions and input. Never have I had so much fun in front of a camera!

Thank you to the staff at iUniverse for making the dream of this first-time author come true! To my editor, Melissa W. Starr, for her excellent editorial advice and encouraging comments along the way.

I cannot forget Nereida Fernandes Fiore, Tina De Angelis, Maria Stamegna, and Rita Pomade.

And most of all, I am deeply grateful to my God Jehovah, who, among many blessings, has given me the gift of writing.

PROLOGUE

The villa was a place of refuge, a paradisiacal retreat tucked in among the verdant hills of the ancient little town of Gaeta, facing one of the most beautiful Italian shorelines along the Gulf of Naples. It was known in the Neapolitan dialect as *À Villete Picerelle* (pronounced pee-chu-rielle), meaning "the little villa."

It was a two-story residence of mustard-coloured stone with white shutters framing the windows of the five bedrooms and two bathrooms within. The southern side French doors, of the dining room on the first floor, opened up to a large *terrazza* overlooking the gulf waters and the seacoast town. Stone pots filled with geraniums, impatiens, petunias, begonias, and marguerites, artfully arranged on the azure tiles, invited the eyes to feast on the bountiful colors swaying in the soft breeze. The aroma of basil and rosemary growing in the small vegetable garden scented the fresh air. It was a welcoming garden.

Caterina Ariosto was wiping clean the wrought iron table on the *terrazza*, where she had just finished serving breakfast to the first guest of the year. April was still early for the tourist season, but the villa had a good reputation, and her three guest rooms were booked mainly through word of mouth.

She bought the villa thirty years ago, restoring it with love and hard work. It now boasted ancient charm and comfort. For guests searching for a place of serenity and genuine hospitality with personal service, the villa would become a home away from home. Many returned yearly, among them, Gustav, the artist who relished capturing the different faces of the gulf on ceramic bowls; Lydia, the writer who typed away feverishly under the canopy of grapevines, and Maria and John, who celebrated their wedding anniversary by requesting the same room they spent their honeymoon in that first year they ever set foot in the villa. All were among the hundreds of people who passed through the villa and enhanced Caterina's life in one way or another. She had met some of the most interesting people here, including her husband, William Newton, an English gentleman ten years her senior.

"Ah, there you are, darling. I found this in the hallway closet while doing inventory," said William, coming out into the morning sunlight. "You don't suppose it belongs to one of our former guests?"

Caterina looked at the large, round box in her husband's arms. It had printed roses on it and a gold-colored cord attached to either side of its cover. It resembled a hatbox. A black wired ribbon was wound across it, sealing the box.

Caterina walked toward William and carefully took the box from his arms. She had forgotten to return it to its former place in her bedroom after storing it temporarily in the hallway closet during her spring cleaning last week.

"No, *amore*, this box belonged to my sister. It contains some of her personal possessions," said Caterina in heavily accented English.

"It is precious, then."

"Yes."

Caterina set the box on the table and sat down. It had been many years since she had last opened it. Perhaps it was best that way. The memories were too painful.

"I will continue with my work, darling." He gave Caterina a warm smile and walked quietly back inside.

Caterina continued staring at the box, and suppressed memories came flooding back, invading her peaceful mind.

Will this box ever find its way into another home, other than mine?

The contents of the box were items that only she and her sister had ever seen. No one else in their family knew of their existence, not even William. Now that her sister was gone, she knew that this box could only be passed on to one other person—a person who did not even know it existed.

Caterina herself had never met this person, did not know what she looked like, where she lived, or what she was doing with her life. She only knew her age and that she was a woman.

Wherever you are, I hope you are happy.

Caterina knew she had no right to look for this woman. She had made a promise. She could only wait as she had been doing for the last two decades for this person to come to her.

And that could mean waiting forever.

CHAPTER 1

Tiziana Manoretti's shoes echoed down the marble hallway as she walked back to her office. Although bone tired, she was happy and relieved the big Cordero project was finally completed. For the last seven years, she'd been working as a mechanical designer for one of the fastest expanding companies in Montreal, Alcore Group of Canada. The engineering firm specialized in building systems to handle the process of bauxite and aluminium production with a focus on increasing production capacity and efficiency.

Two years ago, Tiziana began to occupy the position of head manager on several strategic projects, which granted her a closed office and an attractive salary. This last project, dubbed Cord Nero by her coworkers, had been by far the most demanding.

Swinging the half-open door to her office, Tiziana halted when she saw her boss, Mark Svelitzic, speaking on the telephone by her desk. Standing feet apart with a manila envelope tucked under one arm, he smiled and motioned her in.

Tiziana walked around Svelitzic to her L-shaped desk and sat in her swivel chair. She scanned the pink phone message slips. Nothing pressing. Good, she could leave at a decent hour today and enjoy her Friday evening, something that had become a luxury lately.

Svelitzic hung up the telephone and turned to face Tiziana.

"So, it's finally over!" he said. His smile was infectious.

"Yes, at last." Tiziana couldn't help but start laughing, and once she did, she couldn't stop.

The last few months had been a nightmare. The trouble began when Normand Lemieux, the new shipping employee, sent a critical shipment containing the client's impeller for the plant's main blower for production line C to Algeria instead of Argentina. And this, after Tiziana had spent meticulous hours designing, correcting, testing, tuning, e-mailing, faxing, and losing sleep over the impeller's production.

From the start, Tiziana had found Lemieux uncooperative and quarrelsome. When Lemieux blamed Tiziana for the mistake, he added wood to the fire. Refusing to acknowledge responsibility for his actions and placing it outright on her was the last straw.

What ensued afterwards would long be remembered at Alcore.

"Is he really gone?" Tiziana asked. She heard he had been "dismissed."

"Let's just say you don't need to worry about him anymore. Alex Labonté will be handling the shipping for now." Waving the manila envelope, Svelitzic dropped it onto her desk. It had the name "Brockman" scrawled on it.

"Now that you have nothing to do," he chuckled, "we have a meeting on Monday at 2:00 PM regarding the Brockman project in Australia. We need to discuss the kick-off meeting with the client that's scheduled at the end of next week."

Tiziana nodded. She turned to her agenda and scheduled the meeting in red ink.

Svelitzic checked his watch and headed for the door. He turned back to her and said, "Great work on the Cordero project, Tiziana. Despite the, uh, mishaps, you pulled through as usual. Expect a bonus at the end of the year after your performance evaluation." He smiled, nodded, and left.

With a sigh, Tiziana focused her attention once again on her desk. She spent the next hour organizing next week's work, confirming appointments, and tidying her files. A quick glance at her agenda told her she was having lunch with her best friend, Christopher, tomorrow at their usual restaurant. She could hardly wait to tell him about her bonus. After all, he was the one who had listened to her fume when that idiot sent the impeller to Algeria and tried to blame the mistake on her.

"Algeria! Of all places to send the impeller! You must've had a heck of a time getting it back." Christopher had sympathized with her at the time.

"You should've seen the look on my boss's face after he got that frantic call from the client." Tiziana had shaken her head in disgust. "Chris, the Cordero is a five million dollar project! The mere thought of liability because of consequential damages was enough to cause heart palpitations. And to point the finger at me!"

"You weren't, by any chance, wearing those spiky heels of yours?" asked Christopher, grinning.

"What?"

"Because you're very tall with them on, and next to a short guy ..." Christopher scratched his chin and raised his eyebrows. His grin widened.

Tiziana nearly spat the wine she had sipped from her glass. It's true that Lemieux was a short man, and she was nearly five feet, eight inches with her heels.

Christopher added, "It seems that Lemieux has a hard time accepting a smart chick like you overseeing his work and holding a position he probably feels belongs to a man. What's more, if she's literally breathing orders down his neck to boot, well …"

"Well, what?" asked Tiziana, trying not to laugh.

"Well, I'm glad I'm not short!"

They burst into laughter. It had become their inside joke for Tiziana to ditch the heels when she was dealing with potentially insecure men in the workplace.

Tiziana smiled in remembrance. She was just about to get ready to leave the office when the receptionist informed her through the intercom that her father was on the line.

"Hi, Dad!" she said, smiling into the phone.

"*Ciao, bella.* How did your day go?"

"Great! I finished the Cordero project, and there's a nice fat bonus waiting for me."

"Good girl."

At twenty-seven, Tiziana was still her father's girl. She was an only child living at home with her parents, not uncommon in the Italian culture. She was expected to move out only once she married, and Tiziana was in no hurry to marry.

"What's up, Dad? You sound a little tired."

"Are you finished work, or will you need to be there a while longer?"

"I was just on my way out. Why?"

He hesitated and then said, "I need you with me. Your mother has been taken to the hospital."

"I'm on my way."

CHAPTER 2

Tiziana found her mother in the emergency ward of Montreal General, looking pale and ill. She was lying very still on a hospital bed, her eyes closed. The young doctor who was speaking with her father beside the bed paused as she reached them. Her father immediately embraced her and held her in his strong arms.

"Tiziana, this is Dr. Tremblay," said Steve Manoretti. Tiziana smiled at the doctor and shook his hand.

This was the third time they had been in the emergency ward in the last two weeks. Tiziana's mother, Chloe, had caught a virus last month, and her health had spiralled downward. She couldn't seem to recover or shake off the persistent fatigue. Although April was a busy time in the school year and being around children with special needs could be exhausting, her mother had insisted her profession as a special care counsellor was not the culprit. They all knew, however, that something was not right.

"Your mother lost consciousness today at work," Steve said. He took in a deep breath and looked down at his daughter, whose face was etched with concern.

"Oh, my goodness."

"They also have the results from the last tests taken."

Tiziana felt a tightening in her stomach. She looked from her father to Dr. Tremblay, who now spoke to her.

"Your mother has Type 2 diabetes. She's probably had it for a while, since the early symptoms can be relatively mild. It's possible that because of the virus, we didn't recognize them sooner. However, the diagnosis is clearly diabetes."

Dr. Tremblay turned to her father. "There may be complications, so we'll need to keep her here overnight to better evaluate her condition. We also want her to receive the proper medical attention."

"Yes, of course," said Steve, nodding.

"What kind of complications?" Tiziana asked.

"Patients with diabetes carry an increased risk for heart attack, stroke, and complications related to poor circulation, such as foot problems. There may also be damage to the kidneys and to the nerves, called diabetic neuropathy. It's important, therefore, to further evaluate Mrs. Manoretti's condition."

Tiziana's facial expression must have alerted the doctor to her concern, for she noticed a more reassuring tone in his next words. "Having said this, it doesn't mean that she'll have all or any of these complications. We just want to take the proper precaution, that's all."

Nevertheless, the list of complications sounded scary enough that Tiziana almost wished she hadn't asked. "What can we do to help my mother deal with her illness?"

"I'll be referring Mrs. Manoretti to the diabetes clinic, and I highly recommend that you attend the visits as a family. There's much you can do to help your mother adapt. With the proper knowledge and treatments, your mother can resume a relatively normal lifestyle. But, the adjustments can be difficult in the beginning."

The doctor scribbled a few words in the yellow file folder in his hands before clipping it back to the foot of the hospital bed.

"And one more thing," he added as an afterthought, turning to Mr. Manoretti. "Your daughter and any other children you have should be tested." He then looked at Tiziana. "Diabetes tends to run in families. Therefore, there is a higher risk for you."

"Tiziana is my only child."

"Well, all the more reason then." Dr. Tremblay smiled at Tiziana. "Early detection is the best way to prevent further complications if an illness is present." He looked down at his patient, who appeared to be sleeping, and continued, "I'll return later to check up on her. We won't release her until we're certain everything is under control. We don't want a repetition of today's episode."

"Thank you, doctor," Steve said.

Dr. Tremblay nodded reassuringly before moving on to continue his rounds. Tiziana and her father stood still, absorbing the news. When she turned toward her mother, Tiziana was surprised to see her awake and looking intently at her.

"Mom." Tiziana reached to take her mother's hand and bent down to place a soft kiss on her cheek. "Oh, Mom."

"Hi, beautiful girl." Chloe's voice was low but steady. She smiled at her daughter, looked at her husband, then closed her eyes and sighed heavily.

Steve pulled up a chair for Tiziana, and finding no other one for himself, lowered his tall frame on the edge of the bed. He looked at his wife, and then looked away. Her father seemed suddenly distant and detached. He had a far-off look in his eyes. An uneasy feeling came over Tiziana, but was soon gone when her father turned to her and smiled encouragingly.

"What happened today with mom?" she asked.

"Apparently Derek was acting up. Your mother cleared up the squabble he had with another kid and told me she was feeling light-headed after that. A short time later, she collapsed."

It seemed Derek was always acting up. According to her mother, he was one of the toughest kids she had worked with in her twenty years as a special care counsellor. In addition, he was eleven years old and five feet tall, which was almost as tall as Chloe herself.

"Where was she when she lost consciousness?"

"At her desk. They found her on the floor in her office just after school was out."

"Thank goodness she wasn't driving home!"

Steve nodded solemnly.

Tiziana turned to look at her mother, who hadn't moved. She wasn't used to seeing her mother, a dynamic, energetic woman, drained and listless.

Tiziana reached out and took Chloe's hand again. There was nothing like the image of her mother lying in a hospital bed to remind her never to take for granted the wonderful woman who had raised her.

CHAPTER 3

Tiziana opened the front door to her home and closed it wearily behind her. She kicked off her shoes, dropped her keys on the hallway table, and moved toward the kitchen. Her father had insisted she come home while he stayed at the hospital a little longer. It was now ten o'clock, and she realized she was hungry. She had lost track of time at the hospital, and she hadn't eaten anything for supper.

Opening the fridge, Tiziana stood there staring at the assortment of food. Not much leftovers. Her mother, who loved cooking, especially after taking courses at Tavola Mia Culinary School, had done little of it lately.

My mother has diabetes.

The thought made her sad and angry at the same time.

She closed the fridge and was about to insert two slices of bread into the toaster when the phone rang. Tiziana picked up the cordless phone next to the microwave oven.

"Hello?"

"Hey, Tizzy! I'm glad to finally get a hold of you. Is everything all right? Your cell phone wasn't on." It was Christopher.

"Oh, right. I shut it off at the hospital." Tiziana moved to the living room and curled herself on the couch in the dark. She went on to tell Christopher about her mother.

"Well, at least it's a relief to finally know what's wrong. With the right treatment she'll be back on her feet in no time."

"You're right. It's just that my mom is never sick. It's scary to see her like this." The full import of her mother's situation weighed on her.

"I know."

And he did know. Christopher Pierson's mother had succumbed to cancer when he was twenty.

"Sounds like you got company there." Tiziana heard female laughter in the background. It didn't sound like Katherine.

"Katherine's friend, Tracy, is here. And Peter's on his way over. Hey, why don't you join us? Sounds like you could use some company."

"It's just that I haven't had supper yet ..." Tiziana hesitated. She had planned to hit the sack early.

"No problem, lots of food here. Oh, and Katherine made her famous Tiramisu."

Katherine was Christopher's youngest sister. Tiziana could hear her shouting in the background that she was going to save an extra big piece just for her before the guys cleaned up the bowl. Christopher chuckled and then added, "I'll play my guitar, and we can holler a few tunes. C'mon, I want to see you tonight," he said, playfully.

Really?

"So, are you coming?"

Through the phone Tiziana heard the doorbell ring at Christopher's house. Peter's voice greeted them. More voices blended in cheerful tones, among them Tracy's as she called Christopher back to the group. In contrast, her house was silent and lonely.

"Tizzy?"

"I'll be there in ten minutes."

Tiziana had known Christopher since the day he moved on her street five years ago. He'd been a newlywed and had proudly bought his wife, Victoria, a house in their suburban neighborhood. It wasn't long before he was on friendly terms with her family, exchanging notes on household projects and neighborhood events.

Tiziana recalled several times coming home from work and finding him in the den, deep in discussion with her parents over a glass of wine and cheese. Victoria was never with him on these occasions. She traveled with her friends and did not mingle much with the neighbors like Chris did. She had been raised in the affluent Westmount district and had married Chris without the consent of her parents.

Tiziana would never forget the summer evening when she and her father had found Chris sitting alone on the hardwood floor of his entrance hall looking stunned—a crumpled letter in his hands. He had come home to find that his wife had packed her things and left. Other than his sisters, Tiziana's family had been his main support, since his mother's relatives lived in the Ontario region. Their friendship had deepened.

The divorce had been nasty. Not only had Chris to contend with Victoria's family but their top-notch lawyer as well. In the end, after selling the house and leaving most of the furniture to Victoria, he'd come out feeling bruised and beaten. He then moved back with Katherine, who lived alone in a tiny apartment in the same district. That had been almost three years ago.

Lately, however, Tiziana had noticed a change in Christopher. Although he was naturally easygoing and good humored, she saw a vibrant energy about him that was lacking before. He was physically active and looked fit and healthy. He had cut his shaggy blond hair and took better care of his dress and grooming.

He was no longer heartbroken.

So would he finally notice her?

Christopher opened his apartment door to find Tiziana digging through her purse. Her thick, dark hair fell across her face as she searched.

"I forgot my cell phone. What if my dad needs to reach me?" she asked, frowning up at him.

Christopher put an arm around her shoulder and squeezed it affectionately. "She's going to be fine, Tiz. Your mother is one tough little cookie." He ushered her in and took her leather jacket. The faint scent of her perfume lingered in his nostrils.

Tiziana nodded quietly.

Christopher noted the haggard complexion under her olive skin. "You look tired. How's work these days?"

Tiziana's face lit up. "The Cordero project is finally done. And, guess what? I'm getting a bonus!"

"That's great! You worked hard and you deserve it."

"Tell me about it," Tiziana said, and they chuckled together.

They walked into the living room, where Peter and Tracy were talking. Peter's face broke into a wide smile when his eyes fell on Tiziana.

"Hey, Tiziana." He came forward and kissed her on both cheeks. "Wow, you look good," he said as his eyes scanned her from head to foot.

Christopher stole a glance toward Tiziana, who was smiling back at Peter. She turned and lifted an eyebrow in his direction. He shrugged.

"Thanks, Peter," she said. She then moved to greet Tracy.

Katherine entered from the kitchen carrying a steaming plate piled with lasagna, endive salad, and crusty bread. "Hey, girl!" She gave Tiziana the customary Italian greeting of two hearty kisses on the cheeks and handed her the plate. Katherine was an assistant chef in the reputable Splendido Restaurant known for its fine Italian cuisine, and her cooking was one of the things Christopher loved about living with his sister.

"You look like you need some food," Katherine said as she took the seat next to Tiziana on the couch.

"Smells heavenly." She attacked the lasagna.

"I hear your mother's in the hospital," said Tracy, sitting next to Christopher.

"Yes. They diagnosed her with diabetes."

"My grandfather has diabetes," Peter said.

"The doctor said there may be complications, so they're keeping her overnight."

"They probably just want to make sure they've got everything covered. It must be a relief to know why she's been so sick lately," Katherine offered.

Christopher looked at his sister's face. He knew what she was thinking. With their father out of the picture since they were young children, their mother's death ten years ago had been a painful blow. His other sister, Susan, had been eighteen at the time and Katherine fifteen. He had dropped out of college and found full-time employment in construction work, allowing Susan to continue her studies and Katherine to finish high school. Their mother would have been proud to know that Susan was now a married nurse with a little three-year-old girl named Meredith, after her grandma.

Tiziana finished her dinner as the friends talked about diabetes. Christopher noticed that it was Peter, who, when recounting anecdotes of how his grandfather dealt with his diabetes, had Tiziana squealing with laughter. Christopher was pleased to see Tiziana relaxed and less worried about her mother. He envied the fact that Peter, whose parents came from the same Abruzzo province as Tiziana's dad, could so easily humor her, especially when he threw in those Italian phrases no one else understood.

"Hey guys, what do you say we play a game of Brisc?" asked Peter, pulling a deck of Italian cards from his shirt pocket. "Tizià, let's team up, me and you."

"No way. Girls against the guys," Katherine countered.

"What's Brisc?" asked Tracy.

"Briscola. It's a card game. You can watch me play to learn," Christopher said.

Peter deftly shuffled the cards, and they began playing. As the game progressed, Christopher found himself distracted. Tracy kept whispering questions in his ear, and Peter and Tiziana were interacting in such a way that suddenly made him uncomfortable.

"Hey, Chris, I think this game isn't going so well, eh? You gotta start playing like an Italian," Peter said, reprimanding him.

"You mean cheat," Katherine said.

"Nah, we don't cheat," said Peter, grinning.

"Pete, you're a true Italian, from your vocabulary down to your hairy chest," said Katherine, picking up point cards from the table.

"I happen to know that real women *like* hairy chests," countered Peter. Katherine and Tiziana snorted.

"C'mon, you just don't want to admit it." Peter was looking at Tiziana.

Christopher's discomfort grew after the first round was over. Katherine left to go into the kitchen to refill the cheese and grape platter. Tracy followed. Meanwhile, Tiziana excused herself and went to the washroom. Once alone, Peter turned to Christopher.

"Chris, I need to ask you somethin'. I know you and Tiziana are good friends, but you're not dating her, right?"

Christopher stared at Peter. "No, we're not dating."

"So, you don't mind if I ask her out, or anything?"

"As in a date? Uh … well, if you want to, I guess."

"Great!" Peter said with a satisfied smile. "Cause I like her."

Yeah, I noticed.

Christopher thought of Tiziana. She was beautiful and intelligent. Her world consisted of engineers, high-profile business clients, and CEOs. He was an electrician who did renovation projects. For him, Tiziana had turned out to be a good friend, maybe even his best friend, and he was happy with that. So, if she accepted a date with his buddy, then he should be happy for her. Peter was a good man. Christopher had met him on a construction site, and their friendship had led to opening up their own business last year.

When the women returned, they played a second round of cards. Christopher watched Tiziana closely for the remainder of the evening to see how she responded to Peter's comments. Even after he took out his guitar and started strumming a few songs, his discomfort did not dissipate. Instead, different feelings surfaced, leading him to wonder about the exact nature of his relationship with Tiziana.

CHAPTER 4

"Steve, we need to tell her!" Chloe hissed to her husband as they walked down the hallway from the doctor's office.

"This is not the time or the place," he responded firmly.

"Will there ever be a time or a place?" Chloe stopped walking and turned to face him. "She's twenty-seven years old, for crying out loud! She needs to know the truth, and from us. We owe it to her. It's the right thing to do. You promised—"

"Chloe, that's enough." There was a hard edge to Steve's voice.

Chloe froze and stared at him. Steve tipped a nod toward Tiziana, who could overhear their exchange. He ran his hand through his hair and began walking briskly toward the elevators. He pressed the elevator button several times and paced with agitation. Then he stood with hands on his hips in front of the elevators, shoulders rigid.

"Tell me what, Mom?" Tiziana asked, coming over to stand next to her. Chloe saw her daughter looking in the direction of her father, frowning and observing his every move.

Just then the elevator doors slid open, and Chloe began walking toward the gaping elevator, determination in her step. Tiziana followed. They entered the elevator in silence. Chloe now felt Tiziana's questioning gaze upon her, but she ignored it.

As they exited the building, Chloe said with finality to Steve, who was a few paces ahead of her, "If you do not tell her, I will. Right here, right now."

Steve turned to look at her. Chloe noticed that something in her face made him pause. It was all she needed to see.

"Please." She almost begged.

Steve ran his hand over his face, looked at Tiziana, and then back at Chloe. Chloe knew he was struggling with a decision, a decision long overdue.

"Alright. Let's go home. Tiziana, your mother and I have something to tell you."

"Tiziana," her mother began as she took her daughter's cold hands in hers. They were sitting in the living room. Rays of setting sun filtered through the large bay window, bathing the room in warm light. Tiziana did not feel the warmth. She felt only the palpable tension between her parents, which had increased during the drive home. She was assaulted by frightening thoughts of what they could possibly have to tell her. Were they splitting up? Tiziana noticed they fought more often, but had associated this with the stress of dealing with the changes since her mother's illness.

She saw her mother looking at her father for reassurance, but he was sitting stiffly, arms folded across his chest, waiting to see how she would proceed. A muscle twitched in his jaw.

"Your father and I have something important to tell you and … and we should have told you a long time ago." Chloe took a deep breath.

Tiziana waited.

"Let me start from the beginning," her mother resumed. "When we got married, your father and I wanted a whole slew of children, a whole bunch of beautiful kids to fill our house." She smiled sadly and looked down at their joined hands. "But although we tried everything for almost five long years, I couldn't get pregnant." She stopped and looked up at Tiziana. "We wanted a child so badly, and I started to think of adoption as an alternative. Your father was against the idea at first, but then something happened that changed his mind and changed our lives. He went to his brother Maurizio's wedding in Italy and, while there, found out about a beautiful baby girl who, when born, was being put up for adoption. So we—"

"No." Tiziana removed her hands from within her mother's and stood up. She walked to one side of the room and slowly spun around, shaking her head in negation. Confusion marked her face.

"Are you trying to tell me that I'm adopted, that I'm that baby girl?" she asked in disbelief. She quickly continued, "No, that can't be," shaking her head again as if she misunderstood what she'd just been told. "I mean, people have always told me how I have Dad's mannerisms and that I walk just like him. *Nonna* herself tells me that I'm stubborn just like Dad."

She then turned to her mother, "Or … or how similar we are in personality, Mom, and … and that I laugh just like you, that I have your knack for figuring people out …" She trailed off breathlessly as she looked at the play of emotions on her parents' faces.

Steve stood up and with a trembling voice said, "You are *my* daughter, no matter what's written on any document. Nothing, and I mean absolutely nothing, will ever change that."

"Oh, Tizzy, I know this isn't easy for you to hear, and we're very sorry for taking so long to tell you, but your father is right, this doesn't change—" her mother began as she started to move toward her.

"No!" Tiziana backed away, raising her outstretched right hand. "You can't possibly be telling me that I'm adopted. This ... this story you're telling me, it doesn't make sense—" She stopped abruptly and snapped her head toward her father. He had said the word *document*, and now it struck a new thought in Tiziana.

"Dad, when I registered at school, you always brought my birth certificate. I never saw any adoption papers."

"No, you didn't. We weren't ready to tell you, so I took care of all the paperwork and instructed the school staff not to disclose this information since you were still unaware of the fact," he said in a low voice.

A scene from her college registration day came to mind. She had needed her birth certificate, and when she had asked her parents for it, her father had said he would send it through the mail later, since it was momentarily misplaced. It dawned on her that she was twenty-seven years old and had never seen her birth certificate. Even when it came time to renew her passport, her parents had taken care of most of the paperwork.

Nor had she ever had any reason to doubt her parents, but denial fired through her all the same. "I want to see the documents."

Neither of her parents moved.

"You say I'm adopted," she said, "so let me see the documents."

Steve left the room and returned with the papers. Chloe was now standing by Tiziana. Steve silently handed the documents to his daughter, who stared at them as if they contained a death sentence.

Am I really an adopted child?

She feared the truth.

She took the cream-colored documents. Time had yellowed the edges of the papers, and the creases of the folds were deep. Turning her back on her parents, Tiziana moved toward the waning light by the window. Unfolding the papers, the first thing her eyes locked on was the insignia at the top of the first page.

Orfanotrofio Santa Maria Della Fede.

A quick scan of the documents told her they were in Italian. Since she was a baby, her father had spoken Italian and English, giving her enough knowledge of the language to speak and read it.

Tiziana read the documents carefully, learning that she was born at the orphanage *Santa Maria Della Fede* on March 12, 1980, in Gaeta, Naples. There were other details about her vital statistics. Coming to the bottom of the page, she was disappointed with the omission of the one thing she was looking for, the names of her birth parents. But, of course, that was private information.

Tiziana folded the papers and turned to her parents. "Why didn't you tell me sooner? Were you ashamed of having to adopt me?" she asked in a flat voice. She was no longer sure of how she felt. It all seemed so surreal.

Chloe took Tiziana by the shoulders and, firmly but gently, turned her so she was facing her. Although her mother was smaller than Tiziana both in height and build, she could easily take up a stance that spoke clearly of her authority.

"Ashamed? Oh, Tizzy, you're the best thing that's happened to us! Your father and I finally understood happiness when you came into our lives. We love you very much, and we've raised you to be a happy and successful woman. Do you realize how fulfilled we feel as parents?" Her mother paused and sighed deeply. "The only thing we regret is that we didn't tell you sooner, perhaps when you were much younger and life was simpler to understand."

Steve approached, putting his warm hand on Tiziana's nape with his thumb softly stroking her cheek. It was a gesture he did when she was feeling sad or hurt.

"*Bella di papà,* I held you in my arms a few days after you were born and, at that moment, I became your father. It was the happiest day of my life. I will always be your father. I love you, *cara.* Nothing has changed."

Tiziana nodded and swallowed hard. "I just need some time to digest all this."

Holding the documents tightly, she walked out of the room, but just before she reached the stairs, she turned around once more.

"Why did you decide to tell me now?" she asked.

"Because it would've been wrong to let you go through those medical tests when we knew full well you couldn't have inherited diabetes from me," Chloe said.

"A few medical tests wouldn't have been a big deal."

"No, but it reminded us that you had the right to know. We didn't want you to find out accidentally. Now was as good a time as any." Chloe looked briefly at Steve and then returned her gaze to Tiziana. "And I've grown tired of hiding the fact. Now you know the truth, and I feel relieved."

"You don't feel the same, Daddy?" said Tiziana, picking up on her mother's awareness of her father's silence.

"I don't want anything to change."

Tiziana looked at her father, whose eyes were beseeching her to understand. *But things have already changed, Daddy.*

Tiziana turned and ascended the stairs to her room.

Watching her daughter leave, Chloe remarked, "We should've told her sooner."

"We shouldn't have told her at all," Steve replied.

CHAPTER 5

Tiziana lay on her bed for a full half hour without moving, her hands still clutching the documents and her mind swirling. She hadn't seen this one coming. What twenty-seven-year-old woke up one day and was told, "Oh, by the way, you're adopted."

She remembered a Chinese classmate in high school who had been adopted and who had known of it since she was five. When Tiziana had asked her how she felt about it, the girl looked at her curiously. She was happy, of course. Her parents were great. They had taught her about the Chinese culture, and she even took Mandarin lessons to learn the language. Every year, on the exact day that she had first come to Canada, her family celebrated with the other six families who had adopted their Chinese babies at the same time. It was a part of her family tradition. And this made her feel special.

But Tiziana did not feel special or happy.

Bolting from her bed, Tiziana grabbed her leather jacket, put the documents in her matching purse, and thundered down the stairs.

"Mom! Dad! I'm going out."

Both her parents quickly appeared from the kitchen.

"Where are you going?" they asked simultaneously.

If she weren't feeling so morose, Tiziana would have giggled. Her mother was anxiously fiddling with her necklace, and her father's forehead was heavily furrowed—classic signs of nervousness. They looked at her expectantly.

"I'm going for a walk," she said as she headed for the door. She knew her parents were looking for some reassurance, and although it made her feel selfish, she didn't want to be with them right now. She had heard them arguing downstairs, and their discord was making her more upset.

She slammed the heavy front door and ran down the steps. Her pace only slowed once she turned the corner of her street. Streaks of orange bathed the lower sky as the sun continued its descent. The air was cool and refreshing as it filled Tiziana's lungs with every deep breath she took. Rush hour traffic had passed, so there weren't as many cars on the boulevard.

Tiziana headed south toward the St. Louis River of the Lachine district, in which she lived. Situated on the southwestern part of the island of Montreal, it boasted beautiful property along the St. Joseph Boulevard, where families rode on the bicycle trail, picnicked in waterfront parks, or just watched those who ventured sailing on the lake.

Glittering ripples of water lapped at the rocky shores, which were scattered with the growth of wild vegetation. Tiziana walked along the snaking path parallel to the lake, lost in thought. She loved coming here, especially on her bike, because the scenery was soothing and peaceful. But the longer she walked, the more she realized she needed to talk. Before she became aware of it, her feet were taking her in the direction of Christopher's home. She increased her pace, and twenty minutes later she was climbing up the steps to his apartment building. She buzzed his intercom.

There was no answer.

She tried several more times. She knew Katherine was working at the restaurant, but Tiziana hoped Christopher was home by now. Finally, feeling dejected, she turned and was about to leave when she spotted Christopher's Ford pickup truck pulling up across the street in front of his building.

She watched him climb out, carrying his lunch box in one hand and some papers in the other. He looked weary in his dusty blue jeans and construction boots. Working outdoors the past week had already sun-streaked his dishevelled hair and given a golden hue to his skin. He walked across the street and only noticed her as he reached the sidewalk.

"Hey, Tizzy!" His face broke into a wide smile.

At the sight of him, Tiziana suddenly wanted to run to him and blurt out all that had transpired with her parents. But she just stood there looking at him, frowning and biting her lower lip.

Christopher's smile faded. "What's wrong, Tizzy?"

"Oh, Chris ..."

Tiziana plopped down on the top step. She ran both her hands through her hair and held her head. Chris hurried to sit down next to her.

"Something happen at work?" he asked gently.

She shook her head.

"Your mom? Did she have another episode? Her medication—"

"I'm adopted!" Tiziana blurted out. She raised her head and looked straight at him. She could feel the unshed tears prickling her eyes.

Christopher's right eyebrow shot up. "What?"

"My parents just told me that I'm adopted, Chris. Can you believe it? I can't. I mean, after all these years, they decide I need to know this important but secret fact about myself," she wailed with angry sarcasm. "And so, voila! Out of the blue, I'm told that I'm adopted from a woman who ... who ..." she swallowed hard, "who gave me up after I was born."

"They told you this?"

"My mother said she couldn't get pregnant. They tried for five years and then decided to adopt. My father was in Italy at the time, attending my Uncle Maurizio's wedding, when apparently he found out about a baby who was being put up for adoption. I don't know more than that because at that point I started freaking out a little."

"Yeah, no kidding."

Tiziana dug into her purse and handed the documents to Christopher.

"I was born in Gaeta, Naples, in an orphanage. Not even in a hospital."

She watched as Christopher scanned the documents, knowing he couldn't make much of them since he couldn't read Italian.

"Your birthday's the same," he said.

"Yup, I'm still twenty-seven years old."

"And you're still Italian," he said with a hint of a smile on his lips.

Tiziana managed a lopsided smile. "You know what I was thinking, Chris? I've never actually seen my own birth certificate. My parents have somehow managed throughout the years to keep it hidden from me. I'm still trying to figure out how that was possible."

"That is pretty amazing ... but, Tiziana, not having seen your birth certificate up to this point is not a big deal."

"When my parents avoided showing it to me, I trusted them. I didn't think more of it than that. All along, they were keeping secret the adoption."

"There's nothing wrong with trusting your parents, Tiziana. It's a normal thing to do. You couldn't possibly have known, and besides, maybe there was a legitimate reason for their not telling you sooner."

"No, there wasn't. I asked them. They apologized for that. I got the feeling my mom would have told me sooner, but my dad didn't want to tell me. He said he didn't want things to change. How selfish is that! He thought of himself before me. It was my right to know, even my mom said so!" Tiziana pushed herself off the step and began to pace on the sidewalk in front of Christopher.

"You're right. They should've told you sooner, but that seems to be their only downfall in all this. They sure did a great job of raising you. They really love you, Tiziana."

"If they love me, they should've told me. But they didn't, and that makes me wonder. Are they embarrassed to have adopted me? You know, it's not really popular in the Italian culture to adopt the way it is in the English. Do they consider me a second-class citizen, so to speak, because I'm not from their blood? Did they get me from a … a family who was … oh, I don't know," she gestured in frustration, "abusive or poor and ignorant, or—"

Christopher stood and went to Tiziana.

"Hey, your imagination is going a little wild, now," he chided kindly.

Tiziana turned her head away. Christopher hugged her gently and spoke softly into her hair. "You'll be fine. Look, you just need time to absorb all this and to get used to this new information about yourself. With time, you'll even be able to forgive your mom and dad for not trusting you, the way I had to learn to forgive my dad for leaving us."

Tiziana pulled back to look at Christopher. Darkness had descended on them, and with the streetlight behind him, she couldn't make out his features too well. She was trying to see the shadowed expression on his face when he suddenly let go of her.

"Oh, man. I'm sorry. I'm all dirty, and I must smell worse than an old sock." He looked embarrassed. "I just got off work, and I need a shower badly," he said, backing off.

"It's alright, really." Tiziana had only noticed the warmth and strength of his arms.

"Tell you what. I haven't had supper yet, so how about I go up and shower and then you and I head out to grab something to eat?" He was already grabbing his lunch box and papers.

"Sounds good. I haven't eaten, either," replied Tiziana, noticing his discomfort.

"I'll be down in ten, promise," he said as he unlocked and opened the front door of his apartment building. Before entering he stopped. "Do you want to come in?"

Tiziana shook her head. "I'll wait out here. I need some fresh air."

Christopher nodded and disappeared inside.

Tiziana sat once again on the cement steps as she waited for Christopher.

I've blown it, ranting about my father being selfish to a friend whose father abandoned him as a child.

Soon, the front door of the building swung open, and Christopher appeared in clean jeans and a white shirt. His wet hair was slicked back, and he smelled of Irish Spring soap.

"C'mon, Italian girl. Let's go get us some food and make you smile again." He bounded down the steps and pulled her to her feet.

"How is it that food is always your solution to everything?" Tiziana asked. She was already smiling. Christopher always had a way of making her feel good, despite the crazy things life threw at her.

"Who knows? I may have some Italian blood in me, too," he shot back.

She gave him a sidelong glance, taking in his classic Anglo-Saxon features.

"I think you're fine just the way you are," she said. "Although, there is this eyebrow thing you do ..."

"Don't start with the eyebrow thing," he retorted as the truck picked up speed on autoroute 20 East heading downtown.

CHAPTER 6

Tiziana sat in her office staring absently at the computer monitor in front of her. She was having difficulty concentrating on the tasks at hand, accomplishing little on this rainy Tuesday morning. The Brockman project was underway, and she had specifically requested not to manage it, preferring to design instead, something she loved doing. Designing also allowed her to spend more time assisting her mother, whose health was recovering at a slow but steady rate.

Their team was designing a silo feed and reclaim system—three of them, actually. The silo would be used for storing fluidized aluminium. Tiziana was working on the specific system that would efficiently feed and extract the material from the silo to the plant.

For the past two weeks, though, her mind was spinning with questions regarding her past, her birth parents, and the unknown history of how she came to be adopted. Reaching for her purse in her desk drawer, Tiziana removed the documents that she now constantly carried with her and looked at them again. She had scrutinized every word and memorized all the details regarding her adoption.

When her father asked for the documents, she refused to return them. He had insisted, but she claimed they were hers, and she had the right to keep them. Once, he had even offered to keep them for her in a safe place since they were very important documents, arguing that she would have access whenever she wanted. She shrugged off his offer and, instead, asked him if he had ever met her birth parents. He had responded that her birth mother had only wanted to know that her baby would be brought up by a good family and specifically requested not to be contacted after the adoption, which was in accordance with adoption laws.

"But, Dad, how did you find out that I was being put up for adoption in the first place?" Tiziana had asked.

"Through my brother Maurizio. It was kept quiet because of the woman's circumstances at the time. Her family didn't want her to keep the baby, and they wanted no one to know she was pregnant. I thank God every day that

I came to know of it and that I was able to convince them we were the right couple to adopt you."

"Why didn't her family want her to keep her baby or for others to know she was pregnant? Was she a teenager?"

"All that wasn't important to me." Steve looked away. When he did look at her, his eyes caressed her face. "*You* were the most important thing to me, *bella di papà.*"

"Did *Zio* Maurizio know who she was? Did he know her name? Had he met her?"

"I don't know, Tiziana."

"What about the father? Did he know about his baby?"

"*Basta, adesso.* It's enough," her father said, then walked away.

Her mother hadn't been able to clarify anything regarding her birth parents either, mostly because she did not have the information. Her father had taken care of all the preliminary steps. Instead, Chloe had talked openly of what it had been like to finally fly to Italy for the last time, sign the legal papers, and at last look into the eyes of the most beautiful baby she had ever seen.

"I had a suitcase full of new baby pyjamas and diapers, booties, undershirts, bottles, and all sorts of baby stuff. That moment when I first held you and knew that you were mine, I cried for the sheer joy of knowing I was finally a mother."

As Tiziana listened, she realized that her mother had waited twenty-seven years to tell her all these little details that she had kept hidden until now. At night, Tiziana lay in bed, visualizing all that her parents had told her. But the missing details were haunting her. She wanted to know. She needed to know.

Tiziana stood from her desk and leaned against the tall window of her office. Looking outside, she could see people bustling about their daily activities. June had arrived with the promise of warmer days ahead, and even the steady drizzle couldn't stop folks from savoring the sights of late spring. Summer was around the corner and so was her vacation time. A desire had taken root since the day she was given the unexpected news of her adoption. As she stood there contemplating, it began gnawing at her like hunger pangs after a skipped meal.

Tiziana wanted to go to Naples, to the orphanage in the small town of Gaeta where she was born. She wanted to find her birth parents. She wanted to know who they were and why they had given her up for adoption. Did she have sisters or brothers? And if so, did they know she existed? Were they searching for her too? Imagine finding a long-lost sister! Tiziana briefly fantasized the moment when she would see her for the first time.

Suddenly, Tiziana's mind turned in a different direction. She bit her lower lip as other thoughts invaded her fantasies. What if they didn't want to see her? What if her birth had been a shame to her family? Had her mother been raped?

Does my birth mother hate me?

The intercom buzzed, startling Tiziana out of her reverie. A quick look at her phone indicated Svelitzic was paging her.

Grabbing the receiver, she blurted, "Yes?"

"Tiziana, has Jason spoken to you?"

"Spoken to me?"

"Regarding the changes for the extraction system?"

"Uh … no, I mean, yes, yes he did."

"Well, what are your thoughts? Jason didn't think it might be possible."

"Actually, I haven't looked at it yet. I mean, I did look at it, of course, but I haven't *really* looked at it enough to—"

"Tiziana, come into my office, please."

"Yes, sir."

She replaced the receiver and ran both hands through her hair, holding her head. She was so out of it lately! Her desk was covered with scattered papers, unopened mail and file folders, so unlike the usual organized space to which she was accustomed.

Smoothing down her two-piece Jones New York creamy purple outfit, Tiziana made her way to Svelitzic's office.

"Come in, Tiziana," he said, motioning her to sit on the chair facing him. He watched her as she settled herself and crossed her legs.

Svelitzic leaned forward on his wide mahogany desk. He was a distinguished-looking man in his early sixties whose sharp, intelligent eyes missed few things that took place in the department he overlooked. He had known her since the first day she walked in seven years ago, fresh faced and eager. He'd taken a special interest because she'd been the first female employee on his mechanical engineering team. Over the years, his admiration grew for her tenacity in the face of the challenges that came with working in a predominantly male field. She was his prize employee, and he was fond of her.

"How are things working out with the Brockman project? Is everything well within the team?"

"Yes, everything is fine." Tiziana was unsure of where he was going with this.

"You and Jason working well together?"

"Yes, I like working with him. He's very knowledgeable and helpful."

Svelitzic paused. He tapped his pen on his desk pad for a few seconds and then stopped.

"Tiziana, I've noticed that you're not yourself lately. I'm concerned because in the seven years you've been here, I don't remember seeing you quite like this. As we both know, you've had your difficult moments throughout the years." A hint of a smile touched his lips and then disappeared. "But this seems to be different. You're lagging behind in your work, forgetting appointments, and you're not focused. I know your mother's illness has been hard on you, and if you need more time to assist her, you need only ask and we can rearrange things to accommodate you."

"Thank you, I appreciate your concern and … and I'm truly sorry for not performing to the best of my abilities."

Tiziana looked down at her skirt, where her hands were clasped together. The last thing she had wanted to do was disappoint her boss. She highly respected him, and they had a good relationship. Nevertheless, her dilemma was personal, and although she hadn't meant for it to interfere with her work, as it already had, she didn't want to burden him with yet another "Tiziana crisis."

"Is there something you wish to talk about?" Svelitzic asked quietly.

It was the way he asked that made Tiziana change her mind. He was genuinely concerned.

"It's just that a few weeks ago, I found out about something that's been on my mind ever since. I'm upset with my parents, confused over my dad's attitude, and suddenly my life is not the same anymore. I can't stop thinking about it. I have weird dreams at night, and as you said, it's affecting my work."

Tiziana stopped her rambling when she saw the perplexed look on Svelitzic's face.

"My parents told me I'm adopted," she ended plainly.

Svelitzic stared at her. Finally, he said, "I see … and you had no previous idea—"

"None whatsoever. I'm still getting over the shock."

"I understand."

"Mr. Svelitzic, would it be possible for me to take my vacation in June rather than July? I feel the need to get away to think things over, and … there's something I need to do that's important to me."

Svelitzic looked at her with knowing eyes. Sometimes Tiziana felt he could see right through her. "Let's discuss it with the others at our meeting tomorrow. I don't have a problem with it if you can meet the deadline for the Brockman project. You worked extra hard on the Cordero project, and with everything that's been happening lately, the vacation rest will do you good. If you plan to rest, that is."

Tiziana smiled for the first time since she had come in. "Thank you so much."

Svelitzic smiled back at her. "Alright. Get back to me regarding the proposal changes from Jason."

"Give me an hour and it'll be done.

"Before lunch will do." He nodded in dismissal. Tiziana stood and turned to go.

"Tiziana," he called to her just before she opened the door.

"Yes?"

"Remember that who you are does not necessarily depend on who brought you into this world."

CHAPTER 7

"I've decided to go to Italy," Tiziana announced after dinner two days later. "I want to find my roots, to see where I was born." *And if possible, make contact with my birth parents.*

Steve's coffee cup clattered onto its saucer as he almost dropped it. "What?"

Chloe looked up and smiled.

"I need to do this, *Papà*. I want to know where I come from and why I was put up for adoption," Tiziana replied calmly.

"No. Absolutely not." He shook his head firmly. "You will only come back disappointed. And, as I've already told you, the family doesn't want to be contacted, especially twenty-seven years after the issue has been settled."

"I am not an 'issue.' And how do you know they still feel the same way? People change."

"I doubt it. Let it be, Tiziana."

She was about to speak again when he cut her short. "Why is it so important for you to know, anyway? Haven't we raised you well? Loved you? Cared for you?"

Her father was such a proud man!

"She's right, Steve," Chloe said. "There's nothing wrong with Tizzy taking this trip to see where she's from. She's a grown woman, and she can decide for herself what she wants to do. She doesn't need our permission."

"What about work? Aren't you in the middle of a project?" Steve countered, ignoring his wife.

Chloe picked up her coffee cup and the stray utensils on the table, taking them to the sink.

"I've already spoken to Mr. Svelitzic and to my coworkers on the team. I'll be transferring the rest of my work to Mike, whom I've already put up to speed. I'm leaving next Friday, which gives me enough time to organize everything."

"You've already bought your ticket?" Steve asked, surprised.

"Yes, I'm staying for two weeks at the Villa Irlanda Grand Hotel in Gaeta, Naples, but I was also thinking of visiting *Nonna* in Abruzzo."

Fifteen years after they immigrated to Canada, Steve's parents returned to Italy. They left shortly after Steve and Chloe married. Three years ago, when Steve's father passed away, Tiziana had accompanied her parents to the funeral. She had been to Italy several times during the course of her childhood.

"That's a fantastic idea!" exclaimed Chloe. "Your grandmother will be delighted to see you."

"Why did you choose that hotel?" Steve queried.

"I didn't. The travel agent at Sulano Travel suggested it to me. She said it was one of the best hotels in Gaeta. She had a friend who stayed there last year and gave it great reviews. After she showed me some photos, my mind was made up. The place is absolutely beautiful. Have you heard of it?"

Steve paused. "Yes."

Tiziana observed her father's expression. "You've been there?"

"My brother Maurizio, had his wedding reception there."

"Really? Wow, that's so cool! So tell me, what was the hotel like when you were there?" Tiziana asked, looking from her father to her mother.

"I didn't attend the wedding, Tizzy," said Chloe. She didn't look up from the sink, where she was washing the dishes.

"Why not, Mom?"

"I just couldn't go at the time, that's all." Chloe smiled briefly at her daughter and then resumed scrubbing the pot.

"Are you traveling alone?" Steve said, changing the subject.

"Yes. I asked Katherine, but she couldn't get the time off. It's okay, though. I don't mind going on my own."

"I would rather you go with someone. *Una bella ragazza* like you, alone in Naples, is not a good idea. I don't trust those Italian men, especially in Naples."

Tiziana burst into laughter. Her father could be so overprotective sometimes.

"*Papà*! I'll be fine. I travel for work all the time, remember? And besides, I know how to handle Italian men. I have you to thank for that."

Steve pushed his unfinished coffee to one side and leaned on the table toward his daughter.

"Tiziana, *sei sicura*, are you absolutely sure about this?"

"*Sì, papà*. I really want to do this. And even if I don't ... find them, at least I'll see where I was born."

Steve looked at her for a long time. "*Va bene*," he said at last with a resigned sigh. "If it means that much to you, then go. I can't stop you, now, can I?"

Tiziana kissed her father on the cheek and beamed at her mother, who smiled back at her.

"Okay, then!" she said as she hurried out of the kitchen and bounded up the stairs to her room.

Chloe went to the table and removed the remaining cups, bringing them back to the sink. She glanced at her husband, who sat motionless. He was fifty-seven, and she still found him handsome. His jet-black hair was now peppered with white and had lost only some of its fullness. The few lines on his face enhanced the feature that made it remarkable: his arresting grey eyes that could twinkle with humor or get icy cold with anger.

Lately, Chloe saw more of the ice in those eyes than the twinkle. The tension between them had not ebbed since the time she had insisted they tell Tiziana about her adoption. If anything, it seemed to be increasing. The mention of Maurizio's wedding brought back the unhappy period in their marriage when all their attempts at getting pregnant failed. They had fought often and had been on the brink of separating. Steve had taken several trips to Italy alone visiting his family, while she had stayed behind, waiting and wondering every time if he would return to her. When he did, he would be distant and depressed. She could no longer broach the subject of children or adoption with him. He didn't want to hear it. Just as she was losing hope of bridging the widening gap between them, things changed when he returned from his brother's wedding and told her about the baby from an Italian family who was being put up for adoption. Chloe's heart beat with new hope as she listened to her husband tell her that he wanted to adopt this child and start a family with her.

The months following this announcement had been filled with excitement as they both prepared for this sudden arrival of a baby into their lives. The fragile bond between them had begun to mend as they anticipated becoming parents.

Because the expectant mother had privately consented to give her baby up to the Manoretti couple, the procedure for the adoption was somewhat different than usual, Steve had explained to Chloe. He had taken care of the legal aspect of the adoption: speaking to the authorities and taking several trips to Italy, once with Chloe to the orphanage where the child would be after the birth, and another time with Chloe to meet with an officer of the juvenile court.

Chloe had also done what every expectant mother did. She had occupied her days by preparing the nursery, buying tiny clothes and baby essentials, and reading as much as possible on parenting. The arrival of baby Tiziana had made a new man of Steve and had salvaged their marriage.

Now, however, Chloe felt the same thing happening all over again, and she grappled with the reason she suspected was the cause of Steve's reluctance to unveil their daughter's adoption. This time, though, she would not wait for the miracle of a baby to settle things between them. With more than thirty-three years of marriage under her belt, Chloe felt better equipped to settle things once and for all, whatever the outcome might be.

Or so she hoped.

CHAPTER 8

Propped up on her bed with her laptop, Tiziana searched the Internet for information she needed for her trip. The hotel's Web site gave her its exact location, and she was happy to discover the added benefit of having the bus stop not far from it. There was no way she was renting a car to get around. Italians drove like madmen. She spent the next hour reading up on the history of the hotel and the town of Gaeta.

Her bedroom door was ajar, and she heard a soft knock.

"Come in," she said, still absorbed with the images on her screen. Her hair was tousled, papers were scattered around her on the bed, and her jacket, purse, and a few summer clothes were strewn about. Coldplay was playing on her CD player, and her night lamp glowed in the corner, illuminating the room softly.

"Hey, Tiz. How you doin'?"

Christopher was standing in her doorway. He was dressed in blue jeans and a stylish striped shirt instead of his usual T-shirt. The green and cream colours complemented his skin color and accentuated his lean torso.

"Hi, Chris. You look real nice. Are you going out with my dad?"

Steve Manoretti was a real estate agent and sometimes took Christopher with him when he was evaluating a home for the first time. He appreciated Christopher's eye for detail and architectural layout, which was useful in the appraisal of the property.

"No. I just stopped by before heading out to pick up Peter. We're going to the dealership tonight."

"Please don't tell me he still wants to buy that used Viper," Tiziana mocked.

"I think I've managed to convince him not to," said Christopher chuckling. "By the way, has he called you?"

"If you're trying to set me up with him, forget it. He's sweet and all, but he's sooo not my type, if you know what I mean," she said, rolling her eyes.

Christopher's smile widened. She waved him over. "Come in. I want to show you something."

Christopher went around the bed and sat down on the desk chair he pulled from the mini office Tiziana had set up in the corner of her room.

"I've decided to take a little trip to Italy," she said excitedly. "Check out the hotel where I'll be staying. It's called the Villa Irlanda Grand Hotel."

Christopher looked at the screen and whistled in appreciation. "Looks very snazzy with lots of old European charm."

"Chris, are you wearing cologne?" Tiziana asked before she could stop herself.

Christopher immediately inched the chair back. "Uh ... yeah, Susan got it for me. It's called Acqua di Giò, some fancy Italian cologne. You don't like it?"

"No, no, that's not what I meant at all! On the contrary, it smells amazing on you. It's just that you don't usually wear cologne. You caught me off guard."

She gave him a once-over. "Some girl waiting for you at the dealership, or something?" she teased lightly.

Christopher stared at Tiziana with his chocolate-brown eyes. The intensity of his gaze made Tiziana sit very still. She was drawn into the deep pools of his serious eyes. The warm glow from her lamp illuminated one side of his smooth, clean-shaven jawline, while the other side of his face hid in shadows. She couldn't read the expression on his face, but realized she was beginning to feel warm and flushed. Suddenly, she was aware of her disheveled look, and she consciously ran a hand through her hair.

"I'm glad you like it," he said in a low voice. A moment later, he cleared his throat and continued on a different note. "So, your father was telling me you're leaving next Friday. He didn't seem too thrilled."

"No, he wasn't. I know it's kind of sudden, but I feel I need to do this, whether my father likes it or not. There are a lot of things on my mind lately. The last few months have been hectic, and I need a break, to get away. I'm due for a vacation anyway."

"What's on your mind?"

Right now? You.

Tiziana shrugged noncommittally. "Lots of things." She began to gather her stuff from off the bed. She needed to move away from him. His eyes seemed different tonight, and his presence was almost intoxicating.

"I wish you weren't going alone."

"Like I told my dad, I'll be fine. Actually, I'm looking forward to this time on my own. It'll give me some time to think things through," she said as she hung her jacket in the closet.

Christopher's cell phone rang—the familiar James Bond theme song—which he promptly answered as he continued to watch Tiziana puttering about.

"I just stopped by Tiziana's … uh-huh … okay. I'll tell her. Yup, see you in ten," he finished and flipped the phone closed. He sat there and continued watching Tiziana without saying a word.

"What?" asked Tiziana, now very self-conscious as his warm eyes followed her every move.

"Peter says 'Hi,'" he said with a teasing grin. "I think I could almost hear him drooling." He chuckled as he quickly got up and made his way to the door. This was the Chris Tiziana was used to, not the heavenly smelling man with mesmerizing eyes. She whipped her pillow in his direction as he expertly ducked and dashed out the door.

"See you later, Tiz!" he called out as he bounded down the stairs and out the front door.

Tiziana sat on her bed, then let out a long, slow breath as she flopped backward with outstretched arms. How did her life suddenly get so complicated?

CHAPTER 9

Friday dawned grey and rainy, but Tiziana was buoyant as she packed the last of her toiletries. After a late lunch, her father heaved her suitcases into the car, ready to take her to the Pierre Elliot Trudeau airport. Her mother would meet them there right after school was out at 2:20.

The telephone rang just as Tiziana was about to leave.

"Tizzy, it's Chris. I have to go inspect a job in the east end in Pointe-aux-Trembles. It's a good referral from an important client, and I can't cancel this appointment, but I should be finished in time to make it back to see you off at the airport."

It was now a little past 1:30 and her flight was at five o'clock.

"Okay, I'll see you there."

"Great! I really want to see you before you go."

On the way to the airport, Tiziana thought about the past week. She hadn't seen much of Chris, as they both had been busy with work obligations. However, last night he had called her, and they had spoken at length. She was happy he was coming to see her off.

Tiziana disliked airports, mainly because she traveled often for work and was getting tired of the tediousness of the required procedures, especially after 9/11. The long line-ups for customs, the dreaded random checks, the delayed flights, and the heart-pounding marathons to catch the connecting flights— she had experienced all these before and after a too-brief stay in an exciting city or exotic country.

Today, though, Tiziana didn't mind the airport. This trip was different. She passed the time perusing the bookstore while her father read the newspaper.

At 3:30, when Christopher still hadn't shown up at the airport and it was getting closer to the time when she would pass through the gates, she decided to call him with her father's cell phone. She had forgotten her own cell phone, which was plugged in the corner outlet of her room, recharging its battery. After searching his pockets, her dad apologized. He had left his phone in the car. Her mother, who had joined them, didn't have a cell phone. Tiziana went in search of something she hadn't used in a long time—a phone booth. She finally spotted one and dialed Christopher's cell number only to hear the voice mail come on right away. He must be on another call, she thought. She left a message.

Christopher sat in his truck on highway 40 westbound with his windshield wipers on overdrive as the rain poured down furiously. Stuck in traffic for some time now, he tried to see up ahead and could finally make out the flashing lights of an ambulance and police cars. Darn! Of all afternoons!

He had tried Steve's cell phone and then Tiziana's, but there was no response. He was late, and he desperately wanted to see Tiziana. He had thought of her all night, and after some deliberation had decided to give her something before she left—a letter tucked into a personalized notebook, where she could record her daily thoughts during her trip.

His sister Susan had helped him pick it out. He had just finished a brief conversation with her on his phone when she called to confirm his babysitting Meredith later this evening. Christopher now heard the beep indicating he had a message. After hearing it, his heart sank. Tiziana was going through the gates soon, and he realized he would never make it. He tried Steve's phone again.

Still no response.

He banged his fist against the steering wheel in frustration. His truck had barely moved in the last fifteen minutes. His phone rang, sounding like a beacon, and Christopher lunged for it. He didn't even bother checking who was calling. He only wanted it to be her.

"Hello?"

"Chris, it's Tiziana. I was wondering if you were still coming."

"Tiziana! I'm glad to hear your voice! I'm so sorry about this. I'm stuck in traffic. There's a serious accident up ahead, and we're literally crawling. I really didn't expect this … I don't know if I'll make it."

"It's okay, Chris, I understand. I was worried because it's not like you to be late."

"Aw, Tizzy, I really wanted to see you before you left. Now I have to wait two whole weeks."

"I'll call you when I arrive. We can talk then."

"Tiziana, have a good trip, sweetheart, and … watch out for yourself. Don't forget to call me."

"I won't. I promise."

"I'll miss you," he said softly.

Tiziana did not reply immediately. Christopher could hear her unsteady breathing over the phone.

"I'll miss you, too, Chris."

Forty minutes later, Tiziana was airborne and on her way to Italy. Christopher pulled up just outside the airport's parking lot and watched as her plane flew overhead.

CHAPTER 10

The SWISS Boeing 747 landed smoothly on the airstrip of Zurich Airport. After a long interval, Tiziana boarded another airplane that brought her to her final destination at Capodichino Airport in Naples.

It was now exactly 9:10 Eastern time on Saturday morning. Having traveled all night, Tiziana was eager to get to the hotel. She retrieved her luggage and, after inquiring about transport to the hotel from several airport employees, found her way to the shuttle bus that was to take her 90 kilometres to the Villa Irlanda Grand Hotel in Gaeta.

The afternoon sun in the azure sky was almost blinding, but Tiziana welcomed its brightness and the hot breeze that caressed her face. She stood for a while absorbing its heat. She was here—the land of her birth.

The driver, a man with a weather-beaten face and a generous smile, said, "*Benvenut'à Napoli, Signorì!* Welcome to Naples, Missy!" He assisted her with her luggage.

Tiziana smiled contentedly back at him. "*Grazie!*"

She boarded the tiny shuttle, along with a family with three children and a young couple that looked like honeymooners. The family spoke in the sing-song dialect of northern Italy, and she soon struck up a conversation with them. The honeymooners didn't say much. After a half-hour wait, the driver, who was chatting with a fellow driver, hollered something unintelligible to the officer near the doors of the airport and climbed onto his seat.

They left Naples and took the Via Domitiana, traveling north toward Gaeta. The one-hour ride skirted along small medieval and modern towns, through pleasant, undulating countryside where she caught glimpses of seaside resorts built from ancient Roman villas. Tiziana drank in the scenery of what was considered one of the most romantic coastlines in the world. When they reached the town of Formia, she sat up taller. They were almost at the hotel, which was between Formia and Gaeta. The shuttle bus drove right into the heart of Formia, where it dropped off the honeymooners.

Palm trees were swaying in the sea breeze. She could smell the salt air through the open window. They were stopped near an outdoor market, where a small crowd of men and women were buying fresh fish, cheese, olives, vegetables, and fruit. One particular vendor caught Tiziana's eye. He was having an animated discussion with an older lady dressed exclusively in black. It looked like she was driving a hard bargain because every time he motioned for her to accept his offer, she shook her head. He would then flail his arms until, finally, he threw them up in frustration when she walked away. Before she even stepped off the sidewalk, he picked up the object of their heated discussion—a large, shiny fish—and said, "*Ah Signò! Men'è chista-ca, niscun' to dà!*" She wouldn't get a better bargain elsewhere!

Tiziana laughed heartily. She loved the Neapolitan dialect. It was guttural and passionate. No wonder Pavarotti's most beloved songs were in this dialect. Suddenly, all her fatigue vanished. She was itching to start exploring this part of Italy to which she'd never been. Visiting her father's relatives in Abruzzo had been the extent of her Italian travels. As if the driver sensed her restlessness, the shuttle bus took off again, returning to the main two-lane highway and speeding toward Gaeta.

A ripple of excitement went through Tiziana as the shuttle bus finally passed through the main gateway and came to a stop before the Villa Irlanda's first building. This was the first of the five buildings that made up the hotel complex, each with its own name. This one was appropriately named *La Reception*. The children eagerly clambered down off the bus, followed by their parents. Tiziana disembarked slowly and stared. The complex was magnificent, taking her breath away. She gathered her things, tipped the driver, and entered the Reception, where the family was already registering. While Tiziana waited her turn, she looked around. She was in a long, spacious, bright building that was restored on the ancient rural structure of a Roman villa said to have belonged to the adoptive father of the Emperor Octavian Augustus. A sitting area was appointed with royal blue armchairs; an ancient wall of the Imperial Villa melded with the newer walls of the building.

Two clerks staffed the marbled front desk, a man and a woman in uniformed dark blue suits.

"*Benvenuta alla Villa Irlanda, Signorina,*" said the man, whose nametag read Massimo. He checked her in, and then informed her that, because there was a wedding feast taking place at the Villa this weekend, all their rooms at *La Villa* and *Il Convento* buildings were booked. However, there was a reserved room for her at *La Casa delle Suore*, the Sisters' Residence building, all part of the Villa Irlanda, of course. If she wanted a room with a view of the gulf, it would only be possible on Monday. He reassured her that she would not be disappointed with her accommodations.

Tiziana agreed and was soon escorted by a young bellboy to a ramp that led into the 60,000 square metres of the hotel complex, where the other four buildings were located. As Tiziana followed the bellboy, she was taken in by the impressive historic buildings of *La Villa* and *Il Convento*, their pastel colors making them stand out elegantly against the lush green background. The buildings were all meticulously restored to their original grandeur after the destruction caused by the last world war.

As they passed *Il Convento*, where the dining room was located, Tiziana could hear the clinking of utensils and chinaware above the din of mingling voices coming from a large crowd. A few well-dressed men and stylish women were standing outside, talking and smoking. Tiziana assumed this was the wedding reception to which Massimo had referred.

They passed well-tended gardens, a large solarium, and finally, the stunning twenty-five-metre Olympic-size swimming pool in the center of it all. The walkway led her around the remarkable pool to another smaller pool, a shallow wading pool for children separated from the bigger pool by two olive trees. Tiziana walked slowly through the park with its palm trees, blooming flowers, and verdant lawn, thrilled that she was staying in this stunning complex.

The Sisters' Residence building was on the right side of the smaller pool, facing it. It contained fourteen rooms. The bellboy graciously opened the door of one of them on the first floor for her. He then gave her the key and deposited her luggage near the dresser. Tiziana tipped and thanked him.

"*Con piacere, signorina,*" he replied with a charming smile and left.

Tiziana closed the door and leaned against it. She took the time to study her accommodations. The room was fresh, bright, and inviting, with two windows that let in lots of light. The furnishings were a soft dove grey with teal blue wicker chairs and headboard. The bedspread had a matching teal blue flower print.

Tiziana kicked off her sneakers, peeled off her socks, and padded barefoot on the cool, hand-painted ceramic tiles to where her luggage was waiting to be unpacked. Within half an hour she had organized all her belongings in the dresser and her toiletries in the bathroom.

She put on her shower cap and took a quick shower to wash away the cramps in her sore muscles and the grimy feeling that came with traveling for so long. She donned a baby blue skort and a white cotton tank top. She pulled her thick hair into a high ponytail and applied a sheer gloss to her full lips. With renewed energy, Tiziana was ready to explore the grounds of this expansive property.

But first, she had one more thing to do. Checking her watch, she saw that it was 11:45 back home. She dialed her parents' number and waited, but not for long. After one ring, her father answered. Not a second later, her mother picked up the line with another phone.

"I've arrived at the hotel and everything's great," she said reassuringly. She briefly chatted with them and hung up.

Her next call was to Christopher, but Katherine answered.

"Tizzy, you lucky girl! How is Naples so far?" she cooed. Katherine was one of the most positive and fun-loving girls Tiziana knew, and for a moment she was disappointed Katherine hadn't been able to come with her.

"So far, so good! You're missing out!"

"Please, don't remind me! To think I could've been there with you. Oh, well, can't always get what you want. I'm guessing you also want to speak with my brother, who, unfortunately, just stepped into the shower. He got back from a client not too long ago. Anyway, should I ask him to call you back? He really wants to talk to you."

"Sure. Here's the number. Let him know I'll be stepping out for a bit. I want to check out the hotel property. It's actually, let's see, almost six o'clock over here, and the weather is hot and sunny."

"Would it be alright to wait for his call before you step out? You know Chris; he'll be out of the shower soon. We're going out right afterwards. It's the Grand Prix weekend and there's lots of stuff happening here. Tracy has complimentary tickets to the qualifying session this afternoon, and Chris is excited about going."

"Oh, I see … No problem. I'll wait."

Tracy again. Tiziana had the feeling Tracy was chasing after Christopher. She sat a little too close, laughed a little too loud, and pretty much ignored everyone else when Christopher walked into the room. If Chris noticed, Tiziana couldn't be sure. But with long, sleek blond hair and cornflower blue eyes, Tracy was very noticeable. She actually reminded Tiziana of Victoria, Christopher's ex-wife.

Not six minutes later, the telephone let out a long beep.

"Hello?"

"Hi, Tiz! How's my traveling girl?"

"Great! I can't believe I'm actually here!"

He asked about the trip and the hotel and the weather.

Small talk. What did he really want to tell her?

"Tizzy, I can't talk right now. The girls are waiting for me. I'm going to call you tomorrow, around the same time. We'll talk then."

Her enthusiasm deflated like a pierced balloon. "Fine. Have fun at the Grand Prix."

"You bet."

Tiziana walked out of the room and into the bright sunshine.

CHAPTER 11

The festive music from the wedding reception drew Tiziana to the center of the complex. Leisurely walking around, Tiziana drank in the details she missed on arrival: the neo-classical architectural style of the *Villa* with its Roman columns, arched windows, and balconies, the sweet smell of the flowers mixed with the mouth-watering aroma of the dinner wafting from the dining room; and the cawing of the seagulls reminding her that the beach was just beyond the gates. It felt like being in a small paradise, the ideal vacation spot to rest, meditate, and temporarily forget her world back home.

After touring the lovely grounds, Tiziana decided to walk back toward the sparkling blue waters of the immense pool in the center of it all. She sat on one of the deck chairs, turning it to face the side of the pool to get a better view of the hills behind the complex. Leaning back on the chair, she closed her eyes and let the music welcome her to this country, where life was boisterous and enjoyed to the full. She recognized some of the older classic songs she heard from the live band playing at the wedding. They were the same songs played at family weddings of relatives from her dad's side of the family.

The music brought back happy childhood memories of dancing in both her parents' arms, her mother laughing as her father swung them almost off their feet. That image was so vivid in Tiziana's mind that she could still see the curve of her mother's neck as she flipped her strawberry blond hair away from her flushed face, tempting her father to plant a hearty kiss at its base.

"Iru-la-leru-la-leru-la-leru-la-leru-la-la ..." Tiziana sang along with the chorus as other distant voices from the party were raised in unison to this catchy tune. More memories came flooding back as they ran wildly through her head.

It felt so good to reminisce! Lately, it seemed there hadn't been much to smile about. When was the last time she saw her father embrace her mother affectionately?

Tiziana adjusted herself on the deck chair when something moved in her peripheral vision. She turned her head and saw a man standing but fifteen feet from her. He did not seem to notice she was there, and perhaps for this reason Tiziana allowed herself to stare openly.

The man looked to be in his early thirties and was so impeccably dressed he could have walked off the cover of a *GQ* magazine. He wore a Giorgio Armani pinstriped black suit with a crisp white shirt and silver cuff links. A creamy rose with a small silver ribbon was pinned on the left side of his jacket. Black hair fell full and lush over his forehead, framing a chiseled face that was handsome even from a side profile. The only thing that marred his well-groomed image was the cigarette dangling from his hand.

Tiziana figured he was one of the guests from the wedding, probably a relative because of the rose he wore. He looked pensive as he stood smoking and staring at the mesmerizing waters of the pool. Or maybe he was the groom himself, wondering if he'd made the right decision. This thought made her smile.

Then without warning, the man turned his head and zeroed in on Tiziana, and suddenly she felt like a mouse caught stealing cheese.

"*Buona sera,*" he nodded in acknowledgement. He took a long drag from his cigarette.

"*Buona sera.*"

He looked at her more closely through the haze of smoke he exhaled. "*Lei è americana?*"

"*No, canadese.*"

"Are you here on holiday or perhaps business?" he asked, surprising her with his lightly accented British English and polite but direct manner.

"Both, I suppose," she replied, after giving it some thought.

He continued looking at her, scrutinizing her face unabashedly.

"I'm sorry, I'm forgetting my manners," he said, approaching her. He extended his hand and introduced himself. "Gian-Carlo De Medici."

His hand was warm as it clasped hers firmly. Up close, he even smelled expensive. She noted the TAG Heuer watch and the silver-lined silk tie that matched his outfit perfectly.

"Tiziana Manoretti, pleased to meet you."

"Tiziana," he repeated slowly. "*Un bel nome.* I like that name."

For the first time since she saw him, he smiled. It transformed his face, making him look younger and softening the sharp lines of his jaw. The smoke from his cigarette wafted close to Tiziana's face, and she instinctively waved it away.

"*Scusi*," he said, looking around for an ashtray. Finally, he spotted an abandoned liquor glass on one of the small side tables and extinguished his half-finished cigarette in it.

"I assume you don't smoke. Nasty habit, I agree." He pointed to the chair next to hers. "May I?"

She nodded. "You don't seem to be enjoying the wedding reception."

He paused, looking in the direction of the hotel from which music and laughter still emanated. "I needed some fresh air." He sat down and faced her with his back to the wedding reception.

"Who got married? A friend? A cousin?" asked Tiziana, looking at the creamy rose pinned to his chest.

"Neither." Gian-Carlo looked directly at Tiziana. "She was once my fiancée." He said this without emotion.

"Your fiancée!" Tiziana sat upright in her chair. "And she invited you to her wedding?"

"*Eh sì*, perhaps she wanted to make sure I witnessed what could have been mine. She was tired of playing the waiting game, you see. 'I want to be married,' she said. Well, she got what she wanted. Now, she is married. It's best this way."

"Whom did she marry?"

"My brother."

Tiziana slapped her hand over her open mouth and stared incredulously at Gian-Carlo.

"*Che sarà, sarà*," he said, shrugging nonchalantly.

They were both silent for a few seconds, just staring at each other.

"I wasn't the man for her, and she wasn't the woman for me."

"Well, I don't think she really loved you anyway. In the end, this may have saved you from a loveless marriage."

"Ah, yes, you Americans know all about love," he said with a hint of humour.

"I'm Canadian."

"Same thing." His green eyes twinkled.

"Not really. They *are* two different countries, you know."

"So, what business are you conducting here?" He was smiling again.

"Well, actually I'm here to find out some information about my birth parents. I was adopted when I was a baby, and I was born right here in Gaeta at the orphanage Santa Maria Della Fede."

Gian-Carlo settled himself closer with his elbows leaning on his knees and his hands loosely entwined between them. He was listening intently.

"*Veramente?* You are adopted. So, you are here to play detective? It's not an easy thing to do."

"Yes, I know, but I already came all the way across the ocean."

He grinned. "I'm not sure that's the hard part. The people who adopted you, are they Canadian?"

"My mother is, but my father is Italian from the province of Abruzzo. He immigrated to Canada when he was a child. I grew up speaking English with my mom and Italian with my dad."

He nodded. "Were they good parents to you?"

Tiziana was a little surprised by his question. "Yes, very. The only upsetting thing about my adoption is that I was only told about it a month ago. Before that, I had no clue. So, I'm terribly curious and almost obsessed with searching for my roots. The big question for me is why I was put up for adoption."

"Did it ever occur to you that you may not like the answer?" His gaze was direct and serious.

"Yes, but at least I'll know why."

"How do you plan to find your birth parents?"

"I've just arrived a few hours ago, so I haven't started my inquiry yet. My first stop will be the orphanage, since that's where I was born. Do you know where it is?"

He nodded and pointed toward the northeast. "I say approximately five kilometres from here."

"Do you live in Gaeta?" Tiziana asked, suddenly curious.

"I live in Rome. I'm staying here with a friend."

As if on cue, a stunning blond appeared beside Gian-Carlo. She was wearing a slinky floral dress that moulded her lithe body.

"*Dove ti sei nascosto, amore?*" she said, pouting.

"I was not hiding, only talking to a friend," replied Gian-Carlo in Italian, without looking up at the woman. "Francesca, this is Tiziana. Tiziana, Francesca."

The blond smiled politely, raking Tiziana from head to foot with cool eyes. She slipped her manicured hand in the crook of Gian-Carlo's arm as he stood reluctantly. He shook Tiziana's hand in farewell. His warm eyes caressed her face briefly.

"I hope we meet again," he said in English just before leaving. "I enjoyed our conversation. I should also like to know if you find your birth parents."

And as suddenly as he appeared, he was gone.

CHAPTER 12

Tiziana stayed by the pool, contemplating her conversation with Gian-Carlo. He had been cordial and charming, but underneath his polished, confident look she had sensed loneliness. It was probably this unconscious realization that had made her comfortable disclosing her personal situation to a man who was but a handsome stranger.

She hadn't felt assaulted by his probing eyes. Having worked extensively in the company of men, Tiziana knew firsthand when a man's eyes were roving with wrong intentions. Instead, she felt as if he had been studying her face, much like a doctor or an artist would do. She wondered what had gone wrong with his fiancée, and if he still loved her. It certainly took courage to attend this wedding; although Tiziana did not have siblings, she surmised that his relationship with his brother must not be a close one. At least not now. What kind of a man marries his brother's former fiancée?

Before going back to her room, Tiziana decided to sneak a peek at the wedding party. She was approaching the door to *Il Convento* when it suddenly opened and the bride stepped out with a man. Tiziana almost ducked from view and then sheepishly realized she wasn't doing anything wrong. Nobody knew what she was up to, anyway.

The man who was with the bride must have been the groom, for he held her hand and kissed it as he led her toward one of the tables by the pool. He looked different from Gian-Carlo. He was younger, taller, and more heavily built.

The bride was exquisite in an haute couture wedding dress. It was a creamy white gown with a billowing skirt and a corset with intricate beading and silver threading. She looked young and tall with slender shoulders and chestnut hair piled high to reveal a striking face that looked … familiar. She looked like a model Tiziana had seen in *Vogue* last month. Tiziana moved to get a better look, all the while pretending to observe the scenery around her. The bride turned and smiled at her husband.

It was her! What was her name again? She was popular for the lingerie clothes she modeled.

Mara Quarantini. That was it! Her youthful face with high cheekbones, small upturned nose, and full lips that could turn into a sexy pout, were all recognizable traits. However, what had caught the fashion world's attention had been her refusal to pose topless for a lingerie photo shoot in the streets of Paris. The negative publicity had put her face in magazines around the world, backfiring when it served to heighten her popularity instead. It also landed her a contract with Dolce & Gabbana.

Tiziana tried not to stare and finally began walking in the direction of her room. If she had not met Gian-Carlo, this wedding would have been but a good memory of her first day here in Gaeta. Now, she thought of Gian-Carlo and his sad situation. He was obviously wealthy, and his world seemed to revolve around beautiful women. However, she had seen no affection between him and Francesca. Definitely a lonely but very interesting man. She wondered if she would ever see him again.

From a secluded archway, a distinguished-looking man watched Tiziana. He was in his sixties, although he did not look it, with salt-and-pepper hair and a fit form. He had tracked her every move since he spotted her with Gian-Carlo—the way she talked, smiled, and gesticulated throughout her conversation with him. The man's keen eyes missed nothing. They followed Tiziana as she walked, as if lost in thought, back in the direction he presumed was her room.

Her face stirred feelings he had long buried in his heart, feelings of pain and jealousy—a jealousy so strong it had destroyed his obsessive love for the only woman who, after many years, still haunted him.

CHAPTER 13

Tiziana woke up at seven the next morning, having slept soundly. As her eyes fluttered open and she looked around, she remembered that she was in Italy, in a gorgeous hotel by the Mediterranean Sea. A smile formed across her face, and she stretched like a cat, kicking the bed sheets off her. Today she was going to the orphanage.

After a breakfast of a crisp croissant, or *cornetto*, as the Italians called it, strawberries *con panna*, and a cappuccino, Tiziana went to *La Reception* building and consulted with Julia at the front desk. Massimo was not there this morning.

She could take the bus to the orphanage but then needed to walk through some smaller streets since it was a little out of the way from the bus stop, or she could take a taxi. Tiziana decided to take a taxi. Forty minutes later, she found herself standing in front of an imposing Gothic structure.

It had two tapering pinnacles and a large, round stained glass window in the center between them. Below the window was a statue representing the Virgin Mary that stood in a nook in the stone wall.

She approached the tall, heavy wooden doors set in a pointed archway. An old sign on her right side read, *Orfanotrofio Santa Maria Della Fede*. Tiziana lifted the lion head knocker and brought it down three times.

Her heart began pounding a little faster. She bit her lower lip, ran her hands through her hair, and waited.

I can't believe I'm actually here.

After what seemed like an eternity and no one answered, Tiziana decided to knock again. Just as her hand was about to lift the knocker once more, the door opened slowly with a very audible squeak. A nun stood in the entranceway. She was dressed in a simple nun's habit, a white tunic with a black veil and white underveil, identifying her as belonging to the Dominican order.

"*Sì?*"

"*Buongiorno.* My name is Tiziana Manoretti. I have come to inquire about my birth parents. I ... I was born here and then put up for adoption," Tiziana explained in Italian.

When the nun continued staring at her, Tiziana dug into her purse and handed the documents to her. She looked at them, handed them back, and said, "Follow me."

Tiziana stepped into the cool, dark interior and followed the nun through an austere hallway that led into a larger one. Here she could hear muted voices as she passed closed doors. Occasionally, she caught glimpses of empty class-rooms. *This must be the school section of the orphanage,* she thought.

They came to another set of doors. When they were opened, Tiziana's eyes widened. They stepped into an open tiled courtyard of about forty feet by forty feet. It was square and enclosed by five arches on each side. Situated in the middle of the orphanage, it had no roof. Directly on the other end was another set of doors leading back into the opposite side of the orphanage. It was such a stark contrast to the hallway from which Tiziana had emerged.

The tiles of the courtyard were a colourful mix of mustards, terracotta, and blues, forming a mosaic of the sun in the center.

What interested Tiziana most of all, however, were the children. Thirty or so of them, clad in grey and white uniforms—the girls in tunics and the boys in Bermuda pants—were scattered about. Some of the younger children were playing with a ball, a group of girls were chatting together, and others were skipping rope and singing as they jumped. Two nuns were supervising.

As Tiziana walked across the courtyard, still following the nun, she noticed all eyes turned toward her. She was suddenly conscious of her bright, floral print skirt that flowed to her knees, her strappy summer sandals, and her Guess jean jacket. One little girl with blond pigtails began to walk beside her. Tiziana smiled at her, and the child smiled back. One of the supervising nuns approached them and quietly spoke to the nun who was leading Tiziana. After a brief exchange, the supervising nun turned to Tiziana and spoke.

"*Buongiorno, signorina.* My name is Suor Annunziata." She smiled warmly at Tiziana. "Please, come with me. I will take you to Madre Maria, our Mother Superior," she said in Italian.

Tiziana observed the face before her as being remarkable, not because of classic beauty, but because of radiance and a loving expression. She looked like the grandmother everyone loved.

The little girl with the pigtails now pulled on Tiziana's skirt. "*Sarai tu la mia nuova mamma?* Will you be my new mommy?"

Before Tiziana could respond, Suor Annunziata gently took the girl's hand and rubbed it between her own. "The lady is only a visitor, *bambina.* Now go on and play. Soon, we will be on our way to the museum."

Watching this exchange, Tiziana's eyes stung. Had she not been adopted, would she have grown up within these stone walls like this little girl, waiting for a new mommy to come and take her home?

Suor Annunziata turned to Tiziana and led her to the other set of doors. The nun walked calmly and quietly next to her. Tiziana liked her instantly.

"How many children are at the orphanage?" asked Tiziana.

"We have thirty-three at the moment," replied the nun. "Where are you from, child? You speak with a slight accent."

"I'm from Montreal, Canada, but I was actually born here. My name is Tiziana Manoretti. My mother is Canadian and my father is Italian."

Suor Annunziata's step seemed to falter for a second. Tiziana felt her gaze.

"Have you been here long?" Tiziana asked.

"For most of my life, it would seem. You see, I was an orphan myself, arriving here at the tender age of two. Then, when I was ten, a kind and older couple adopted me. My mother was a nurse, and so I learned her trade." She paused. "I was working at the hospital when both my parents died, my mother from heart disease and, shortly after, my father from a broken heart. I was an orphan again, so I sought solace within these walls. I knew it was my calling. The good Lord wanted me here because the children needed me. I've never left since the day I came back."

She smiled kindly at Tiziana. "Are you looking for solace, child?"

Tiziana looked deeply into the nun's eyes. Orphaned twice! She couldn't begin to imagine what that must have been like. She had parents who loved her and who had raised her well.

"No. I just want to know who my birth parents are." After a brief pause, she added, "Is that wrong?"

"No, my child, it isn't. But it doesn't always mean it's the best thing to do."

Before Tiziana could ask her what she meant, they came to a stop before a door. Suor Annunziata knocked and they were immediately beckoned in. It seemed Madre Maria was expecting them, probably having been advised of her visit by the first nun.

Tiziana walked into a medium-sized room that resembled a simple office. Sitting behind a massive wooden desk was a nun with a lined face and sharp, dark eyes. The tall, large-boned nun stood and motioned Tiziana to take a seat.

"You may go now, Suor Annunziata," said Madre Maria in a strong, resonant voice.

The door closed quietly behind her, and Tiziana realized she was now alone before this impressive woman, who exuded authority and strength. She almost gulped audibly.

"What can I do for you, my child?" asked the Mother Superior, sitting down on her wooden chair.

Tiziana handed the documents across the desk to the Mother Superior. "I have come to inquire about my birth parents. Twenty-seven years ago I was born in this orphanage and then put up for adoption."

"What is your name?"

"Tiziana Manoretti."

If Tiziana's name meant anything to Madre Maria, she did not show it. She took her time to read the documents before her.

"*Signorina* Manoretti, we have a policy at the orphanage that does not allow us, without proper consent, to divulge any information whatsoever to the child or to the family adopting the child. You must understand, we not only respect the wishes of our clients, but we also guarantee full protection of privacy. Most birth parents want to remain anonymous. Bringing up the past can be painful."

Tiziana was prepared for this. "I fully understand your position. I was wondering if you could pass on a message from me to my birth parents. Perhaps now, after all these years, they may wish to know me."

Tiziana would not be deterred by the Mother Superior's scrutinizing gaze.

"And what is your message?"

Tiziana retrieved a sealed blue envelope from her purse. In it was a simple letter addressed to her birth parents, telling them that she was doing very well and that she wanted only to meet them and to thank them for choosing to give her life. She handed the envelope to Madre Maria, who reluctantly took it.

"I cannot promise you anything. I will verify our files, and if the names of your birth parents are therein stated, which they may not be, it may then be possible to contact them. However, I will need to consult with the law if I am authorized to do this."

"Are you telling me that you may not have their names on record?" said Tiziana, clearly surprised.

"Precisely."

"Can you please verify the file for me? I need to know if I should take different measures to find them."

The Mother Superior looked her squarely in the eyes. "*Signorina* Manoretti, your file is twenty-seven years old. It is archived and stored in our basement. Surely, you are not asking me to go digging at this moment to retrieve it."

"Should I return at a more convenient time?"

"No need. I have your letter here. There's not much else you can do but wait."

Why is this woman brushing me off?

"I will call Suor Teresa to escort you back."

Tiziana knew enough about negotiating tactics to realize she would not get any further with the Mother Superior. "That won't be necessary. I can find my way. Thank you for your ... help." Tiziana quickly stood, and before the Mother Superior could say anything else, she left.

As Tiziana walked briskly back toward the doors that led her into the courtyard, her mind was racing. She was disappointed, frustrated, and angry. Was it possible there was no record of her birth parents' names? How could she find out? And, if that was the case, what was she to do now? Did the Mother Superior know who they were? Was there someone who had seen them and remembered who they were? Tiziana knew this was a long shot, but she was far from giving up.

Suor Annunziata suddenly came to her mind. She was a nurse. Had she been here twenty-seven years ago and taken care of her when she was a newborn or even possibly assisted her birth? In any case, the woman was friendly and compassionate. Tiziana wanted to speak with her again. It was possible that Suor Annunziata might have information that could help her find her birth parents.

With renewed determination, Tiziana almost ran down the hallway. She must find Suor Annunziata.

CHAPTER 14

The Mother Superior watched as the spunky young woman left her office. She stared at the closed door, remembering the look on the woman's face when she told her there may be no record. She glanced down at the envelope still in her hands. This was a case she had not yet forgotten, even after twenty-seven years.

Throughout the course of the thirty-five years she had been here, Madre Maria had seen many scandals involving illegitimate babies. The women, especially, would run to the sanctuary of these walls, and she, née Maria Roccia, daughter of a peasant family, would "fix" the problem. The worst and most notorious cases were the noble families, whose secrets were deeply buried here. The most pitiable were the underprivileged, who at times were cast into terrible situations without fault of their own: an abusive husband who left his battered wife pregnant for the eleventh time, a pretty slip of a girl raped by the town bully, or the naive young girl who was left pregnant and quickly forgotten by the rich landlord's son.

Madre Maria's mission in life was to provide a safe place and an education for the unwanted children and to find them a good home whenever possible. She herself had been rescued by her uncle, a priest, who had taken it upon himself to have her trained and educated by the nuns.

Madre Maria got up from her chair and went to fetch Suor Teresa.

"Please retrieve this file from the archives," she said, handing the nun a piece of paper with a name written on it.

Yesterday, Madre Maria had received a phone call from one of her benefactors—a powerful man well respected in the political and business community—who made secret contributions to the orphanage, no doubt to ensure continued silence on her part. Thinking he wanted to make a donation, she was surprised when he gave her specific instructions regarding a woman named Tiziana Manoretti. If this woman visited the orphanage requesting information, the Mother Superior was not to divulge anything concerning the past. Moreover, she was to inform him immediately if this occurred.

Close to an hour later, she was flipping through the contents of the retrieved file. She put the blue envelope Tiziana had given her into it, thinking that it was a shame it would never be read. Opening her bottom desk drawer, she put the file under some other documents and then locked it.

Madre Maria took a deep breath and picked up the telephone. She dialed the number the benefactor had left for her yesterday.

"*Pronto?*" said a male voice.

"*Sì, pronto.* This is Suor Maria from the orphanage. The young woman came today. You can rest assured that she knows nothing. I made sure of that."

"Very well. I am pleased. You can expect … ah … an extra donation this year."

"Thank you, *Signore.*"

How she loathed this man! Subtly using charity as a bribe. From as far back as she could remember, he made use of his family name and wealth to get what he wanted. May God Almighty forgive her for complying with the wishes of this conniving man.

CHAPTER 15

After she left the Mother Superior's office, Tiziana managed to find her way back to the courtyard, which was now empty. She took the doors that led her to the front part of the orphanage. Walking down the hallway, she boldly looked into rooms where the doors were ajar and knocked on others. Finally, she spotted a nun in one of the rooms that looked like a small library.

"*Scusi*, I'm looking for Suor Annunziata. Can you tell me where I can find her?"

"She went to the museum with the children."

"Which museum?"

"*Il Museo Diocesano.*"

Tiziana scrambled to get her pen and a scrap of paper from her purse. She scribbled the name of the museum.

"Can you please tell me where it is?"

"Next to the Duomo of Gaeta."

"Thanks!" replied Tiziana, already heading out of the room.

As she exited the orphanage, Tiziana consulted her map and saw that she needed to head further south. She set out at a steady pace, but after thirty minutes wished she had worn her running shoes rather than her new sandals. Although still early morning, the sun's heat was already strong, causing Tiziana to remove her jacket. It was going to be a hot one.

Tiziana walked along Via degli Olivi down to Via Maresca, and still no sign of a bus. Remembering that it was Sunday, she figured the bus schedule would be slow, especially since in Italy nobody rushed anywhere. She nearly jumped out of her skin when a group of teenagers in a convertible sports car hooted and shouted for her to join them for a fun day at the beach. Hot and dusty, she was almost tempted to accept, but waved them off. Their rowdy excitement reminded Tiziana that she was on vacation, and a day at the beach would be refreshing.

At last, Tiziana saw a taxi and flagged it down. It pulled to a stop next to her, and Tiziana saw that another passenger was in the back seat. It was an older, heavyset woman dressed all in black, including the handkerchief on her head.

"Where are you going?" asked the grey-haired taxi driver in a strong Neapolitan accent.

"To the Museum *Diocesano*."

The taxi driver nodded and consulted with his passenger. "My client says that if you don't mind sharing the fee for the ride, you can join her. We're going in that direction."

"Great!" Tiziana opened the door and slid onto the seat next to the woman, who nodded at her without smiling. She had thin, pursed lips, a bulbous nose, and coarse facial hair on her chin. Clutching her purse to her ample bosom, she sat looking straight ahead.

They rode in silence for a few minutes, when the woman suddenly spoke to Tiziana in Italian. "What is your name?"

"Tiziana Manoretti."

"Are you going to church, *signorina Manoretti*?"

"Uh … well … no, I'm actually going to a museum."

"The Diocese Museum is part of the Duomo of Gaeta, which is the main church of the town," the driver explained to Tiziana.

"Oh, well, then I guess I am going to church," replied Tiziana, smiling sweetly.

"*Molto bene*," said the woman, as if that made a difference to her. "And you believe in God?"

"Yes." Tiziana figured this woman to be a devout Catholic.

"*Brava*," said the woman, satisfied. After a brief moment, she added, "Are you married?" She was staring at Tiziana's hands.

Tiziana caught the taxi driver's eyes through his rearview mirror. Grinning, he winked at her, obviously enjoying the exchange between her and the woman.

"No, I'm not. Why?"

The woman ignored her question and continued her inquisition. "Do you like children?"

Tiziana thought she heard a snort from the taxi driver. Was he laughing? She glanced at him in the mirror again and saw his eyes full of mirth. He seemed to be shaking his head ever so slightly.

Am I missing something here?

"Yes, I love children," said Tiziana, raising her eyebrows at the taxi driver, who shrugged back.

"*Bravissima*," said the woman with a glint in her eyes. "And I'm sure you can cook, too, *vero*?"

The woman still hadn't cracked a smile, and although Tiziana sensed she was satisfied with her answers thus far, she felt like a clueless schoolgirl trying to pass a test.

"Yes, I can cook."

The woman's thin lips moved upward in a crooked half smile. She nodded several times, her large nose flaring. "Yes, yes, you will do just fine. But you are a little too skinny. You need more fat."

The taxi driver's shoulders moved up and down in conjunction with his silenced guffaws. Tiziana looked in bewilderment from one to the other. She was clearly not in the know here. Just then, the taxi came to a stop before the San Francesco Church, a Neo-Gothic structure built in the form of a cross with a nave and two aisles.

"Giuseppe, the door, please," said the woman to the taxi driver, as if he were her son.

The driver got out of his seat and came around to open her door. Before she stepped out, the woman turned to Tiziana and asked, "Where do you live?"

"Oh, I don't live here. I'm a tourist."

"Which hotel?"

"The Villa Irlanda." Tiziana instantly regretted her answer the moment it came out of her mouth as she saw the driver gesturing emphatically for her to be quiet.

"*Bene*. My son Giacomino would love to meet you. He needs a wife, you understand? My Giacomino is a good man. Sant'Erasmo, our patron saint, has answered my prayers. *Brava. Brava.* I will see you later." The woman patted Tiziana's hand as if sealing a deal.

Tiziana's eyes widened in disbelief, but before she could utter anything to the contrary, the woman heaved herself out of the taxi and strode purposely toward the church. The driver got back into his seat, shaking his head openly, as he turned to look at Tiziana with a huge smile on his face.

"You knew all along what she was up to, didn't you? Why didn't you say anything? And please don't tell me her son is actually going to show up at my hotel! Hey, wait a minute. She didn't even pay her part of the fare!"

"*Signorina*, you are not the first, and I assure you, until her good-for-nothing-son gets a wife, you will not be the last." He turned in his seat and resumed driving.

"You mean she's done this kind of thing before?"

"Uh-hmm. Even before you flagged me down, *Signora* Pepina had already spotted you."

Tiziana sat back in her seat. She thought of the way the woman had fired questions at her, and suddenly, the absurdity of the whole thing had her giggling. Before she knew it, she was laughing hysterically with Giuseppe.

As their laughter subsided, Tiziana noticed they were now in the old quarter of Gaeta. They turned onto Via Duomo and rode up the hill until Tiziana spotted the impressive bell tower of the Duomo. A few minutes later she was walking toward the left of the church, where Giuseppe indicated would be the Diocese Museum. Here, paintings from the thirteenth to the eighteenth century were on display. She spotted the school bus and assumed it was the one that had brought the children from the orphanage.

Tiziana saw a nun in a white tunic with a black veil and hurried up to her.

"Suor Annunziata!" she called out. The nun turned, but it was not Suor Annunziata. She looked around and scanned the small crowd. Giuseppe had informed her that the museum was only open from nine to eleven, and her watch indicated it was already close to eleven. She would wait outside to be certain she wouldn't miss Suor Annunziata. She was not disappointed. After a few minutes, Tiziana saw the kind nun smiling as she guided her group of children back toward the bus.

Quickly, Tiziana moved to where Suor Annunziata could see her. "Suor Annunziata, I need to speak with you, please."

The nun stopped and then moved toward her.

"Yes, child, what is the matter? You look distressed," said Suor Annunziata with concern etched on her forehead. She was holding the hands of two young children.

"I'm fine, but I need to ask you something that's important to me. Were you at the orphanage when I was born there?"

Suor Annunziata's face lost its look of concern and became shadowed. "It was a long time ago, *cara*. What did Madre Maria tell you?"

"Nothing. Absolutely nothing. There may not even be a record of my birth parents' names in the file. Do you remember who they were? Do you know *anything* about my past that can help me find them?"

Suor Annunziata seemed lost in thought for a moment, then she whispered, "You remind me so much of her ..."

"Who? My mother?" Tiziana clutched at the nun's sleeve. "Do you know who she is?"

Abruptly, the nun backed away and motioned for the children to start walking.

"I must go now. The children are waiting. You must address all your inquiries to the Mother Superior. I cannot help you." She hurried with the children toward the bus. Once there, she turned and looked sadly upon Tiziana before boarding. The bus roared into motion and drove away, leaving Tiziana standing alone, staring after it.

Tiziana spent the rest of the afternoon idly walking the streets of downtown Gaeta, contemplating the events of the morning. When hunger pangs set in, she had a *panino* filled with *prosciutto cotto*, goat's cheese, and aragula leaves, washing it all down with Acqua Minerale San Pellegrino. She finished her meal with a strawberry and lemon gelato.

She strolled along the narrow, cobbled Piccolo Alley, browsing through its shops and chatting with the friendly shopkeepers. One of them, named Anna, insisted she visit the *Montagna Spaccata*, the Split Mountain Sanctuary. After deliberating the matter, Tiziana bought a pair of sturdy flip-flops to give her feet a break from the new sandals, which were killing her toes. She wanted to walk up the mountain and enjoy the sights without having to worry about inflicting further pain on her feet. After all, she was on vacation, she thought, as she wandered the winding streets of this hilly resort town. It was a splendid, sun-bursting day with only a few puffy, cotton-ball clouds riding the sea-blue sky.

Tiziana didn't regret her decision. She followed the precise directions that Anna, a native of Gaeta, had given her. It took forty-five minutes to walk to the entrance of the mountain and up to the sanctuary. Just before reaching the sanctuary, Tiziana stopped to admire the various souvenirs displayed by several vendors. She saw the usual postcards, religious relics, and rows of colourful trinkets and knickknacks. Tiziana carefully chose several postcards and a magnet to add to her growing collection on the fridge at home. The magnet was made of hand-painted ceramic with a view of Gaeta jutting out into the sea. She also bought a small wooden fishing boat typical of those used by the fishermen in Gaeta, for Svelitzic, her boss, whose favourite sport was fishing.

Tiziana continued on her way, along with a few other tourists. She was curious to visit the mountain, which, according to legend, split three times after the death of Christ. Tiziana entered the Chapel of San Filippo Neri and descended the narrow stairs between the split rock mass. Anna had told her to watch out for the large handprint on the right side of the rock. The legend stated that a Turk, who did not believe that the rock had split at the death of Jesus, touched the rock and said, "If this tradition is true, then let this rock become liquid." That was when the rock liquefied and made an imprint of his hand.

Tiziana spotted the imprint and touched the smooth rock. She read the sign beneath it and wondered how much truth was in the legendary tale of the unbelieving Turk. She continued to the bottom of the stairs to the small chapel. To the left was another staircase that led up to a small lookout with a magnificent view of the Tyrrhenian Sea as seen from between the split rock. Tiziana stared out into the sea, breathing in the saltwater air and reflecting on all that had transpired in the last few months. Up here, the wind tugged at her hair and the crashing waves below were rhythmic and stimulating. It felt wonderful to savour the sights and sounds of nature.

After a half hour, Tiziana made her way back and left the church. This time she wanted to go down to the *Grotto del Turco*, just to the right of the church. She paid the small entrance fee and carefully began to descend the several hundred steps down the open cave. The flip-flops made the long, steep descent a little more precarious. The further down she went, the more deafening the crashes of the pounding waves became against the boulders and rocks jutting out between the wide split of the mountain. The strong scent and feel of the saltwater mist and the echo of the roaring waters were exhilarating. Tiziana made it to the bottom, where a few adventurous young men were walking on the massive boulders and rocks closest to the mouth of the split, where the waves boomed. Tiziana stood on a boulder and enjoyed the invigorating scenery and the sensation of being at the bottom of a monstrous cave. She closed her eyes. She was happy she had come.

Finally, she made her way back to the hotel, weary but content. She kicked the flip-flops off her aching, blistered feet, removed her skirt, and crawled under the bed sheets for a late afternoon siesta. Her last thought just before falling asleep was that Suor Annunziata knew a great deal more than even she had expected.

CHAPTER 16

Tiziana woke up slowly with a pounding headache. She moaned and rolled over as the pounding got louder. It took her a while to realize the pounding wasn't just in her head. Someone was knocking insistently on her door.

She got up groggily, slipped on her skirt, and staggered to the door. She opened it cautiously. Through swollen eyes she saw Gian-Carlo standing in front of her, looking fresh and handsome in blue jeans and a pink and green striped shirt. His hair was gelled and fell in random locks away from his face. He chuckled at the sight of her.

Oh, my goodness! Tiziana could only imagine the picture she presented. Her hair was all over the place, she was sweaty from sleep, and her skirt was inside out and crooked.

"Don't laugh at me," was all she could croak out. She turned and staggered back to the bed, where she sat down heavily, holding her pounding head with both her hands. She was a little dizzy.

"Looks like a bad case of jet lag. May I come in?"

Tiziana nodded slowly, and Gian-Carlo walked straight to the telephone on the desk and dialed the reception. He spoke rapid Italian into it. He hung up, pulled the chair toward Tiziana, and sat facing her.

"I think I was out too long in the sun."

"Did you go to the orphanage?"

"Yes, but for some reason I don't think the Mother Superior liked me very much. I didn't get much information. But I spoke to one of the nuns there who gave me the impression she knew who my mother was."

"And?"

"She didn't want to tell me anything either." Tiziana rubbed her eyes and stifled a yawn.

"Well, your search has just begun. Don't give up. Tomorrow I will contact a friend of mine who works at the juvenile court. Now listen, Tiziana, you will take a shower, and I will take you out tonight. I'm having supper with my cousin, Stefania, and she wants to meet you."

"Where's Francesca?" asked Tiziana, eyeing the open door as if she expected the blond bombshell to walk in at any minute.

"She returned home," he answered with a controlled smile on his face. It seemed he was trying not to chuckle.

Just then, a bellboy knocked on the open door. He was carrying a tray with a pitcher of water, two glasses, and a little plastic cup with two pills in it. Gian-Carlo took the tray, thanked the bellboy, and proceeded to pour Tiziana a full glass of water. He gave it to her with the pills and instructed her to swallow. Tiziana didn't argue. Anything to make the pounding go away. The water was cool and refreshing, and she gulped down the whole glass. Gian-Carlo took the glass from her hand, placed it back on the tray, and gently pulled her up by the arm, guiding her to the bathroom.

"*Forza.* C'mon, a shower will wash away all the fatigue, and you'll be as good as new. I will wait for you in the lobby. Take the time you need."

He closed the bathroom door behind her. Tiziana locked it, slowly stripped off her clothes, and stepped into the shower. The lukewarm water was invigorating, and the pounding in her head began to subside. She didn't really feel like going out tonight, but the option of staying alone in her room or in the dining room wasn't exciting either.

Gian-Carlo looked around the room. He spotted Tiziana's purse, took it, retrieved her wallet, and carefully searched through it. He noted her address and her personal business card. When he saw a photograph of Tiziana with her parents, he stared at it for a long time, memorizing the faces. Then he put the photograph and the wallet back where he found them and the purse in its original place. He scanned the room again, and this time saw the documents he was looking for on the bureau next to the bed. He took out a small digital camera from his pocket, and with efficiency and precision, took photos of each page. Just as he was about to leave, the telephone beeped. He hesitated only for a moment before picking it up.

"*Pronto?*" he said.

There was a pause and then, "I think I have the wrong room number."

"Who are you looking for?"

"Tiziana Manoretti."

"This is her room, but she's in the shower at the moment. May I ask who's calling?"

Again there was a pause. "I'm Christopher. Who're you?"

"Gian-Carlo, a friend of Tiziana."

"Really? She's never mentioned your name to me before."

"I will leave her the message that you called. Does she have your number?" Gian-Carlo asked in a pleasant tone, choosing not to get involved.

"Yes. I'll be waiting for her call."

"Very well. Ciao."

Gian-Carlo wrote Tiziana a message on the writing pad he found in the desk and left it on the bed, where she was most likely to see it. He chuckled at the explaining Tiziana would probably need to do when she spoke to Christopher. He wondered if he was Tiziana's *ragazzo*. He hadn't found any photos of a possible boyfriend in her purse.

Gian-Carlo walked out of the room and headed for the reception area. He needed access to the Internet. He wanted to do a little investigating.

Tiziana finished her shower, toweled herself dry, and peeked out the bathroom door to make sure Gian-Carlo was gone. She walked to the front door, locked it, and then went straight to her closet to see what she was going to wear. She chose her capri jeans with beaded back pockets, a black and red halter top, and comfortable but dressy thong sandals. She blow-dried her hair to a lustrous sheen, then applied some light foundation to tone down her red cheeks and some liner to her eyes, emphasizing their grey-green colour. A touch of red gloss to her lips completed her look. After a last glance in the mirror, she added hoop earrings. She was attaching her watch when she noticed the note on the bed.

Christopher had called while she must have been in the shower and Gian-Carlo had answered. Uh-oh.

Tiziana dialed Christopher's number and waited. There was a busy signal. She hung up and paced the room. She decided to call back in a few minutes. She quickly tidied the room and then tried calling again. Still busy. It was now almost 8:00 PM. Gian-Carlo was waiting for her. She could always try later. Tiziana grabbed her purse and was searching for her cotton cardigan when a knock sounded at the door. Thinking it was Gian-Carlo coming to fetch her after her long prep time, she swung the door open with a smile.

Standing before her was a short, paunch-bellied man with thinning hair and watery eyes.

"Are you Tiziana Manoretti?" he asked with a Neapolitan accent.

Tiziana was frozen in place. "Yes ..."

"*Mamma mia!* My mother was right. You are a gorgeous woman!" he said with his eyes widening and greedily devouring her from head to toe. "It's me, Giacomino. My mother said you'd be waiting for me." He glanced at her purse. "Perfect timing, huh? I'm gonna take you out on the town like you've never—"

Tiziana shut the door, locked it, and leaned against it. Once the surprise of finding Giacomino at her door wore off, she began to feel the laughter welling up inside her. She covered her mouth so he wouldn't hear her hilarious snorts.

You've got to be kidding me! This can't possibly be real.

Giacomino pounded on the door. "Hey, *bella mi*, don't be shy. Giacomino will take care of you. C'mon out, now."

The telephone beeped. Tiziana hurried to it. Gian-Carlo's familiar voice asked if she was ready to come down to the reception desk.

"I'll be right there!" Tiziana found her cardigan, swung the purse on her shoulder, and opened the door. Giacomino moved aside as she came out, his face registering surprise and pleasure as he looked her over again. Ignoring the man breathing audibly next to her, she made sure the door was locked before she set out on a brisk walk toward the reception area. Giacomino hurried along, panting as he tried to keep up with her long strides.

"I think there's a misunderstanding." Tiziana spoke over her shoulders as she whipped along the walkway. "I already have a date and ... a boyfriend."

"Wait up, *aspetta,* Tiziana! No need to play hard to get. A boyfriend? But you have me, a real man. Come with me and ..." he was breathing hard now "... I will show you a good time."

Tiziana reached the reception area, where she spotted Gian-Carlo speaking with Massimo. Gian-Carlo turned at the sound of her clicking sandals on the marble floor and did a double take. Tiziana could only imagine what he saw. With hair flying back, she was almost running toward him with a pudgy, panting man in tow.

"Ah, there you are, *amore*! Are we all set to leave?" Tiziana grabbed Gian-Carlo's arm the moment she reached him and hung on. She could feel her face was flushed and her body warm from her hurried walk. Giacomino stopped several feet away and stared with open mouth as he tried to catch his breath.

Gian-Carlo gave Tiziana a questioning look and caught on when she silently pleaded with her eyes.

"*Sì, amore mio.* I've been right here, waiting for you. And here you are looking absolutely gorgeous!" he replied with flourish, obviously enjoying the game she was playing. He swung her in the direction of the doors and raised his hand in a sign of farewell to Massimo and Giacomino.

Once in the parking lot, he looked down at her with a wicked grin and said, "So, are you going to tell me what that was all about?"

CHAPTER 17

Tiziana and Gian-Carlo were still laughing as he manoeuvred his Mercedes Benz CLK 350 convertible into the small parking space in the old quarter of Gaeta. Tiziana had recounted this morning's episode with a full, detailed description of Giuseppe, the taxi driver, and Signora Pepina, the matchmaking mama.

Gian-Carlo cut the engine and opened the door for Tiziana. Taking her hand, he put it in the crook of his right arm, leading her across the street and into a small alley street named Vico del Cavallo. They entered the restaurant Antico Vico, and the friendly manager greeted Gian-Carlo by name. The restaurant was unlike any Tiziana had seen. It had originally been a stable but was now restructured with arch openings and a vaulted ceiling with fresco images. The largest fresco was along a full wall. It was a colourful and eye-catching scene of the supposed last meal of King Francesco II of Bourbon before the siege of Gaeta.

Antico Vico was now synonymous with "right off the boat" fresh fish and seafood platters, along with the traditional cuisine of Gaeta. If the aroma was any indication of the taste of the food, then Tiziana knew she would dine well.

They were escorted to a table where a couple were having an animated discussion. When the woman turned and saw them, her whole face lit up with pleasure. She and her male companion stood to greet them. Gian-Carlo kissed the woman on both cheeks and hugged her, introducing her as Stefania, his cousin. The attractive woman came forward and amiably kissed Tiziana on both cheeks. Gian-Carlo shook the man's hand and introduced him as Urs Wehtingen, Stefania's husband.

"Gian-Carlo told us how he met you by the pool yesterday when we were at the wedding," said Stefania smiling, as they all took their seats.

Gian-Carlo pulled out a chair for Tiziana.

"Yes. I had just arrived, and I decided to enjoy the festive music and the view by the pool."

Stefania had a beautiful, brilliant smile with small, straight teeth and translucent, glossy lips. Her fine-boned facial features were framed by short, cropped blond hair, professionally styled and streaked with chocolate-colored undertones. She had a casual chic look that complemented her refined yet easy manners.

"It's a good thing, too, because he finally stopped moping when he returned to the wedding reception," added Urs with a teasing grin aimed at Gian-Carlo.

Urs was a pleasant-looking man of average build with wavy, shoulder length hair and engaging brown eyes.

Gian-Carlo smiled and addressed Stefania. "Well, was I right? She has the look, doesn't she?"

Stefania was closely observing Tiziana's face. She gently took hold of Tiziana's chin, turning her face both to the left and to the right as she scrutinized her cheekbones, temples, forehead, nose, and eyes. Stefania gave Gian-Carlo a knowing look.

"Oh, yes, I think you're right this time."

"Right about what?" asked Tiziana, clearly intrigued.

"About the perfect face for what we've been searching," Urs said.

"You didn't tell her anything, did you?" Stefania turned to Gian-Carlo, who shrugged and kept smiling.

"You see, Tiziana," Urs explained, "Gian-Carlo is a professional photographer."

"The three of us own a company named PictureMe! Studios. In the last year, we've been working on a special portfolio of all our best photographs," Stefania added.

"But there's one set of photographs Gian-Carlo wants to shoot that will capture the sixties and seventies look of the movie star Emmanuela Del Verde. You may or may not be familiar with her," Urs continued.

Tiziana shook her head, although the name did sound somewhat familiar.

"We still haven't found the suitable model, though," Stefania said.

"Until now," finished Gian-Carlo, looking at Tiziana like the cat that swallowed the bird. Tiziana opened her mouth, but nothing came out. She was stunned. The three friends paused expectantly and then burst into laughter.

They proceeded to elaborate on their project, explaining to Tiziana what they'd accomplished thus far. Tiziana listened attentively throughout the four-course meal that consisted primarily of appetizing mussels, the famous Neapolitan buffalo-milk mozzarella and tomato salad, followed by the delectable main dish of *frutti di mare* linguini served with Muscat Oppidum of Terracina, a chilled dry white wine.

She learned that Stefania was a professional makeup artist and hair stylist, and Urs was a professional costume designer. Together with Gian-Carlo, they started *PictureMe! Studios* ten years ago.

"Why the English name?" asked Tiziana, sinking her teeth into the tender and succulent calamari.

"We work on an international level," said Gian-Carlo, modestly. His cell phone rang just then, and he excused himself before answering it, walking to the back of the restaurant for privacy.

"Who is Emmanuela Del Verde?" asked Tiziana.

"She was an Italian actress in films throughout the late sixties and seventies. Her best films, though, were the ones from the early eighties. She starred with Mastroianni in *La Zingara* and *La Passione d' Esmeralda*, just to name a few of her movies. She was known for the passion and the intensity she brought to the screen," said Urs.

"*La Passione d' Esmeralda* sounds familiar. I think my father has that one in his Italian movie collection."

"Emmanuela Del Verde was also Gian-Carlo's mother and my aunt," said Stefania with a hint of sadness.

Tiziana stopped chewing her olive and stared at Stefania.

"She was killed in a car accident when Gian-Carlo was twelve. She was only thirty-nine. It was the most tragic day of his life. He simply adored his mother. She would bring him with her on the movie sets, and he loved to watch her act. She had a vibrant personality and could make any character she was playing come to life."

"How terribly sad for Gian-Carlo," Tiziana said quietly.

"I think you remind him of her," said Stefania. Tiziana remembered how Gian-Carlo had studied her face when they first met.

"Was she your mother's sister or your father's?"

"Emmanuela was my mother's middle sister. My mother is the eldest. I grew up in Switzerland, where I met Urs and where my parents still live. The youngest of my mother's sisters lives here in Gaeta."

"What about Gian-Carlo's father?"

"He remarried and lives in Rome. Gian-Carlo has a step-brother, Massimiliano, who was married yesterday."

"Oh, I see."

"So, are you going to do the photo shoot or not?" Gian-Carlo's voice came from behind her as he took his seat.

"I've never done this kind of thing before. I have no previous experience modeling. I don't know," said Tiziana uncertainly, wondering if she could live up to their expectations.

"What do you do for work?" Urs asked.

"I work as a mechanical engineering technologist in an engineering firm, usually managing projects in which I oversee the design of machinery used in the production of aluminium and bauxite."

The three friends looked at each other.

"Beautiful *and* intelligent? She's the one," said Urs.

"Definitely," agreed Stefania.

"You owe me for helping you escape Giacomino," said Gian-Carlo, grinning mischievously.

"Giacomino?" said Stefania and Urs simultaneously, turning to Tiziana.

Tiziana moaned and mockingly clutched her heart while Gian-Carlo began telling the tale of Tiziana's nearly arranged marriage.

"Barely arrived and already they want to snatch her away into marriage," said Gian-Carlo, smiling.

Toward the end of the meal Stefania asked Tiziana, "How long are you here in Gaeta?"

"For at least a week. Then I'd like to visit my grandmother in Abruzzo."

"I'm giving a Nia class here tomorrow before I return to Rome. Would you like to join me?"

"What's Nia?" asked Tiziana, wondering if it was an art class.

"It's an exercise class, sort of. It's one the latest movements in the field of fitness. I think you'll like it." Stefania went on to explain she was a brown belt instructor, trained in Switzerland, and one of the first to offer this type of exercise in Rome. Since she was in Gaeta for a few days, she had organized a class for friends who were interested in knowing more about this growing exercise trend.

"I'd love to join your class," said Tiziana, pleased to have been invited.

They left the restaurant at eleven thirty, satiated and content with the evening and the pleasure of each other's company. The night was balmy with a dark, velvet sky sprinkled with glittering stars. They decided to digest their rich meal by walking on the beach. The girls removed their sandals and the men followed suit, rolling up their pants as the cool water lapped at their feet. Gian-Carlo and Tiziana talked about their work, their family, and their childhood, learning more about each other as the night progressed. He was an attentive listener, and it seemed that he could detect her feelings just by looking at her facial expressions.

"Can I ask you a personal question?" Gian-Carlo asked as they strolled behind Stefania and Urs.

"Yes."

"Who is Christopher?"

Tiziana sighed deeply. "That's a complicated question right now." She paused. "Let's just say he's my best friend."

"Your best friend? Ah … you Americans don't know a thing about love. A man and a woman cannot be best friends."

"You've never been best friends with a woman, then?"

He laughed. "Not really."

Tiziana hoped he wasn't laughing at her.

He was still smiling when he said, "Tiziana, it's been my experience that one or the other in the relationship will always tend to view the friendship as more than what it is. If not pursued, those feelings will turn into unrequited love, and that is the worst type of love there is." He stopped talking, and after a moment he said in a serious tone, "It will eventually destroy the friendship."

Tiziana's head was bowed as she listened to Gian-Carlo. She strolled along the beach, her toes digging into the cool, wet sand and her thoughts far away.

"Tiziana," he said softly, taking her hand in his.

She lifted her head and blinked back tears.

"How long have you loved him?"

"I don't know. It just … happened," whispered Tiziana. She had never voiced her feelings regarding Christopher, and until now had not realized how deeply she felt for him.

"How does he feel about you?"

"I know that he … he loves me … as a friend, that is. He's a big part of our family. He's the son my parents never had. We helped him through a rough period in his life when his marriage ended in a bad divorce. So we're close. His sisters are like my sisters."

"Does he know how you feel?" Gian-Carlo was still holding her hand.

Tiziana shook her head.

"It's time to stir the pot, don't you think?"

Tiziana raised questioning eyebrows at Gian-Carlo.

"*Per la miseria!* You Americans are truly clueless," he said, laughter spilling forth again.

Tiziana let go of his hand and put both her hands on her hips. "I'm Canadian, *Signor Italiano.*" She swung a playful punch toward his shoulder, but he moved and began jogging toward Stefania and Urs.

"*Eh, ragazzi,* wait up! I'm being attacked!"

"Not so fast, Casanova!" said Tiziana in hot pursuit.

It was past midnight when Gian-Carlo drove her back to the hotel. They walked slowly on the pathway leading to her room. The buzzing song of the crickets and the fragrant, pungent smell of the garden flowers accompanied them.

"I'm returning to Rome tonight. I'll call you tomorrow regarding the photo shoot, *va bene*?" Gian-Carlo was standing with Tiziana in front of her door.

"I still can't believe I've agreed to do that."

"It'll be fun, I promise. Now get your beauty sleep." He pulled her close and kissed her on the forehead. "*Buonanotte, Tizianella*," he whispered and then was off into the night.

In just a couple days she had aroused the interest of a handsome stranger for a reason she could not fully detect, she had been propositioned for marriage, and she had been offered a modeling job with a professional photo studio.

Her life just kept getting more complicated.

Chapter 18

Tiziana was ready to crawl into bed when the telephone beeped.

"Pronto?" answered Tiziana.

"Tiziana?" It was Christopher.

"Chris! I tried calling you twice earlier, but your line was busy." She felt guilty for not trying to return his call during the evening.

"I've been calling all afternoon. Where've you been? You were out with that guy?"

Tiziana could hear he wasn't pleased. "Yes. I was out with friends. I had a great time."

"You never told me about this guy friend of yours in Italy."

"That's because I met him on Saturday when I arrived. I was sitting by the pool and he was at his brother's wedding here at the hotel, and we started talking and became friends."

"And the next day he's in your hotel room while you're taking a shower? This guy doesn't waste time, does he?"

"It's not like that! You're making more of this than it really is. You don't even know anything about him."

"I know he's interested in you."

"And what's wrong with that? It's not like I have a boyfriend waiting for me back home."

"I'm interested in you."

"Of course you are! We're good friends. But it's not like we're dating, is it? The last time I checked, you cut our conversation short because you were going out with Tracy."

There was silence on the other end.

Christopher finally spoke. "I'm sorry about that. It was unintentional."

Tiziana knew by the tone of his voice that he meant it. "Okay, if you say so." What else was there to say?

"Tiziana?"

"Yes?"

"Do you like this guy?"

"His name is Gian-Carlo."

"You didn't answer my question."

"I like him as a friend. Nothing more." She couldn't explain to Christopher that she felt good in Gian-Carlo's company. He wouldn't understand.

Christopher let out a deep breath. "I'm so happy to hear that."

"Why?"

"Because I'd like to think there's a chance for us."

"A chance? I don't believe in chances, Chris. If you want something to happen, you make it happen." Had she really said that?

Again there was silence. Tiziana held her breath.

"I miss you, Tizzy. You're so far away."

"I'm right here, Chris." Missing her was not enough. She knew a coworker who missed her cat when she went on vacation.

"It's not the same. We're talking over the phone. I want you here with me."

"Right now I need to be here. It feels good to be in Italy, in Gaeta, the town of my birth. I'm enjoying my time off, the sun, the people, and the food. I don't remember the last time I had such a great vacation, and it's only been two days."

"I'm happy you're enjoying your trip, Tizzy, honestly. I was just thrown off when I heard that guy—Gian-Carlo's voice answering your phone. It was the last thing I expected."

Tiziana wanted to change the subject. "I went to the orphanage today," she said, using a different tone.

"Right! I'm sorry, Tiz. I forgot to ask you all about that. Tell me, how did it go?" Tiziana knew she could count on Christopher to be interested in what meant a lot to her. It was one of the many things she loved about him.

Tiziana told him about her meeting with the Mother Superior, how she followed Suor Annunziata to the museum, her encounter with Giacomino's mother, and her escape from Giacomino himself. They talked for an hour, finally discussing different alternatives in her search for her birth parents. It felt like old times.

"Gosh, Tizzy, I wish I was there with you, sharing your experiences."

"And have me miss the opportunity of meeting Giacomino?"

Christopher chuckled. "Right, wouldn't want you to miss that."

Tiziana yawned and was surprised to see that it was after two in the morning. "Oh, my gosh, Chris, it's so late! I need to get my sleep or I'll look terrible tomorrow for the photo session."

"What?"

Shoot!

"Uh, it's nothing, really."

"What's happening tomorrow, Tiziana?" Christopher sounded serious again.

"Well, Gian-Carlo, he's kind of a renowned professional photographer, and his company, which includes his cousin and her husband, very nice people, I met them tonight, well, they're building a portfolio of their best photographs and they want me, of all people, I can't imagine why, to pose as a sixties movie star who apparently I resemble." Tiziana was a little out of breath.

"Yeah, that's nothing, all right," he mumbled.

"We'll talk tomorrow?" asked Tiziana, ignoring his muted remark. "I promise to call back if you don't find me here."

"Sweet dreams, Tizzy."

"Good night, Chris."

Tiziana replaced the phone receiver, sighed deeply, and got into bed. The phone beeped again.

"Pronto?"

"Tizzy?"

"Yes?"

"I just wanted to say … be careful tomorrow."

"I will." A pause. "Chris?"

"Yes?"

"You need to trust me."

"I know. I know. It's those Italian men I don't trust."

Tiziana smiled. "Good night, Chris."

Maybe the pot was getting stirred after all.

CHAPTER 19

Christopher hung up the phone slowly and slouched farther down in his easy chair. He laid his head back and stared up at the ceiling, his legs sprawled and his arms limp on his chest. He needed to think things through. He thought he had it all worked out in his mind, but the distance between him and Tiziana seemed to complicate things. She was thousands of miles away from him in another country, on vacation by the Mediterranean Sea, meeting Italian men who wanted to dine and photograph her. He, on the other hand, was here working long hours and missing the beautiful face of the girl who actually enjoyed listening to the stories of his days on the job site.

Christopher stood up and made his way into the kitchen, where he replaced the cordless telephone. It smelled wonderful. Katherine was whipping up a batch of chocolate chip cookies, another benefit of living with a sister who loved to bake goodies instead of buying them.

"When are those going to be ready?" asked Christopher, eyeing the globs of mixture that Katherine was dropping onto the cookie sheet.

"Six minutes," answered Katherine. She pointed her chin toward the oven. "I think the first batch might be ready, though. Can you check?"

Christopher peeked through the oven's window. "Looks ready to me." He grabbed the oven mitts, opened the oven, and retrieved the cookie sheet.

"You can have as many as you want. I'm making them for you," Katherine said.

Christopher leaned on the kitchen counter and looked at his youngest sister affectionately. "For me? What's the occasion?"

Katherine looked at him from head to toe and tried to hide her smile. He realized his hair was sticking up on ends, probably from raking his hands continuously through it while he'd paced anxiously waiting for Tiziana's call, which never came. His shirt was sticking out of his jeans and he was barefoot.

"You want the give-it-to-me-straight version or the beat-around-the-bush one?" Katherine asked, as she opened the oven and shoved a second cookie sheet into it.

Christopher folded his arms across his chest. "Since when do you beat around the bush?"

"All right. I'm feeling somewhat sorry for you. It became clear to me from observing you this weekend that other girls don't interest you. Why do I say that? Well, Tracy practically threw herself at you, and you dodged so far I thought you were going to sprain a muscle. Then, there was that girl at the Grand Prix counter who gave you V.I.P. treatment, hoping to fish you in, but you didn't bite. The *only* girl who makes your heart beat faster is now in sun-drenched Italy having a good time, and you're finally panicking."

"Finally panicking?" Christopher's right eyebrow shot up.

"And don't you know it. The question is, Chris, what are you going to do about it?"

Christopher pushed himself off the counter and went to the refrigerator. He took out the milk carton and poured himself a cup of milk. He was silent as he returned to stand in the same place, holding his cup and eyeing the golden cookies cooling on the stove top.

"What's holding you back, Chris? You've got to start swimming again, so to speak. So, you nearly drowned with Victoria. That's over and done with. You've dipped your foot in, but it's about time you take the plunge again." Katherine expertly scooped up the cookies with a spatula and placed them on a plate. She pushed the plate toward Christopher.

"Kathy, she's in Italy. And I'm here. I can't talk to her over the phone. I tried and I botched it." He took a cookie, dipped it into the cold milk and devoured it in two bites. "These are delicious, by the way." He took another and did the same thing.

"So, you're giving up? That's not like you. How important is your relation-ship with Tiziana? You think you'll be good friends forever? Eventually, things will change. Either you will be the cause of that change or she will."

Christopher turned to look at his sister and smiled. She sure had a way of getting straight to the heart of the matter. He wiped the cookie crumbs from his mouth and set down his empty cup.

"You should talk. Whatever happened to Matt?"

"He didn't want kids." She shrugged. "Why should I start a relationship with someone who isn't compatible with me? She smiled sweetly at him. "What do you want, Chris?"

He couldn't change the subject. She was too sharp. Her words echoed in his head. What *did* he want?

"Look, Chris, just be sure you're not giving her mixed messages. If Tiziana is the one you want, then tell her. She shouldn't have to guess. If not, then back off, that's all."

Chris looked at his sister closely. "You know something I don't?"

Katherine laughed. "I've got eyes. I know you, and I know Tiziana. That's enough."

Chris looked down at the floor. He was vacillating. Even his youngest sister could see he was struggling with his emotions. He needed to make a solid decision.

"Thanks for the cookies, sis … and for the kick in the butt," he said as he headed for the front door.

"If you mess up, I'm really gonna kick your butt," Katherine said in a low voice, but he heard it clear enough. He smiled to himself. He slipped on his running shoes and was out the door.

Christopher bounded down the steps of his apartment building. The evening was still young. Maybe he could talk Peter into a game of pool. He felt the need to work the tension out of his body. He was tucking his shirt into his jeans and heading toward his truck when he heard his name being called.

"Hey, Chris!" Ten-year-old Matthew was bouncing a soccer ball on his knee. "You wanna come play with us?" Two other boys, Justin and Timothy, were standing nearby, watching eagerly.

Christopher changed direction and began walking toward the trio.

"Don't you boys have school tomorrow?"

"School's almost out. Only ten days left," answered Justin, grinning.

Christopher smiled. He checked his watch. It was half past eight and still light out.

"All right boys, show me what you got!" With lightening speed, Christopher manoeuvred the soccer ball away from Matthew and started kicking it up and down, on his knees and in between the boys' legs, challenging them to take it back.

Half an hour later, after many whoops and kicks and running around, Christopher sent the boys home. They left laughing and jostling each other as they headed to the same apartment building Christopher lived in.

Christopher watched them leave. As he stood on the street, his heartbeat slowing down, a tune popped into his head. It was rhythmic, making him move his hands to a drum beat. Suddenly, he sprinted after the departing kids, up to his apartment, and straight to his room. He took a blank piece of paper and started writing furiously.

CHAPTER 20

Tiziana woke up the next morning with the beeping of the telephone. She moaned and threw the pillow over her head.

I'm supposed to be on vacation and allowed to sleep in.

After five beeps, she groggily got up and answered.

"Tiziana, I woke you, didn't I?" It was Stefania. "*Scusa, bella,* but Gian-Carlo asked me to tell you that the photo session will be postponed to tomorrow. Something came up that he needs to take care of. Did you still want to join me for the Nia class? I'll be giving the class in an hour."

Tiziana had completely forgotten about the Nia class. "Yes, I'd like to try your class," she said, suddenly awake.

"I'll pick you up in half an hour."

"I'll be ready."

Tiziana took a quick, invigorating shower. She pulled her hair into a high ponytail and dressed in a black Nike sport tank top and matching stretch pants. She grabbed her tote bag and threw in a change of clothes, her wallet, and a small towel. She could buy a bottle of water later. Tiziana made it to the reception building just in time to see Stefania pull up in her cute red MINI Cooper.

"So tell me more about Nia," said Tiziana as they sped along Via Lungomare Caboto. The morning air was refreshing through the open windows, while the sun's early rays bathed her in comforting warmth.

"The word *Nia* stands for neuromuscular integrated action, which you will probably forget the minute you start doing it. Simply put, Nia is a holistic fitness program based on the principle of the joy of movement. It's a fusion of various techniques, and it integrates well the expressiveness of dance, which I think you'll really love. The workout is done barefoot, by the way, and you go at your own rhythm and timing, expressing yourself as you move. It's a lot of fun. But beware of one thing."

"What's that?"

"It's addictive!"

Stefania had rented a dance studio at *Il Centro del Movimento Danzarte*, where the class would be held. It was a large, well-equipped room with mirrors, a sound system, and sprung floors. A few women were already there, and Stefania introduced Tiziana as they entered the room. One of the women, a singer-songwriter named Maria, had been to Montreal, and Tiziana struck up a conversation with her. By the time the class was about to begin they were ten in all, nine women and one man, Mauro Giuliani, a hair stylist well known for his artistic hair creations on Rome's fashion runways.

Stefania explained at the outset that today's routine would be focusing on connecting to the sensations of "dynamic ease."

"What this essentially means is that we want to achieve a workout of energetic balance and harmony without the strain of effort or pain. You'll see what I mean as we go along. Remember to move at your own pace," she said.

Throughout the workout, Stefania continuously instructed them to listen to their bodies, to get in touch with their feelings, and then to express these feelings—whatever they may be—directly in their movements.

In the first stage of the routine, Tiziana focused on following the basic simple steps and enjoying the uncomplicated movements of the different parts of her body. She began to be aware of her feelings when the movements called for dynamically pushing against a mountain, whipping something away, or banging on drums. Tiziana flung her arms, whipping and pushing with all her strength. The images of her confrontations in the workplace and recently at home flashed before her, and instinctively she pushed with her arms and whole body to fling them away. This made her feel overwhelmingly liberated and surprised when tears stung her eyes. Then they did the same movements but with ease, caressing the mountain, gently tossing a ball, or tapping lightly on drums.

As the workout progressed, Tiziana began to laugh as her imagination came to life when Stefania told the class to dynamically catch butterflies, then to flutter easily through light clouds. Next, she asked them to swim dynamically in the sea and then fly easily through space, calmly floating away. Tiziana felt like a child again as she lost her initial self-consciousness and danced playfully around the class, past the others, who were moving around in abandon like her. The soul-stirring music encouraged her as sweat trickled down her whole body. She was breathing hard and her heart beat loudly and steadily. Her body felt languid and relaxed by the end of the workout as they finished with stretching movements to soothing musical notes.

Tiziana gulped down the remaining water in the bottle Stefania provided for her just before the workout. She observed the others as they talked about the

Nia workout and chatted with Stefania. Maria walked over and, after exchanging e-mail addresses, kissed her goodbye. Mauro Giuliani came up to her and shook her hand in farewell. His T-shirt was wet with perspiration, and Tiziana tried not to giggle as she recalled him hopping unrestrained during the freestyle part of the workout. She wondered now what she must have looked like, running and skipping around the room, pretending to snatch imaginary colourful butterflies that made her think of summers in the park with her mother.

After the last members of the group trickled out, Stefania and Tiziana left together.

"I can't remember the last time I had so much fun exercising! Actually, it didn't even feel like I was exercising," Tiziana said.

"I know, but wait until tomorrow. You might ache a little everywhere."

"I must admit, it's very different from the usual workouts I do. I felt like a kid again."

"That's good. The great thing about Nia is that there's no such thing as a perfect move. You focus on finding your body's way of expressing itself, much the way children do, with pleasure and joy."

"Thanks for allowing me to experience that." Tiziana suddenly realized just how calm and relaxed she felt. The constant ache in her shoulders, from the strain of working long hours on the computer, was gone.

"I only guided you, *bella*. You allowed yourself to experience the dynamic ease," Stefania replied with her brilliant smile.

They were outside the building and walking to the car when Tiziana spotted a bar where she could buy a bottle of water to quench her thirst.

"Would you mind if we made a quick stop to pick up some water?"

"Not at all."

Tiziana and Stefania entered the bar, where mouth-watering aromas instantly invaded their senses. The smell of cappuccino, biscotti, and plain, white dough pizza topped with olive oil and rosemary, cut into squares and served on wax paper, was so tantalizing they decided they couldn't pass it up.

Tiziana made her way to the commercial wall-to-wall refrigerator at the far left side of the bar, which contained an assortment of drinks. She retrieved two bottles of San Pellegrino Acqua Minerale and was weaving her way back in between the tables to where Stefania had ordered two squares of pizza when a familiar voice stopped her dead in her tracks.

"Tiziana, is that you?" The voice was loud with a strong Neapolitan accent.

Even before she turned around, Tiziana knew who it was. Giacomino strutted toward her while he winked to his buddy, who stood looking on sceptically.

"Ehhhhh, so we meet again, *bella mi*! It's too bad our first date didn't work out, but that's all right. I'm a patient man. No hard feelings, huh? We could give it another try, you know. Giacomino will be there for you anytime you wish, and I mean anytime you wish."

He spoke like a salesman buttering up his client, only without finesse. On closer inspection, Tiziana could see that he wasn't as old as he first appeared. He could be in his thirties, but his unkempt look and watery red eyes suggested the misuse of narcotics. Tiziana almost felt sorry for him. No wonder his mother was desperate to marry him off. She probably thought marriage was the solution to his troubles.

"Uh ... no, thank you. I have to go. *Ciao*." Tiziana turned and went straight to Stefania, who was sitting on a barstool looking amused.

"Hey, Giacomì! You know this *bella ragazza*?" asked the owner of the bar, standing on the other side of the counter. He was eyeing Tiziana, who hadn't changed from her exercise outfit. She imagined what she must look like with wisps of hair escaping her ponytail. Her cheeks were probably two splotches of vivid rose from all the twirling, skipping, and dancing she had done.

"Are you kidding me? We were almost engaged!" bragged Giacomino. "She and my mother had a one-on-one, you know, between women." He gestured like a man who was familiar with the ways of women. "And everything was arranged, right Tiziana?"

Tiziana felt every single eye in the bar on her. She felt hot and could feel her face turning an even brighter shade of red. Gaeta was a small town, where most folks knew each other, and although she didn't really care what they thought, she wanted to set the record straight. Engaged to Giacomino! Obviously, the people in the bar knew Giacomino and were now wondering. Because of his speech they were curious about her relationship with him. She had to attempt to let Giacomino understand once and for all she had absolutely no interest in him.

None whatsoever.

Tiziana faced Giacomino squarely. "No. You couldn't be more wrong. Nothing at all was arranged with your mother. I simply shared a taxi ride with her, and she asked me a few questions. I'm sorry, but as I already told you last night, this is a big misunderstanding. I have absolutely no interest in dating you. And besides, I'm already interested in someone else." Tiziana threw in the last statement in hopes that he would get the picture.

"So it's true about you dating De Medici's son?" asked Giacomino, somewhat deflated.

"What?" Tiziana was momentarily flustered.

"The senator's son, Gian-Carlo, I saw you with him yesterday, all cosy together when you left the hotel. You're his new *ragazza, vero?*"

Tiziana remembered how she had run to Gian-Carlo when Giacomino had pursued her. She turned to Stefania, who looked at her with sudden understanding. If Tiziana denied she was Gian-Carlo's girl, then Giacomino would know she wasn't really dating, thus giving him enough reason to pester her further. On the other hand, if she claimed to be Gian-Carlo's girl, she would be acknowledging in public a rumor that wasn't true.

"We need to get moving, Tiziana," said Stefania, tapping her watch. She slid off the barstool and motioned for Tiziana to follow her.

Gratefully, Tiziana smiled and shrugged at Giacomino. She turned to head out the door when the owner cleared his throat and said, "*Signorina,* I believe you still have to pay for those." He indicated the water bottles in her hand.

"Oh! Yes, of course." Tiziana wanted to hide her head in her large tote bag as she dug for her wallet, promptly paid for the two water bottles, and zipped out of the bar to meet Stefania, who was already waiting outdoors.

"Oh, my goodness! That man doesn't give up!" exclaimed Tiziana as she reached Stefania.

Stefania chuckled and handed Tiziana the aromatic pizza wrapped in wax paper. Tiziana almost forgot the incident the minute she bit into the soft bread. She closed her eyes as she savoured the pizza, remembering she hadn't had breakfast. She opened them, still chewing with relish, and saw Stefania looking behind her at the bar. Through the windows, Giacomino, his buddy, and the owner were all staring at them.

The two women momentarily looked at each other and then burst into hysterical giggles. Stefania quickly put her arm through Tiziana's and steered her toward the car.

"Let's go before they decide to kidnap you," she said.

"Kidnap me? Whatever for?" said Tiziana, continuing to munch on the delicious pizza.

"Ah, *bella*, there's a naivety about you that is so refreshing. We shall try to capture it on photo. It's what makes you so endearing. Gian-Carlo saw it right away, that day by the pool when he first met you."

"Really?" Tiziana had been called many things before, but never naïve.

Stefania and Tiziana chatted easily as they hopped into the car and drove back to the hotel.

"Gian-Carlo has arranged for a taxi to pick you up tomorrow morning at six to drive you to Rome. Bring an overnight bag just in case the shoot lasts for more than one day," Stefania informed Tiziana just before dropping her off.

"Okay, cool," Tiziana replied, beginning to feel excited about her adventure to Rome.

"*Cosa*?" Stefania asked, not fully comprehending.

"It's an expression, meaning 'it's fine,'" Tiziana said, smiling.

Stefania nodded. Then with a kiss and a wave, she drove off into the brilliant mid-morning sun.

CHAPTER 21

From just outside the reception building, through the open doors, Tiziana could see Julia at the front desk checking out the family with the three children who had arrived with her on Friday. It seemed so long ago they had been on the same shuttle bus heading to this hotel.

Tiziana stepped into the cool interior of the reception area. She stopped to say goodbye to the family.

"*Signorina* Manoretti, how can I help you?" Julia asked with a cordial smile.

"I was wondering where I could rent older movies featuring the actress Emmanuela Del Verde."

"Let me get that information for you. Any movie in particular?"

"*La Zingara* and *La Passione d'Esmeralda*, if possible, but any other movie starring that actress will do."

Julia typed on the keyboard of her computer. Five minutes later, she picked up the telephone and dialed the number of a movie rental shop. After a brief exchange that alternated between Tiziana and the clerk on the other end of the line, it was arranged that three movies would be brought directly to the hotel for Tiziana's viewing.

"Thank you so much!" Tiziana said. As to when exactly they were going to be delivered, that was another matter. Italians' view of time was different from North Americans'.

Once back in her room, Tiziana showered and changed into shorts and a tank top. She felt relaxed and calm. Her cheeks had a youthful pink glow and her muscles were still languid. The Nia class had been a revelation. She hadn't realized how stressed she had felt in the last six months. Her work, her mother's illness, her changing relationship with Christopher, and the sudden announcement of her adoption had all weighed heavily upon her.

An image of chasing butterflies in the park with her mother flashed clear and bright in her mind, making her smile. Her mother loved butterflies. When Tiziana was a child, her mother would read beautifully illustrated books about the different species of butterflies to her as they cuddled together in bed.

On impulse, Tiziana picked up the telephone and dialed her home number.

"Hello." It was her mother's tired voice.

"Hi, Mom. Did I wake you?" It dawned on Tiziana as she glanced at her watch that it was a little past 5:30 in the morning back home.

"Tizzy, darling, how are you enjoying your trip?" Although Tiziana sensed her mother was happy to talk to her, her voice was feeble.

"I'm having a wonderful time. I've made new friends, and I love being here. Gaeta is such a charming and picturesque little town. The people are friendly, and the food is delicious."

"I'm glad to hear it. I knew you would love Gaeta. I did. I still remember clearly the day when I came to get you and bring you home," said Chloe, wistfully.

"Mom, how are you feeling? You sound more tired than usual."

"My body must still be adjusting to the meds. I'm not sleeping as well as I used to. Besides, it's the end of the school year, and I'm due for my vacation. Don't worry about me, Tizzy. I'm fine otherwise."

Her mother's work required a lot of energy, especially when implementing behavioural programs with her students. Somehow, though, Tiziana was not convinced this was the main cause of her mother's fatigue.

"Where will you and Dad go for your vacation this year?" asked Tiziana, thinking how much her mother needed it this year.

Chloe hesitated before answering. "We're not certain yet. With everything that's happened, with my health, that is, I ... we haven't decided yet."

Tiziana sat on her bed and listened to her mother's voice, unsteady, tired, and lacking its usual jovial tone. For the last two months, Tiziana had pushed away the gnawing feeling that her parents' marriage was suffering. The tension between them wasn't only about uncovering the adoption issue. Tiziana sensed there was more to it but didn't know what it was.

"Maybe you could rent a chalet up north for a week and take it easy, just the two of you. What does Dad say? What does he want to do?"

"We're not sure yet."

"Oh ... okay. Is Dad still sleeping? Can I talk to him?"

"He's not here. I ... I think he's downstairs."

Tiziana was afraid to ask why her father, who usually woke up around 7:00, was not in his bed at 5:30. There was an awkward silence and then Tiziana said, "Mom, next time I come back to Italy, I'm going to take you and Dad with me. We'll make it our family vacation."

"That would be wonderful, sweetheart."

"I love you, Mom. I'm sorry I woke you. Try to get some rest. I'll call again."

"I love you, too, Tizzy."

Tiziana heard the click as her mother hung up the phone. In the silence that followed, a sudden anxiety gripped her. Something was definitely wrong between her parents, and Tiziana felt a growing anger toward her father. How could he treat her mother this way when she was dealing with a new illness?

Then guilt plagued Tiziana, who had thought only of her feelings when the adoption had been revealed. She hadn't truly thought about what it must have been like for her parents to suffer because they couldn't have children. Going through the decision-making process of adoption must not have been easy, either. Perhaps she should not have come to Italy so soon. If she were home, she could discern what was going on instead of having to guess from a distance. She had no siblings with whom to speculate and share her suspicions and feelings. There was only one person who was close to her parents and with whom Tiziana felt she could discuss such a personal matter.

Christopher.

CHAPTER 22

Tiziana wanted to talk to Christopher. It was possible that he may have noticed or knew of anything amiss between her parents. Tiziana checked her watch. It was almost six o'clock back home, and Chris would be rising for work. On the second ring, he answered with a deep, sleepy voice.

"Good morning, beautiful." The way he said it made Tiziana's heart beat a little faster.

"How'd you know it was me?" asked Tiziana, settling down to a comfortable position on the bed.

"Who else would be calling me at this hour? I was lying here, dreaming about you, when I heard the double ring of the phone. I knew it was you." His voice was lazy and very relaxed.

"You were dreaming about me? Hmmm ... I hope it wasn't a nightmare."

Christopher chuckled softly. "On the contrary, sweetheart, it was one heck of a good dream."

"Well, are you going to tell me what this dream was all about?"

"I'd rather show you. But, since you're not here, I guess you're going to have to wait," replied Christopher, this time sounding more like the teasing friend she knew so well.

"Darn, I hate waiting."

"So do I." He let out a sigh. "So, Miss Supermodel, how was the photo shoot? I'm green with envy at the thought of some other guy photographing you."

Tiziana explained the change of plans and the fun she had during the Nia class. This led her back to thoughts of her mother and the reason she was calling Christopher so early this morning.

"Chris, I need to ask you something important. I just finished speaking to my mom and ... I don't know ... I honestly feel like something is wrong between her and my dad. I can't quite put my finger on it. I think it started sometime before my mom got sick. It's like there's this distance between them. My mom seems upset and sad, and my dad ... well ... like he's frustrated and angry all the time." Tiziana sat up. "Chris, have you noticed anything? Do you see a change in my parents? Or am I just being paranoid here?"

There was silence on the other end.

"Chris, if you know anything, please tell me. I don't like secrets."

Chris let out a long breath. "Yeah, I did notice that things are different lately with your parents. Your dad seems ... distracted and ... well, basically unhappy about something. I went by your parents' place yesterday, after I tried calling you at the hotel, and was told that you left with Gian-Carlo. I was kind of worried," he cleared his throat, "so I asked your parents if they knew him. Your mother certainly didn't, but your father had this strange look on his face. When he told me that he didn't know Gian-Carlo, I ... well ... I think—"

"What? What do you think?"

Christopher hesitated before he said quietly, "I think he lied to me."

"Lied? Why would he lie?" Tiziana was stunned. "I only met Gian-Carlo three days ago by coincidence, and he definitely did not know me or my family."

"All right, but you asked me what I thought, and that's the feeling I got. I could very well be mistaken. Maybe your parents are just going through a rough spell in their marriage. All couples fight about issues they don't agree with. This adoption topic, for instance, it's a big deal in their lives, and they each see things differently. It's not unusual."

"You mean the fact that my mom was so adamant about telling me, while my dad wasn't at all?"

"Right. Things regarding their kids are always a hot debate among parents. The way I see it, your parents both have strong feelings about you and what concerns you, but that's also because they love you and will express it in different ways."

Tiziana rubbed her eyes hard. "Chris, I asked my mom if I could speak to my dad, but he wasn't sleeping next to her. She gave me the excuse that he might've been downstairs, but she didn't offer to go tell him I wanted to talk to him. That's not like my mom."

"So, he may have decided to sleep on the couch last night, and you just happened to call early this morning, putting your mom in an awkward situation, so to speak. If that was the case, your mom wouldn't have wanted you to know, and with good reason."

"I've never seen my dad sleep on the couch," replied Tiziana, this time rubbing the spot between her eyes.

"It can happen, occasionally, when couples are angry with each other, Tizzy. Parents can hide things from their kids when they have to because they don't want them involved or worried, but it certainly doesn't mean they've stopped loving each other."

"Maybe you're right. Maybe I'm making more of this than I should." Tiziana rose from her bed and walked in front of the window. She could see the shimmering waters of the pool. She could hear Christopher starting to move around in his room too.

"You need to get ready for work, don't you?" Tiziana was already somewhat relieved from the anxiety of her parents' situation.

"Yup. As much as I love talking to my dream girl, I have to hit the road before traffic starts. I'm working in the East end today."

"Okay, dreamer, have a good one then."

"The best part of my day will be over the minute I no longer hear your lovely voice, *bella* Tiziana."

"Chris." Tiziana stopped in her tracks. She forgot everything else as Christopher's words echoed in her mind.

"Tizzy, I wish I could burn this phone because the distance between us is killing me. I want you here. I want to look at your beautiful face and tell you things I can't over the phone. I miss you like crazy. I'm counting the hours till you come home to me." He took a deep breath. "But, I'm a patient man. Just promise me one thing."

"Yes?"

"Promise me you won't give your heart away to some charming Italiano."

"Too late. I've already been safeguarding it for someone special," said Tiziana, deciding on the spot to risk telling him what she had been afraid to.

"What?" Christopher whispered.

"That's right. My heart is already taken. It belongs to someone with warm chocolate eyes and blond hair that I'd love to run my hands through. He also does this eyebrow thing …"

"Tizzy!" Christopher said. She could hear him walking around and then heard the shower spray turn on. "Are you serious?" She could see him in her mind's eye, running his hands through his spiky, messy hair—an unconscious gesture when he was restless.

"Very serious, Chris," Tiziana said softly.

"Ah, Tizzy …"

Tiziana felt spurred to continue, now that she had decided to start. After all, she felt he had given her permission by speaking to her like a Romeo. "Oh, and that new cologne you wear, it smells soooo good on you it makes me want to get very close, so close, in fact—"

"Tiziana, please, not over the phone, it's too hard! I'll never make it to work today."

Tiziana giggled. "Oh, all right. I wish you weren't going to work, then."

"Forget work, I wish you were here." He let out a frustrated sigh. "Don't have too much fun without me, sweetheart. I'll be waiting for your next phone call. In the meantime, I'm taking a cold shower."

Tiziana laughed. "All right. Bye, Chris."

"Bye, love." There it was again, that sexy drone in his voice.

The moment the line went dead, Tiziana put her hot forehead against the cool glass of the window. Then, as the extent of Christopher's words hit home, she let out a whoop of joy and exhilaration. Twirling in a pirouette toward the bed, she let herself fall backwards on it.

Was she dreaming, or had Christopher just told her that he was in love with her?

CHAPTER 23

Tiziana spent the rest of the afternoon at the beach, soaking in the heat of the June sun, and cooling off with a long swim in the salty sea. She tried reading a novel, but images of Christopher's face distracted her, making her mind wander. She imagined the moment she would talk to him again, how she would run into his arms when she would see him after two full weeks of absence. She had longed to reveal to Christopher how she felt about him, how wonderful he made her feel! Suddenly, she wished he was here with her.

After a while, the soft crashes of the frothy waves on the sandy shore, the gentle breeze caressing her skin, the whisper of rustling palm leaves, and the lull of the afternoon hour caused her to doze peacefully for almost an hour on the beach. She woke slowly from obscure dreams of her mother running toward her but never reaching her. Then Chris appeared, looking so dashing that she almost didn't recognize him. He opened his arms to her when, suddenly, someone called his name. Turning, Tiziana could see Tracy motioning for him to join her. Chris apologized to Tiziana, telling her he would be back. Then he dashed off. Even in her dreams, Tiziana felt a sinking feeling as she stood there waiting. Then, out of nowhere, Giacomino was next to her, begging her to play a card game of Scopa with her. He no longer had a pot belly, and he appeared to be younger. She agreed to play cards with him, waking after losing two rounds.

Rising from the lounge chair, Tiziana gathered her things and brushed the sand off her legs and feet. The late afternoon sun glinted off the shimmering crystalline sea in a blinding glare. Tiziana put her T-shirt and shorts over her bathing suit and headed back to the hotel. Before going to her room, she stopped by the reception desk and requested the use of the hotel's computer to access the Internet. She wanted to look up information on adoption in Italy as well as the location of the courthouse in Naples, where the next step in her search for her birth parents would take her. Tiziana still held some hope that the Mother Superior at the orphanage would do her part in transmitting her letter, if at all possible. However, she needed to exhaust all her options for the best probability of finding them.

After indicating to Tiziana where the computer was, Massimo pulled out a bag from under the desk and handed it to her.

"The movies you asked for have arrived," he informed her with a smile.

"Oh, thanks! Please add the expenses to my account."

Tiziana dropped the bag of movies in her beach tote. She found her way to the computer, sat down, and typed several key phrases in the Google search engine. She quickly found the information she needed. The city juvenile court that oversaw the handling of adoption cases for the region of Naples was in the city of Naples. She jotted down the address on the back of a business card in her wallet. She wondered if Gian-Carlo had contacted his friend at the municipal court.

As she continued her research, Tiziana read that prospective adoptive parents who wanted to adopt an Italian child must legally reside in Italy and have been married for at least three years.

Tiziana scrunched her forehead in thought. Her parents had been married close to five years when they had adopted her. However, they had never resided in Italy. Or at least she didn't think they had. Or maybe the law had changed since the time of her adoption. She also noted that her adoption had been taken care of fairly quickly, since, according to the Italian government's Web site, it could take up to three years to finalize the whole procedure. Could it be different in the situation of a mother who had made plans to give up her child for adoption soon after its birth?

Tiziana was so caught up with learning more of the details of the legal aspect of adoption in Italy that only the grumbling of her stomach managed to convince her it was time to get going. So she pulled out scraps of paper from her wallet to scribble the names of Web sites set up to aid adopted children who want to find their birth parents. The longing to know who her birth parents were was stronger than ever after having spent a few days in this beautiful region of Italy. Here, in the hometown of her birth, she felt closer to them, somehow. During fleeting moments, as she passed men and women on the streets, she sometimes wondered if one of them could possibly be her mother or her father. Would they cross each other, unbeknownst of the true nature of their relationship? She felt so close and yet so very far from any discovery.

Tiziana returned to her room. The garden was quiet, except for some guests who were heading to the dining room for an early supper. Most Italians dined in their homes or made their way to the restaurants after sundown. Tonight she would order a dish of spaghetti *alla Carbonara*. Her mouth began to water at the thought.

Once in her room, Tiziana wanted to take a shower and order her meal before settling down to watch the movies. But curiosity beckoned her. She retrieved the movies from the bag and decided to give the DVD player a quick check. She familiarized herself with the remote and set up the first movie to play. As it began, Tiziana watched with interest.

Emmanuela Del Verde was certainly a captivating actress. She was very expressive, conveying emotions so convincingly with every feature of her face and with both bold and subtle body language. Tiziana caught certain expressions that made her think of Gian-Carlo. He had inherited her full lips and the same way she curved them, whether in pleasure or disgust. In *La Passione d'Esmeralda*, she played a woman who fell in love with an Indian man, much to the chagrin of both their families. It didn't matter that he was from one of the richest families in India. She was originally from a little village in Tuscany, and they were from two different worlds. Although they tried to make the relationship work, her Indian lover gave in to the pressures of his family and culture, leaving Esmeralda alone, heart-broken. Finally, in despair, she committed suicide.

It was one of those highly dramatic movies with the crescendo music so typically Italian, much like an opera, that Tiziana was bawling by the time it ended two hours later. She felt like a baby, but she couldn't help the feelings of sadness that Del Verde had evoked in her with her riveting performance. The image of Del Verde's face filled with pain when her character discovered her lover's betrayal was still engraved in Tiziana's mind. She was drawn to that beautiful face and could not put it out of her mind. The additional knowledge that Del Verde had died tragically, leaving her young son behind to mourn her loss, brought fresh tears to her eyes.

As Tiziana sat on her bed hugging her knees, still in her beachwear, with fine sand between her toes and salt on her skin and hair, she wondered what on earth had possessed Gian-Carlo to think that she was in any way similar to that larger-than-life movie star.

CHAPTER 24

Chloe dug her hands into the soft, cool earth as she knelt beside her rock garden under the mid-June sun. She gently threw back the wriggling worm that came up with the loose, moist dirt. Styrofoam boxes filled with white begonias, orange impatiens, and rust-colored marigolds sat next to her. She picked up one of the boxes and carefully pried the tender flowering plants from it. Next, she separated the individual plants and began transferring them to the garden. She chose the perfect spot for each one, added new, rich soil and patted it down firmly around the base of the plant on the garden bed.

She worked methodically, finding solace and comfort in the familiarity of the fragrant soil beneath her fingers, in the vivid colors of the flowers, and in the warmth of the sun on her arched back.

Stopping to wipe the sweat from her brow, Chloe took a deep breath. She was more tired than usual, again. The sleepless nights were catching up to her. Her medication—had she taken it this morning? She couldn't recall. She should have rested when she returned from work today, but her bare garden had beckoned.

It was therapeutic being close to nature and the beauty it offered. Here, in her garden, she felt closer to God. She could talk to him about her feelings, her struggles to adapt to her new illness, and her anxieties about the communication barrier that was, once again, causing a widening gap between her and Steve. The one major obstacle to their happiness was the different ways they each dealt with the hard challenges of life. This difference had surfaced early in their marriage when she couldn't get pregnant. She had remained positive, always hopeful, as they explored the various options the medical community gave them at the time.

Steve, on the other hand, had retreated into a cocoon of misery, choosing to escape when things looked hopelessly bleak. Those several trips he'd taken alone to Italy had shut her out from the deep disappointment he experienced at their failure to conceive. They had survived that extremely trying period in their marriage only when Steve had finally consented to adopt. Now, however,

Steve was troubled by the fact that their daughter had been told the one thing he adamantly had chosen to keep a secret—her adoption. He had never elaborated as to why he felt this way, but the years of working with children who did not voice their feelings, but acted them out instead, had honed Chloe's perception. She was keenly observant, gathering insight with patience and wisdom. It was not enough to have this instinctive feeling, to suspect, because ultimately a confrontation would be necessary to deal with the issue. Chloe also knew that the time had come to finally deal with this issue—an issue that was also utmost on Steve's mind.

Just after Tiziana left for Italy, she had overheard Steve on the phone with his brother Maurizio. Against her better judgment, she had approached the door that led to the den from the laundry room where she was and peeked around the corner. Her husband was sitting on the edge of the couch, deep in an animated yet hushed discussion. She couldn't make out much of the conversation in the rapid dialect Steve was speaking. She caught Tiziana's name several times and once even her own. She had quietly moved back into the laundry room to continue folding the pile of socks and underwear.

Chloe gathered her garden tools and stood slowly. Her knees cracked and her back ached, but this physical pain was tolerable compared with the emotional pain she was experiencing lately. She felt as if she was losing her husband again, losing him to the isolated sanctuary he'd built around himself.

After the happy years they had spent following Tiziana's adoption, Chloe had forgotten how much effort, patience, and long-suffering it had taken to be compassionate and understanding when Steve withdrew from her. This time, though, Chloe wasn't certain she had the energy to put up with it. Her efforts to discuss with him their situation and his unfair animosity toward her were thwarted at every turn. She felt worn out and taken for granted. Things needed to change. Her health was suffering. She was heading for a burnout.

A car door slammed, its sound bringing her thoughts back to the present. She turned to see Steve walking toward her, unsmiling, looking fatigued and burdened. He kissed her on the cheek.

"The garden looks nice," he said, looking over the two hours of work she'd spent to make her garden come alive with color. Indeed, the splashes of bright colors among the rocks were a cheerful sight.

"Thank you."

"Here, let me help you with those." He stooped and gently took the cart containing the tools from her hands. He threw in the empty Styrofoam boxes and then hauled the half-empty bag of soil under his other arm while still holding his briefcase.

"C'mon," he said to Chloe as he headed toward the garage, leaving her with nothing to carry.

Chloe followed him. She watched him striding to the garage, tall and strong. A familiar Bible verse came to mind, clear and hopeful: "Love bears all things, believes all things, hopes all things, endures all things. Love never fails."

CHAPTER 25

The taxi arrived fifteen minutes late the next morning. The driver was a quiet, middle-aged man who stayed focused on the road and nothing else. It suited Tiziana just fine; she sat with her head laid back and her droopy eyes shaded by a black cap emblazoned with the Alcore Group company logo. Her muscles ached from the Nia workout and from the swimming she did yesterday.

A little over an hour later, the blare of honking European cars making their way through early morning traffic signaled their arrival in Rome. They seemed to be in the center of the city. The taxi made its way through narrow, cobblestone streets and finally stopped before a glass-fronted studio in a building whose historic architecture would have some of today's architects drooling. The palazzo was of Renaissance style, large and spacious with columns, arches, and intricate mouldings. Three side-by-side poster photographs of fashion models were suspended from the ceiling on display in the large left window. The steel-grey sign on the right window of Picture Me! Studios indicated to Tiziana she had arrived at the right place.

Before Tiziana could retrieve the money to pay her cab fare, a young man sitting behind the reception desk of the studio came forward and unlocked the front door. His blond hair was short with spiked bangs, and he wore a fitted, striped pink shirt with designer jeans. He approached the taxi driver and handed him enough Euro dollars to cover the fare more than sufficiently. Then he graciously opened the car door so Tiziana could step out.

Extending his hand, he smiled and said in a cheerful tone, "*Ciao, Tiziana. Mi chiamo Alessio*. Welcome to Picture Me! Studios."

"*Grazie*," Tiziana replied, wondering again what she had gotten herself into.

The entrance of the studio was modern. The curved glass desk was accented with black, white, and steel-grey office furniture and accessories. It had a minimalist look with clean lines. Occasionally, there was a splash of red: the pillows on the black couch, the tulips on the coffee table, and the binders on the desk.

Alessio offered Tiziana coffee, which he brewed from the espresso coffee machine in the mini marbled bar set up on the right-hand corner. There were also fresh fruit, biscotti, and *cornetti* to accompany her steaming cup if she so desired. She sat on the leather couch sipping her coffee and observing as Alessio returned to his desk to make a phone call. He announced her arrival to the person on the receiving end. Excellent customer service was an important part of the Picture Me! photo experience, Tiziana noted, and she smiled thinking she would not have expected any less from Gian-Carlo.

"I have just informed Flavia of your arrival. She is from Spa Diva Centro Benessere next door. She will be taking care of you this morning before the photo shoot," said Alessio in careful English. He did not look a day older than twenty, but his courteous manner and friendliness were simultaneously professional and endearing. Tiziana finished her coffee and wiped the remaining crumbs from the biscotti off her lips. She wondered what other surprises Gian-Carlo had in store for her.

The front door opened and a woman stepped inside. She greeted Alessio warmly, and when she spotted Tiziana, she immediately smiled. Alessio came around from his desk, kissed her on the cheek, and made the introductions. Flavia Amato owned the prestigious health spa two doors down from the studios. Apart from the immaculate white gold-trimmed aesthetician's jacket worn long over her flared black pants and the sleek chestnut hair pulled back into an elegant chignon, her manners and warmth defined her as an unpretentious, confident person. Her hyacinth-colored eyes were sincere and sparkled with interest in a face seemingly untouched by makeup. Her skin was clear and smooth with a small mole on her upper lip that brought attention to her full lips. Hers was an unforgettable face.

"Gian-Carlo wants to speak with you sometime this morning," Alessio said to Flavia.

"I know. I'll give him a ring as soon as I have a moment. Tell him *mia mamma* sent him her homemade *pizzelle*."

"Are there any for me?" Alessio asked hopefully.

"Only if he shares," Flavia replied, smiling as she escorted Tiziana out of the studio. As they walked the few steps to her spa, Flavia elaborated, "Gianni and I grew up together. When I visit my mother, she occasionally prepares *pizzelle*, which are flat, wafer-like cookies. My mother adds her fig marmalade to form a cookie sandwich of sorts. They're his favourite."

"My grandmother used to make *pizzelle* when she lived in Canada, and she taught my mom to make them, too," said Tiziana, nodding in memory of how good they tasted straight off the griddle.

"*Vero*, Gianni did mention to me that your father is Italian."

Flavia unlocked the door to her large health facility. She led Tiziana into a reception area tastefully decorated in earth tones. It was spacious, elegant, and inviting. On the left, two Natuzzi couches in dark chocolate tones faced each other. Between them was a low table embellished with an oval black bowl containing smooth, flats rocks. On the wall of this section, Tiziana saw a mural fountain, its water trickling down the tiled mosaic scene of a summer garden.

"A gift from Gianni," Flavia explained.

"It's a beautiful work of art."

On the right side of the room was the long, S-shaped reception desk. The spa logo was painted in calligraphy script on the taupe wall behind it. Two empty chairs behind the desk were a testimony to the early morning hour. Flavia's and Tiziana's shoes echoed on the beige- and mushroom-coloured granite floor, which was highly polished, leading the eye to follow it into the narrow hallway. The fragrance of essential oils lingered in the air, and a soothing piano piece was playing from the surround-sound audio system. Flavia opened one of the doors in the hallway into a cozy, honey-coloured room with dimmed lighting.

"I've been instructed to pamper you. Ideally, I would love to have you for the day, but Gianni only allotted me two hours, so I've decided the best thing in such a limited time would be a full-body seaweed exfoliation followed by a Swedish massage. Does that sound good to you?"

Sounds amazing! And kind of intimidating ...

"I've never had that done before," said Tiziana, biting her lower lip and looking uncertainly at Flavia.

Flavia abruptly stopped unfolding the towel that was in her hands and stared at Tiziana.

Tiziana wondered if she was the first to step into this spa who had never been fully exfoliated before.

"I'm sorry. It's just that your expression ... you reminded me of someone," said Flavia, still looking at her intently.

"You mean, I'm not the first to be fully exfoliated?"

"What?"

"Nothing! Whatever you wish to do, I'm all for it."

"*Allora, va bene!* You're in for a treat."

Flavia was right. Tiziana did enjoy the treatment, even though she was totally naked and being scrubbed down by a stranger. Flavia's professionalism and bedside manners were impeccable, putting Tiziana at ease as she expertly manoeuvred the warm, fluffy towels, uncovering gradually and working with gentle but firm hands. She was skilled in her trade and chatted easily with Tiziana, asking general questions about her life in Canada. The calm and relaxing ambiance of the room, followed by the soothing massage, made for an intimate setting. Tiziana found herself disclosing the life-altering events of the last few months—her mother's illness, her adoption discovery, and her feelings for Christopher.

"The most difficult thing is to love someone who takes your love for granted. If your friend has moved on from his past marriage and is now ready to commit, then your relationship will prosper; but if not, it will be like having a third party between you even though she is not physically present. It's the lingering effects of a past relationship that can be intrusive and sometimes even destructive. *Mi spiego?*"

"Yes. Even Gian-Carlo told me that a man and a woman could never be best friends. It would turn into unrequited love."

Flavia stopped her movements for a moment. "Did he? How interesting ..." She resumed the massage without elaborating.

"How long have you known Gian-Carlo?"

"Since I was four and he was six. My mother used to work for the De Medici family, taking care of the household management and helping to raise Gianni since his mother was often away during her filming. And his father, well ... he's involved in politics and is a busy man. Gianni and I often played together as children. After school we would spend hours exploring nature with my older brothers. I was a tomboy, and I followed them everywhere."

Tiziana couldn't imagine the stylish woman as a tomboy. "What was Gian-Carlo like as a kid?"

"He was always getting us into trouble! He had quite the imagination. His mother laughed it off as a passing phase in a boy's life, but not his father. Signor De Medici seemed to disapprove of Gianni's behaviour constantly. In retrospect, I think that Gianni yearned for his mother's attention and would willingly go against his father to attain it." Again, Flavia's hands slowed for a second and then continued.

"Stefania did tell me that Gian-Carlo was very close to his mother and was deeply affected by her death," Tiziana said softly.

Flavia took a deep breath. "Yes. When Gianni and I heard of her accident we were at a friend's home. We were young. I was only ten and he, twelve. Signor De Medici came to get us, and we went directly to the hospital. Just before she died, Emmanuela asked to speak with Gianni alone. She ended up dying in his arms. Afterwards, he was inconsolable. Something changed in Gianni that day. He didn't even want to sleep in his home. He stayed with us for two weeks until his father came to take him home, nearly threatening him when he refused to leave."

"Perhaps it was too difficult for Gian-Carlo to return to a house where he knew his mother would no longer enter. Having no brothers and sisters of his own, he probably found comfort in your family," Tiziana reasoned.

"Yes. He liked being around my brothers, and my parents love him dearly. Emmanuela always said Gianni liked being with me, especially, because I was the sister he wished he had. She lost a baby girl through a miscarriage when he was seven."

"Oh, how sad." Tiziana understood how painful it was to desire a sibling and the loneliness that came with being an only child.

"Emmanuela almost ended her acting career when that happened. She was well along into her pregnancy, and Gianni was absolutely ecstatic for the baby's arrival. Then, she fell ill and went to stay with her sister in Naples. I was only a child then, but I remember Signor De Medici not allowing Gianni to see her, and only once he received news of the miscarriage did he send for Gianni. Gianni never talked about that visit in Naples with his mother except a few years ago. His mother mourned the loss of that baby so fiercely that she was bedridden for weeks, refusing to eat or leave her room. Gianni told me that one night he heard her crying, and so he went and laid down next to her. Then she whispered to him, 'I named her Tiziana. She was so beautiful, your baby sister, *tua sorellina, Tiziana.*' Gianni said he could never forget how she moaned that name over and over again in her sorrow. Then one day, three weeks later, she got up, took a shower, and went back to Rome. It was shortly after this that she starred in *La Passione d'Esmeralda,* winning her worldwide acclaim. It was her best performance to date."

"I can see why. I saw the movie last night and I couldn't take my eyes off her. It's a real tearjerker," replied Tiziana, recalling the intensity of emotions on Emmanuela Del Verde's face.

Flavia agreed. "I began to see the movie in a different light after I found out about the baby girl she lost."

"And now I understand why Gian-Carlo likes my name. He told me so on the first day we met."

"Hmm-hmm," Flavia said distractedly. She completed the massage, washed her hands, and sat down next to Tiziana, who was still lying on the couch.

"Were you also at Gian-Carlo's brother's wedding?" Tiziana asked.

"No. I wasn't close to Gianni's fiancée. I don't think she approved of my close relationship with him, and frankly, I knew she wasn't the right woman for him."

"I didn't think so either after Gian-Carlo told me she went off and married his brother. But their relationship must have caused a rift between you and Gian-Carlo, no?"

"Somewhat."

Tiziana and Flavia stared at each other without saying more. Tiziana wondered if her question had been too direct. She had the distinct feeling that Flavia's feelings for Gian-Carlo were much more than just sisterly.

"Well, how did you like your treatment and massage?" Flavia asked.

"Mmmm. Wonderful."

Flavia nodded and smiled. "Stay on the couch as long as you like. When you're ready to leave, get up very slowly." She stepped toward the door. "I'll be just around the corner, in my office."

"Thank you, Flavia."

"*Prego, cara.* Oh, and that's for you," she said, pointing to a small gift bag in the corner near Tiziana's clothes. She left quietly.

Tiziana lay on the couch for a while, thinking of her conversation with Flavia. The more she learned about Gian-Carlo, the more she liked him. She wondered about the true nature of his relationship with Flavia.

Tiziana began to hear voices in the hallway and noticed the spa was coming alive. She also realized she was getting cold, lying naked under the towels. She rose slowly and dressed. Gingerly, she opened the professionally wrapped burgundy and gold gift bag. Inside, there was a complete miniature line of European body products along with an exfoliation sponge—unlike any she had seen. *How thoughtful of Flavia.*

She gathered her things, opened the door, and went in search of Flavia.

CHAPTER 26

Flavia sat at her desk and looked over the events lists that Clara, her reception-ist, had given her yesterday. She wanted to book the fall conference in Belgium before her calendar filled up. She dropped her pen on the desk and leaned back against her chair. She wondered what Gianni was doing in the fall. Did it make a difference? She supposed it always would.

Flavia thought back to her tumultuous relationship with Gianni throughout the years. As they were growing up, Flavia and Gianni had been known as the inseparable duo, until the year his mother died suddenly. That's when things began to change. Gianni's rebellious behaviour caused his father to send him to a private school in Milan, where his son's tactics stayed out of the prying eyes of the media. Flavia saw little of Gianni—although much to her father's shock, she would occasionally escape by train to meet him—until the summer Gianni was twenty and showed up on her family's doorstep.

That summer turned out to be the most memorable and heartbreaking for Flavia, for soon after it ended, Gianni announced he was leaving. He wanted to explore the world, to get away from his father's controlling hand. Flavia had begged him not to leave her, but there was a restlessness about Gianni, an urge to run away. He was gone for five long years in which Flavia had but a handful of postcards as a witness to some of the places he had lived. He visited her and called. And every time, it seemed that their relationship continued from where they'd left off, but it was not enough.

"He's squandering his time and his money," Flavia's father had said. "Move on with your life, Flavia."

"He'll come back to me," she would say.

After the five years Gianni did return, but his restlessness remained. His life had no direction. There was no career filling his days. It was only when he went to visit a friend in the United States that he felt inspired by a photographer he met there. He had discovered his passion for the art of photography and was driven to pursue it. However, their on-and-off long-distance relationship was beginning to wear on Flavia. She was now twenty-five and wanted to marry and start a family. Gianni had other plans. He was making a name for himself in the world of fashion and marketing. When he gave her no indication he wanted to settle down, she took up work at a prestigious health spa in Tuscany and mastered the best techniques under the tutelage of a smart and ambitious woman. That's when she began dreaming of opening her own health spa.

Gianni eventually opened up Picture Me! Studios and she, Spa Diva. When she started dating Roberto, Gianni's reaction finally confirmed what she had discovered painfully throughout the years about where she stood in his life.

"He's not the man for you, Flavia. You'll never be happy with him."

"He's a good man, Gianni. Besides, he loves me."

With hands on his hips and a brooding face, he replied, "You're making a mistake."

"I'm thirty-two! And you're too busy living your own life!"

"I'm just not ready, Fla, I told you this," he said, his lips set in a firm line.

"No, Gianni," she said, brimming with anger, "you're ready for your photography, ready to search for a person you may never find, but you're not ready to fully share your life with me." She had shaken her head in defeat. "My father was right, I should've moved on with my life a long time ago instead of waiting like a lovesick puppy."

"You've said enough."

Mara Quarantini had entered into Gianni's life, and she and Gianni had gone their separate ways. They had remained friends, but it was a strained friendship. When Roberto had proposed two months ago, she had hesitated. To her horror and that of her family, her decision was influenced by the instincts of her heart, by the feelings that had taken root years ago. She could not consent to marry Roberto.

"Hey, Flavia!" Tiziana's voice penetrated Flavia's thoughts.

"Ah, there you are. Ready for the photo shoot?"

"Ready as I'll ever be."

CHAPTER 27

Alessio escorted Tiziana from the lobby through a wide hallway to the rear, where the studios were located. Two men were creating a set, transporting a cream-colored sofa to the center of the large space and draping it partially with a hanging curtain. Stefania was in the midst of the activity along with Urs, but Gian-Carlo was nowhere to be seen.

"There you are!" Stefania's face lit up when she spotted Tiziana. She had a way of making one feel like the most important person in the room. Pulling Tiziana forward, Stefania introduced her to Nunzio and Domenico, affectionately called Mimmo, the extended team of Picture Me! Studios. They each shook her hand vigorously, exchanged a few words, and returned to their work. The atmosphere in the room was cheery as the men joked and fooled around while they worked.

Stefania led Tiziana to a large dressing room equipped with two large mirrors framed with spotlights above a long bureau fully stocked with makeup, creams, and hair-styling products. Several short-backed chairs were scattered about. To her left, a wall-to-wall rack was filled with an assortment of costumes and clothes with a separate upper shelf for wigs and outrageous hats. The right wall contained floor-to-ceiling black shelves full of colourful accessories neatly organized. Tiziana caught glimpses of scarves, boas, smaller hats, jewellery, hair accessories, belts, and shoes. To the far end of this wall was a door that opened into a bathroom with the typical sink and chair found at hairdresser salons. By the entrance, where they stood, was a small sofa with a side table and a magazine rack.

"We're very excited because we've just landed a contract with Bellini," said Stefania as she walked into the room.

Tiziana's eyes scanned the room with interest, and they were immediately drawn to the wall space between the two mirrors, where a black and white poster of Emmanuela Del Verde hung. It was taken from an upward angle, giving the viewer a partial side profile of her face and shoulders. She looked stunning. Her light green eyes looked into the distance, and her slightly opened mouth hinted at a smile. Tiziana could see reflections of Gian-Carlo in her features.

"Let's see if we can capture that look," said Stefania, following Tiziana's gaze. In the next forty minutes, after Tiziana stripped and donned the thick terry robe provided for her, Stefania washed her hair, settled her in a chair in front of one of the mirrors, and proceeded to style her hair, copying the hairdo Emmanuela Del Verde wore.

"So how do you feel this morning?" Stefania asked.

"Relaxed. Flavia massaged the ache out of my muscles," Tiziana answered, remembering how she had danced in the Nia workout.

"Flavia has golden hands. We all run over to her spa after working hard on a special shoot."

"She's an interesting person. She told me a little about her childhood with Gian-Carlo."

"She and Gian-Carlo are very close. We thought that maybe they would finally get married, but life can be complicated sometimes."

So I guessed correctly about Flavia and Gian-Carlo.

"Maybe Gian-Carlo views her more like a sister since his mother miscarried and his hope for having a sister was lost."

Stefania stopped the blow-dryer and looked at Tiziana in the mirror. "Miscarriage? I never knew my aunt to be pregnant or to have lost any baby."

Tiziana was momentarily caught off guard, but looking at the puzzled expression on Stefania's face, she realized that Stefania truly had no clue regarding any miscarriage her aunt may have suffered.

"Oh, I must have misunderstood. It must have been Flavia's mother who had a miscarriage."

Tiziana did not say much as Stefania finished her hair and moved on to apply her makeup. She mulled over the things Flavia had spoken about. It may not be relevant that Stefania, who was a close family member of Gian-Carlo, did not know about the miscarriage.

She glanced in the mirror and her eyes widened. What a transformation! The eye makeup was bold, outlining her luminous grey-green eyes so they became the focus of her face. Her cheekbones were highlighted with shades of bronzed powder, giving them a sharper contrast, and her full lips were a ruby red with a luscious sheen. Her dark hair was in loose, shiny waves that rippled to her shoulders in a classic sixties look. Instinctively, she looked up at the poster and then stared at herself in the mirror. She could now see a resemblance in the upper facial area, especially the eyes.

"They say we have seven people in the world who resemble us. It looks like you've just found one, *vero*?" Stefania tucked in a loose hair behind Tiziana's ear. Then she rummaged through her jewellery section to find Tiziana a pair of studded earrings.

Once Stefania was completely satisfied with Tiziana's face and hair, she selected a small bottle containing scented and tinted almond oil, a concoction she had put together. She applied the oil over most of Tiziana's body, especially the arms and legs.

"Flavia must have given you the exfoliation treatment. Your skin is silky and smooth."

Next, she pulled out of the rack a black, tight-fitting cashmere dress. It was worn off the shoulders and had a wide waistline belt of the same material emphasizing an hourglass shape. The skirt moulded her hips and fell to just below the knees. A pair of black, pointy high-heeled shoes completed the outfit.

"Gian-Carlo was right about your size," said Stefania, nodding as she studied Tiziana from head to foot.

Before Tiziana could say anything, Stefania opened the door and motioned for her to follow. Tiziana took a deep breath and went out into the studio. Gian-Carlo was standing in front of his Hasselblad camera mounted on a tripod. He wore a plain black T-shirt with black pants and Puma sport shoes. He was directing Mimmo to adjust the position of the panel reflectors and photogenic umbrellas. Tiziana noted the powerful artificial window light and soft boxes. She stood nervously trying not to bite her coloured lips. Gian-Carlo turned and stood still, staring at her for what seemed a lifetime. Then he approached her slowly and continued to stare. The expression on his face was unreadable. His nostrils flared as his eyes searched her face. There was a vibrant energy about him that was palpable.

"*Vieni con me, Tiziana.*" Gian-Carlo took her by the hand and positioned her on the sofa in the center of the studio. From that moment on Tiziana felt like she'd stepped into another world. He spoke to her, indicating how he wanted her to move as he snapped picture after picture. He himself moved with lightening speed. He knew exactly what he wanted from her and succeeded in obtaining the results he desired as he checked his camera and the computer screen, adjusted the lighting, and coaxed different expressions from her. He praised her when she followed his directions precisely, and after a while, Tiziana understood what he was looking for and became more adept at doing it.

Stefania appeared every few minutes to touch up her makeup and hair. Throughout the course of the morning, she changed outfits three times, and the setup changed according to the theme Gian-Carlo chose. He worked tirelessly, and Tiziana admired the easy manner he used with her and the team. It was evident he loved the art of photography and was talented in his field.

By early afternoon Tiziana was showing signs of fatigue, and Gian-Carlo ended the session. She gratefully went into the dressing room, changed into the terry robe, and learned the laborious task of removing heavy makeup. It felt like a mask was coming off. She munched on the platter of food Stefania brought her, appeasing the hunger that had developed after the surprisingly hard work of posing and modeling. Stefania left the studio for an hour. Tiziana could hear the others moving quietly in the back studio. Exhaustion hit her as she lay on the sofa to rest. She fell into a deep sleep as she lay curled up on her side, a lock of hair falling across her face.

Gian-Carlo knocked on the dressing door. When he heard no response, he opened it to see if Tiziana was still there. Upon seeing her sleeping on the sofa, he quietly entered and crouched down beside her. His eyes caressed the sleeping face, whose features he had memorized, and he gently swept the lock of hair back from her face.

He marveled that only three days ago they had met because he had chosen to be present at a wedding he initially would not have attended. After searching so long, it was she who had come to him, from across the ocean no less. She was different from the others, and he knew it because she was the one. He knew because instinctively it felt right this time, and soon he would know for certain. For one thing, although she probably realized he was wealthy, she did not expect anything from him. He'd nearly laughed the evening at Antico Vico Restaurant, when at the end of their meal she'd retrieved her wallet from her purse to pay her share. Only after she noticed Stefania discreetly indicating to her that it was all right did she put it away. She was independent, funny, and smart, and she had responded to their offer to model with modesty. He liked being in her company and listening to her stories about her work and her family. There was a naiveté about her that he found refreshing and alluring.

The only one who knew of his quest was Flavia. He wanted to delve deeper into this matter with her, but since their separation more than a year ago, too many things had come between them. He missed her. He wanted to put his pride aside and crawl into the safe haven of her friendship, but he had left her one too many times.

He looked once more at Tiziana's face. Finally, after so many years, could he put his mind at ease and fulfill the promise he had made to a person he still craved was alive?

Chapter 28

They ended the day with a late supper at Stefania and Urs's apartment, situated in the Trastevere quarter just south of the center of Rome. The apartment was an eclectic mix of family-owned antiques and stylish but comfortable modern furniture. Stefania whipped up a quick meal of *spaghetti con aglio e olio*, a green salad served with crusty bread, and a platter of cheese and sliced fruit.

Tiziana agreed to stay on for the night in their guest room. She wanted to spend the next day touring Rome. She decided this when they'd driven by the monumental Piazza Venezia, the focal point of the city, and then on to Via dei Fori Imperiali, passing by a breathtaking sight—the Colosseum. Outlined in the indigo sky with powerful spotlights, the ancient architectural structure stood out majestic and colossal in the heart of Rome. Tiziana had stuck her head out of Gian-Carlo's car as her eyes devoured the romantic sights and sounds of Rome in the evening.

The center of the city had been alive with zooming cars, crowds of beautiful young men and women sporting the latest fashions, and tourists flocking to the piazzas. She caught glimpses of them enjoying dinner outdoors and listening to musicians entertaining them with romantic Italian songs over the cascading waters of the famous sculpted fountains.

She called Christopher that evening on his cell phone.

"Pierson speaking," he shouted into his cell phone. Tiziana could hear the loud background noise of drills and electric saws. *He must be on the work site,* she thought.

"Tiziana, is that you?"

"Yes, Chris! And guess where I am?" She could hardly wait to tell him.

"Hold on, I can barely hear you." She heard Christopher moving and the work sounds fading a little.

She told him she was in Rome and wished he was with her. She caught bits and pieces of his conversation, and after ten minutes decided to end their shouting match. Christopher had said he'd been happy to hear from her and that he missed her. Tiziana concluded she would have to be content with this for now. Tonight, more than ever, she missed him too.

During his lunch break, in between a mortatella sandwich and gulps of cold water, Christopher told Peter about Tiziana's phone call.

"She's in Rome," he said, biting a chunk off his rapidly diminishing sandwich.

Peter whistled in appreciation. He bit into his own panini and watched Christopher with a sly smile on his face.

"What?"

"You like her, don't you? I mean, *really* like her."

Christopher smiled sheepishly. "Yeah, I do."

"How long have you liked her?"

"Too long before I realized it." Christopher popped the last bite into his mouth.

"Did you tell her?"

"We spoke yesterday morning."

"Oh, boy," said Peter, shaking his head.

"What?" Christopher froze, suddenly wondering if Peter still had feelings for Tiziana.

Peter put a calloused hand on Christopher's shoulder. "Don't worry. I know she's off limits for me. But she's in Italy, man. Italian guys don't waste time, if you know what I mean."

Christopher thought of Gian-Carlo, how he had been in Tiziana's room while she showered. Instinctively, his gut clenched.

"She seems pretty sincere about her feelings for me," Christopher replied. A vision of his ex-wife, Victoria, packing her suitcase for yet another vacation with her so-called friends flashed before him.

"Yeah, I'm sure she is. But she's in Rome, the city of lovers, on vacation, all alone—"

"And your point is?"

"Don't waste anymore time." Peter looked at Christopher, his half-eaten panini momentarily forgotten in his hands. Christopher stared back at his friend. He nodded.

As Peter resumed eating, he said, "Hey, did I tell you about the time my sister went to Italy?"

"No." Christopher started on his slice of chocolate marble cake. He braced himself for another long-winded family story.

"Well, she had this guy she liked over here, but by the time she came back from her trip, she was madly in love with some guy over there whose neck I wanted to wring when I found out. Anyhow, she—"

"Pete, your sister is ten years old."

"My point exactly! You see what I'm talking about …"

The following day, Stefania accompanied Tiziana on a mini tour of the city. They began by visiting the Colosseum, waiting in line for over half an hour inside the stoned arched entrance—a wait Tiziana felt was worth every minute once she stepped into the amphitheatre. She felt suddenly small and insignificant amidst the large ruins both below her and rising above her. She slowly turned and looked all around her at the four orders of the Colosseum's columns, which were partly intact. She and Stefania walked around the amphitheatre, snapping photos in various nooks and shaded arched corners. Stefania proved an interesting companion; she threw in tidbits of history and entertained Tiziana with stories of the photo industry.

Later, as they strolled past the intricately detailed Arch of Constantine—a reflection of the Romans' great building skills—and into the Roman Forum, Tiziana felt transported in time. With a little imagination and the descriptive maps in her hands, she could envision the ruins of broken columns, statues, and walls turning into temples, churches, and Roman political houses, into which the Caesars, emperors, and victorious Roman generals once walked.

Tiziana thought of Christopher, who loved to build with his hands. How he would have been fascinated exploring these famous architectural wonders with her. Maybe one day she would return with him.

After a quick lunch, Stefania headed to work, leaving Tiziana on Via Del Corso, where she shopped to her heart's content. She bought a few skirts and tops on sale along with a pair of patent-leather brown pumps. She allowed herself to splurge on a stunning chestnut brown Nuovedive satchel bag, which even on sale cost a small bundle. It was made of Italian calf leather, stamped to look like crocodile—a worthy investment that would last years and flatter her wardrobe.

Tiziana finally turned onto the fashionable Via Condotti, which led her right to the breathtaking Piazza di Spagna, its steps bursting with colourful flowers up to the Church of Trinità dei Monti. She sat on the steps along with other foreigners, watching the throngs of Italians and tourists milling about. She munched on the fresh coconut and juicy peach she had purchased from a street vendor. She stayed there for an hour, resting and savouring the feeling of having nothing to worry about except what she was going to eat for supper. She struck up a lively conversation with a group of French students, even exchanging e-mail addresses with a young woman who was studying engineering.

At dusk, she wearily disembarked the bus that took her back to the Trastevere quarter and, after getting lost only twice, managed to find Stefania's apartment, where the two women talked fashion as Tiziana unwrapped her latest purchases.

Gian-Carlo arrived an hour later and insisted on driving her back to Gaeta, although she reassured him she would be fine taking the train back. He wouldn't hear of it.

He sped on the highway, driving silently with Zucherro's music to accompany them. He was brooding again, reminding Tiziana of the first time she set eyes on him by the pool at the Villa Irlanda Hotel. Every so often he would turn and look at her without saying a word. She wanted to ask him what was on his mind but refrained from doing so. Instead, she thought of her plans for tomorrow. It would be Thursday, and she needed to go to the juvenile court. They were nearing the end of the week, and she was no closer to finding her birth parents than when she first arrived. She also wanted to visit her grandmother and relatives in Abruzzo.

"Gian-Carlo, have you spoken to your friend at the courthouse in Naples?"

"Yes. His name is Luca Terrucci. You can ask for him, and he should be able to assist you." He pulled a business card out of his shirt pocket and handed it to Tiziana. "Are you going tomorrow?"

"Yes. I should be leaving early in the morning."

"Very well. I will tell him to expect you."

"Thank you."

Tiziana saw that the business card was Gian-Carlo's. It had his studio and cell phone numbers on it. Luca Terrucci's name was written on the back of the card.

"Don't hesitate to call me if you need anything," Gian-Carlo said.

When they arrived at the hotel, he parked his car, walked her to her room, and bid her farewell by kissing her hand.

"*Buona notte, cara*," he said quietly. And then he left before she had a chance to respond.

CHAPTER 29

Tiziana woke up late the next morning. By the time she got organized and took the train to Naples it was early afternoon. She entered the juvenile court with hope and a measure of trepidation. Would they also turn her away empty-handed, or would she get the information she needed?

Tiziana followed Gian-Carlo's advice and asked for Luca Terrucci. However, he was not available to see her at the moment. She was told to wait, and after doing so for forty minutes, Tiziana inquired once again. She was given the same response. The man at the reception was not too accommodating. He didn't smile and went about his work with a bored look on his moustached face. She decided to forgo waiting for Mr. Terrucci since the man could not give her a specific time of availability. Instead, she asked where she could get information regarding legal proceedings for adopted children from Italy. He directed her to another department with yet another reception area, this time with a few people waiting ahead of her. As Tiziana observed the rate of the service, she calculated it would be another forty minutes before she would be served.

She noted the irony that Italians sped, ran through red lights, and honked other drivers out of their way, hurrying along to jobs where service to the public was always in slow mode.

Tiziana finally presented her papers to the woman at the reception desk and was surprised when she took them to an official, Julio Mondi, who called Tiziana into his office promptly. Good! No more waiting.

Julio Mondi was a short man with dark hair and dark eyes. He motioned her to take a seat and began to look over her papers. Turning to his computer, he typed in her name and waited. Tiziana couldn't see the computer screen, but she observed his typing and where his fingers stopped on the documents she knew by heart. She could see he was doing a systematic search by using her adoptive father and mother's names and any other information he deemed pertinent. He kept frowning as he looked at the screen every time after he pressed the Enter key. He put on his glasses and returned to the documents, flipping through them more than once. As he did this, he would occasionally look at her.

"*Un momento, per favore,*" he said at last and left the room.

Tiziana waited another thirty-five minutes. She sighed in exasperation. She'd been here for more than two hours and accomplished nothing! The door opened and Julio Mondi returned with another official, who was tall, grey-haired, and very serious.

"*Signorina Manoretti,*" the second official addressed her in Italian. "Where did you get these documents?"

Tiziana was a little surprised by his forthright manner. "My parents gave them to me," she replied in Italian.

"That would be Stefano Antonio Manoretti and Chloe Allen Manoretti?" he stated, reading the names directly from the documents and mispronouncing her mother's name.

"Yes." Tiziana was beginning to get the distinct feeling that something was wrong.

"Did you know that these documents in your possession are falsified?" His grey eyebrows rose in question.

"Excuse me?" Tiziana's heart slammed against her chest.

"These documents," he waved the papers in the air, "are not legal. They are counterfeit. Therefore, we need to keep you here for questioning. You do realize, Signorina Manoretti, that this is a crime. You may have been illegally smuggled out of the country as a child, perhaps without the knowledge or consent of your birth parents."

For the next half hour, she was scrutinized by two pairs of peering eyes and barraged with questions. She was asked her full name, address, occupation, her parents' full names, address and occupations, how long she had lived in Canada, and how long her parents had lived in Canada. When they began asking information regarding her father's family, Tiziana played stupid. No, she wasn't aware of the exact location of her grandparents in Italy, and no, she did not know her father's relatives too well since she'd only been to Italy a few times. Once the questioning became tedious and too personal and her heart stopped beating hard, Tiziana mustered up the boldness to speak her mind.

"*Signori,* as far as I'm concerned I have done nothing wrong and neither have my parents, who know that I'm searching for my birth parents. After all, I'm the one who came here to *you* with these documents. Therefore, before we proceed any further, I would like to make a phone call."

Tiziana's mind was in turmoil. Although she truly could not believe her parents capable of such an act, she was beginning to question what were the true circumstances surrounding her birth and adoption.

Both men looked at her. Tiziana thought she saw the grey-haired man's eyes narrow.

"*Va bene*," he said and pointed to the phone on the desk.

Tiziana waited for them to leave, but they showed no sign of doing so. She retrieved Gian-Carlo's business card from her purse and dialed the number, praying he would answer.

On the third ring, he did. "*Pronto!*"

"It's Tiziana. I have a problem. I'm sitting in an office at the juvenile court being questioned, interrogated more like it, because they say that my documents are false. I have been here for some time now, and I need you to advise me."

There was silence on the other end. Then he said, "What is the name of the official questioning you?"

Tiziana looked at the grey-haired man and politely asked him his name.

"Giuseppe Cagliardini," he said with authority.

Tiziana repeated the name to Gian-Carlo, who said, "Tiziana, I want you to stay there until you hear from me again, understood?"

Tiziana looked at the two men, whose eyes hadn't left her. "I don't think I'm going anywhere right now. But how will you reach me?"

"Don't worry, I'll reach you," he said with confidence and determination.

Tiziana believed him.

CHAPTER 30

Gian-Carlo was sitting in his father's office when he got Tiziana's phone call. He'd been there half an hour and already he was angry with his father. It was no secret among Gian-Carlo's close friends that he did not get along with his father. As a matter of fact, he loathed him.

Eduardo De Medici was a businessman involved with politics for as long as Gian-Carlo could remember. He held the office of senator in Rome and was known as a proud, hard man whose charm and good looks wooed both men and women alike to support his cause. He was well respected and came from a noble family in Naples, from a long line of ancestors who had built an empire in the olive oil industry. At sixty, he was still physically fit and had his share of discreet affairs, never allowing any of them to interfere with his work or position. The only weakness in his life had been Emmanuela, the woman who had nearly cost him his sanity and his career. She had been strong willed and independent, two traits he had finally broken until she eventually pushed away from him, forever.

Gian-Carlo was pleased to see the surprise on his father's face today when he walked into his office, unannounced. He had thrown a file onto his desk without a word, waiting for him to open it.

"What's this?" Eduardo asked, pointing to the file with his chin.

"I need your opinion."

"Since when do you need my opinion on anything?" Eduardo asked with a hint of sarcasm.

"Well, in this case, *you* are the only one who can enlighten me."

Eduardo held Gian-Carlo's gaze, scrutinizing his son. Gian-Carlo folded his arms and stared right back, giving nothing away. Eduardo picked up the file and opened it. He looked through the series of photographs, scanning them quickly. Then he closed the file. It was not quick enough, though, for Gian-Carlo had noted the hardening of the jaws, the flaring of the nostrils, and the beads of sweat that appeared on his father's forehead.

Eduardo looked up and, to Gian-Carlo's dismay, smiled. A charming, false smile that had no positive effect on Gian-Carlo. "Well, it seems that you're getting quite good in your field. Congratulations."

A pause.

Eduardo then leaned forward and with a look of concern that did not reach his eyes said, "You really miss your mother, don't you? But this obsession with her … it's getting unhealthy, don't you think?" There was a hint of mockery in his words.

Rage began to build up in Gian-Carlo. How dare he turn this around! No wonder his mother had run away from him that fateful night. In her desperation to leave quickly, she had met with death when her car crashed only five kilometres from their home. He had witnessed the fight that night, had heard snatches of their heated conversation. Flavia had rung the doorbell in the middle of it, and he had been reluctant to go with her until Emmanuela had ordered him to leave the house. What happened shortly after he left he would never know for certain because it was two hours later when his father came to get him and Flavia to take them to the hospital.

Gian-Carlo was about to hurl a scathing remark at his father when Tiziana called from the juvenile court. Eduardo turned his chair sideways and stared out the window dispassionately, feigning disinterest. Gian-Carlo knew he was listening attentively to his clipped conversation. The name "Tiziana" was sure to have perked his ears.

"What's the problem?" Eduardo asked after Gian-Carlo hung up.

"None of your business," replied Gian-Carlo, getting out of his chair and marching into the hallway. He dialed Luca Terrucci's cell number and waited.

As soon as he answered, Gian-Carlo barked into the phone, "Luca, have you met with Tiziana Manoretti, whom I referred to you?"

"No. As a matter of fact, I waited for her this morning, but then I got involved with an important case. I haven't heard from her at all. Is she still coming?"

"She's there at the juvenile court being interrogated by Giuseppe Cagliardini because he claims her documents are false. What the hell is going on?"

"Cagliardini, you say? Let me look into it. There … may be a misunderstanding. I'll call you as soon as I find out what's going on."

"Luca, that girl better walk out of that court soon, you hear?"

"I'm on it, Gianni."

"Thank you."

Gian-Carlo hung up and took a deep breath. He walked back into his father's office and found him by the bookshelf next to the door, flipping the pages of a book.

So you couldn't help yourself from eavesdropping.

"I'm leaving. Before I go, I have one thing I want to say to you."

"Just one thing?" Eduardo lifted an eyebrow.

Gian-Carlo looked deep into his father's eyes. "I know your little secret."

He saw fear flash in his father's eyes, and then it was gone. But it was confirmation enough. Gian-Carlo grabbed the folder with the photographs on his father's desk, turned, and left the office.

Eduardo listened to the retreating footsteps until they were gone. "Not for long, my son. Not for long." After all, he was a master at taking care of delicate issues.

He thought of the photographs in the folder he had just seen. His son was well known for his use of shadow and light to create stunning artistic portraits with a sense of drama and mystery. And he had outdone himself again. Eduardo could still see the young girl's face with her smouldering eyes and cascading retro waves partly in shadow, looking far off. It was such a close resemblance to Emmanuela—a resemblance so striking it had jolted Eduardo. Gian-Carlo's photographic skills and keen perception had captured the features of the woman who still haunted his dreams. It was not so much the polished glamorous look or the sultry ruby lips, but the vulnerability in the smoky eyes, the strength of character in her gaze—and then again, the opulent appeal of a simple girl. It was enough to make Eduardo understand that whatever knowledge Gian-Carlo had, it could easily serve as a bomb if he used it against him in anger.

He had waited too long. It was reported to him on several occasions that his son had been seen with a woman known as Tiziana Manoretti. It appeared she was his latest girlfriend, although there was no concrete proof of this except for their being in each other's company. Eduardo even had photographs showing them walking out of the Grand Villa Irlanda Hotel with her arm around his and again walking together on the beach late in the evening. The photo that disturbed Eduardo the most was the one where Gian-Carlo was kissing Tiziana on the forehead just outside her room door.

He whipped around, threw the book in his hands on his desk, and sat once more on his chair. He adjusted his tie, smoothed his hair back, and took a deep breath. He reached for the telephone and dialed with rapid punches a private number in the Supreme Court of Rome.

A deep male voice answered.

"I need a favour," Eduardo De Medici stated calmly.

CHAPTER 31

Luca Terrucci strode down the hallway toward Giuseppe Cagliardini's office. Something was up and he needed to find out what was going on.

On Monday, Gian-Carlo, whom he knew since grade school, had called him and left a message. He had returned Gian-Carlo's call yesterday and hadn't been surprised with the request to verify certain records. This was the fifth time Gian-Carlo asked him to do this. And in every case there had been no records. Terrucci had asked Gian-Carlo what exactly he was searching for. "A woman who I believe may have been adopted" was all Gian-Carlo would offer as an explanation. The difference this time was that Gian-Carlo actually provided him with photographs of adoption documents.

"If you have a copy of the documents, then you already have all the details, and you know for certain she has been adopted," Terrucci had said.

"I'm still missing the names of her birth parents."

"You know that's confidential information, Gianni."

"It's very important to me. The information is for me alone. It's a personal matter."

"It always is." Terrucci sighed heavily.

"You will understand once you get the information. Afterwards, you can be the judge as to whether you want to disclose it to me or not."

Terrucci had been unable to look up the information right away, and now he wondered who this Tiziana Manoretti was. Gian-Carlo had been very upset over the phone, indicating this woman meant something to him.

Cagliardini was not in his office and, after some thought, Terrucci guessed him to be in Mondi's office. He knocked on the office door and was ushered in. Three people were sitting in silence—Mondi, Cagliardini, and an attractive woman he assumed was Tiziana Manoretti. She seemed to look at him suspiciously.

Terrucci came forward and offered her his hand. "Tiziana Manoretti, *vero?* I'm Luca Terrucci. I heard you needed my assistance."

Tiziana stood and shook his hand. "Yes! Thank you. I have come to inquire about how I could locate my birth parents since I was adopted from the *Orfanotrofio Santa Maria Della Fede* in Gaeta. But I am now told that my documents are false and that my adoptive parents possibly committed a crime, that they"—she turned toward Cagliardini—"may have smuggled me out of the country."

Terrucci looked over at Cagliardini and could see that he was hot under the collar. This was a serious accusation, and if this woman had any connection with the De Medici family, the heat would become a blazing fire.

The palpable tension in the room was interrupted by Cagliardini's secretary, who knocked urgently on the door.

She spoke a little out of breath. "Signor Cagliardini, *Judice* Berdinelli would like to speak with you immediately."

Cagliardini excused himself and left promptly. He wasn't expecting a call from Judge Berdinelli and wondered what it was about. Perhaps the judge had heard of his new promotion. What an honor to be singled out by a judge in the Supreme Court of Rome! He increased his pace. Once in his office, he sat down and punched the flashing button on his phone.

"Giuseppe Cagliardini speaking," he said in his most authoritative voice.

"Cagliardini, it's *Judice* Berdinelli. It has come to my knowledge that you have a young lady by the name of Tiziana Manoretti in your courthouse, am I correct?"

Cagliardini froze in place. "Yes, sir."

"I would ask you to please return all documents to her and to stop the … so-called investigation. She is part of a special case that was handled by a different legal procedure years ago, which is why you may have thought the documents to be false. No such thing in our courts, Cagliardini, you understand?"

"Of course, sir, of course, I understand perfect—"

"Very well. Tell the young lady that we cannot help her any further and send her on her way."

"Yes, sir, right away."

"One more thing, Cagliardini. Rest assured that the discreet manner in which you deal with this case will not be forgotten."

"Thank you, sir. You can count on me," Cagliardini replied with renewed confidence.

"*Arrivederci.*" The line went dead.

Cagliardini sat at his desk for a few seconds, trying to absorb what had just occurred. *Judice* Berdinelli's last words rang in his mind. Well, he had better take care of the matter quickly.

On the way back to Mondi's office Cagliardini realized no one other than he and Mondi knew of the investigation under progress with Tiziana Manoretti. So how had *Judice* Berdinelli found out and in such a short period of time? Then he remembered *Signorina* Manoretti had made one phone call. Whomever she spoke to must have taken action.

Now, there remained one question. Who was this young woman, this special case, with connections all the way to the Supreme Court?

Who on earth was Tiziana Manoretti?

CHAPTER 32

Luca Terrucci accompanied a frustrated Tiziana from the courthouse into the gloomy afternoon outside.

"I still don't understand why no one will answer any of my questions," she lamented to Terrucci. "It seems all my efforts are thwarted at every turn."

"These things take time, sometimes years, and there's a lot of effort involved. Your birth parents may have gone through great lengths to make sure you wouldn't find them. Maybe your birth mother was very young, didn't know who the father of her baby was, and has since moved on with her life. She probably has a family or even a prominent career. This kind of discovery for them could cause much pain and problems. Or perhaps they're no longer alive."

"I hadn't thought of that."

"What I'm trying to say is that you may never find them. I have seen many such cases. If you've had good adoptive parents, then consider yourself blessed."

"Yes, I do.... I understand."

"In any case, you're here on vacation, no? Enjoy our beautiful country. Go to the beach, do some shopping ... You are young and beautiful and should be having fun," Terrucci said and smiled at her encouragingly.

Tiziana smiled back, shook his hand and bid him goodbye.

As Tiziana turned to leave, Terrucci's coworker Gerardo was entering the building. Terrucci saw him watching Tiziana's backside admiringly.

"Who's that?" Gerardo asked.

"Hands off, Gerardo. She's a friend of Gian-Carlo De Medici."

"It's interesting you should mention that."

"Why?"

"Because she reminded me of someone, but I couldn't quite grasp who until you mentioned De Medici."

"What do you mean?"

"Don't you think she resembles the actress Emmanuela Del Verde?"

Terrucci's head snapped sideways to face Gerardo. "You think so?"

"Yeah, the way she bit her lower lip just before she left, that sexy expression, you know, that draws you to look at her mouth," said Gerardo, nodding knowingly.

Terrucci turned to walk back into the building, "You're such a nutcase."

Gerardo followed him, defending his case. "C'mon, I know women! And Del Verde was famous for the way she moved and bit those luscious lips …" He continued enumerating all the things he loved about that actress until Terrucci waved him off.

"I've got work to do and so do you. Now move it, and don't bother Leandra on the way to your office." Terrucci chuckled as he watched the gigolo sauntering straight toward Leandra's desk.

Once in his office, Terrucci sat at his desk and began a search using his computer. There was absolutely no record of Tiziana's birth or adoption, and yet the papers had been drawn from this very juvenile court. The signature on the papers was from an official who no longer worked at the juvenile court. He had died a few years back from cancer. Cagliardini had dropped the case like a hot potato the minute he returned from his brief conversation with *Judice* Berdinelli. Even Mondi had registered surprise at this sudden termination in procedure.

Terrucci called Gian-Carlo and explained what had transpired. "I didn't do much. Cagliardini stopped everything after receiving a call from *Judice* Berdinelli. I don't know if that had anything to do with it, but he wouldn't answer any of Tiziana's questions afterwards and ordered me to escort her immediately from the building."

"I see."

"Gianni, I searched everywhere. There is absolutely no record with Tiziana or her adoptive parents' names."

"What about the official who drew the papers?"

"He's dead. Cancer."

Gian-Carlo was silent for a few seconds. He then cleared his throat and said, "Thank you, Luca. I'm grateful. Where did Tiziana go? Did she tell you?"

"She mentioned she was taking the train back to Gaeta."

Flavia's shoes echoed as she walked through the quiet photo studio toward Gian-Carlo's office, situated deeper in the back end of the studio. Flavia knew he liked this corner, where he could be away from the hub in the front. It was his space, where no one disturbed him if the door was closed. Alessio had indicated to her that she would find him here. She slowed her pace as she approached his open door, noticing he was deep in thought as he stared at a folder of photographs. She cleared her throat and smiled at him when he looked up.

Gian-Carlo closed the folder and smiled back at her. "Come in."

Flavia walked in and sat down on the chair directly in front of him. She saw his eyes travel from her face down the length of her and then back up to her mouth.

"I received your father's invitation to his twentieth anniversary bash," she said.

Gian-Carlo continued staring at her. She could see he was scrutinizing her, peering at her in a way that made her wonder what he was thinking. Then his eyes became warm as they lingered on her face. She remembered this look. She swallowed hard and crossed her arms, waiting for him to respond to her comment.

He leaned back in his chair. "Does that mean you're planning to attend?"

"I'd like to."

"With Roberto?"

"Roberto? No ... we're no longer together." Although she hadn't personally told him, she was certain he knew.

"I saw you with him last week."

"Oh," she nodded in understanding, "he came by to pick up a gift certificate for his sister. We went for lunch afterwards." She did not elaborate further. She could see he was digesting this information.

Gian-Carlo's hand reached for his shirt pocket. Flavia hid her smile when his hand came up empty, and he started opening desk drawers searching for what she suspected were cigarettes. She disliked his smoking habit. At last, he stood and reached in his back pocket, pulling out a packet of gum. Tearing the wrapper, he shoved the stick in his mouth and chewed.

"I haven't smoked in three days," he said. "*Cavolo*, it's driving me insane." He ran a hand through his hair.

"You can do it, Gianni."

The smile he gave her lit up his face. Flavia smiled back. For a moment she felt like she was back in the days when he had such smiles only for her, and she couldn't ever imagine they would one day become scarce.

"Well, I was hoping you would take me with you," she said.

"Where?"

Flavia frowned. "To the anniversary party."

Gian-Carlo's smile faded. "I'm not going, Fla."

"You're not attending your father's anniversary?"

"No."

Flavia looked away for a moment. When she turned back to him, her lips were set in a straight line. "Gianni, this anger toward your father ... it needs to end. Stop living your life in the past. Let it go. Even she would not have wanted this ... this bitterness between you and your father."

"I don't need him in my life."

"But you're letting him rule it!" She stood up and paced the room. After a minute of silence, she said, "Let's go together, Gianni. I'll be by your side."

He looked down at his desk. "I'll be away that weekend."

"Surely you can rearrange your pla—"

"It's personal, Flavia. I'm planning a trip to Canada." He looked at her as if daring her to say anything.

She stood rooted as she absorbed his words. "You think she's the one."

"Yes."

What more was there to say? It wasn't the first time nor would it be the last. She couldn't contest his consuming desire to search. It was his mission in life. It ruled out everything else.

Including her.

CHAPTER 33

Tiziana called Christopher from the train station. She was hoping he might be home since his work schedule varied depending on the job he was doing. A little voice answered.

"Hullo?"

"Hello, it's Tiziana. Is this Meredith?"

"Tizzy! Hi, it's me, Mewedith!" Christopher's niece responded with squeals and enthusiasm, immediately lifting Tiziana's mood.

"Well, hello sweetheart! I'm so happy to speak with you. Are you having fun playing with your aunty?"

"We made play dough today. Are you still in a plane in the clouds or did you get off already?"

Tiziana laughed. "I landed a few days ago. And now I'm in a country far away, but I will come back at the end of next week, and then I'll tell you all about it."

"Uncle Chris, too, is taking a plane to Towonto. He's going with Tchwacy. She's nice."

Tiziana thought she misunderstood. One of the trains arrived, its hissing wheels momentarily drowning out the sounds around her. "Uncle Chris is taking a plane with Tracy, sweetheart, is that what you said?"

"Yeah, he's leaving to—"

There was a fumbling of the phone. It crashed to the floor and Tiziana winced.

"Hello?" Katherine's breathless voice came on the phone.

"Katherine, it's Tiziana." She could hear a shushing in the background as Katherine whispered to Meredith, who was now wailing because she wanted to finish talking to Tiziana.

"Oh, hi! How are you? How's Italy so far?"

"Fine. Kathy, Meredith just told me that Chris is going to Toronto with Tracy. Is that right?" She was in no mood for small talk. Not after Chris had acted like her Romeo.

"Is that what she said? No, no, no," Katherine gushed. "She must have over-heard us talking about planes and traveling. Tracy was here and she explained to Meredith how she works for Air Canada and all that. You know Meredith," Katherine said, laughing. "That child has an amazing imagination!"

"Hmm-hmm ... I see." Tiziana felt uneasy. After briefly chatting with Katherine, who kept ignoring her niece's protests to give her back the phone, Tiziana hung up. She walked idly around the train station and then headed back toward the phone booth. This time she dialed Christopher's cell number. After three rings, a female voice answered. It was not the voice she wanted to hear.

"Hello!" Tracy's high-pitched voice came through along with the cacophony of outdoor traffic.

"Hi, Tracy. Tiziana speaking. Is Christopher around?" *And why are you answering his phone?*

"Uh, well ... he stepped out of the truck to pick up something for work. Can he call you back?"

Didn't Tracy realize she was calling long distance? "Not until much later. I'm at a phone booth right now waiting for the train to take me back to Gaeta, so he won't be able to reach me."

"Oh, okay. I'll let him know. He's driving me to work, and he's supposed to return to the job site afterwards."

So he left work to drive you to your office. What a gentleman.

"Okay, bye then." Tiziana hung up before Tracy responded. She didn't care if it was rude. If she wanted confirmation that something was going on, she had it. Christopher and Tracy were together at this very moment. He'd gone out of his way to drive her to work, she was in his truck answering his cell phone, and if anything Meredith said was true, they were also traveling together. That spelled intimacy to Tiziana. Tracy worked for Air Canada and frequently received com-plimentary tickets. It allowed her to travel to Toronto to visit her family and friends. Sometimes Kathy joined her. Was it Christopher's turn to visit her fam-ily, so she could introduce him as her ... *Oh! I can't even say it!*

Ugh! Stop it, Tiziana!

This could be just one big misunderstanding, or so she hoped, although now she was so upset, so angry, she couldn't think straight. It had been a frustrating day, and she wanted to get back to the hotel. She needed to swim in the pool or run along the beach to think things over and sweat the tension out of her body.

By the time Tiziana returned to the Villa Irlanda Hotel, it was evening and pouring rain. She ran to her room, not caring that the rain soaked her hair and clothes and pounded on her face. She fumbled with her key, opened the door, and switched on the lights.

She gasped at the sight before her and covered her mouth to stifle the scream that was on the verge of spilling out.

Someone had broken into her room and left a chaotic mess. Her clothes were strewn all over the floor, her bed was almost stripped, and the contents of her toiletry and makeup bags emptied out. On the mirror was a chilling message written with lipstick: GO HOME TIZIANA.

Tiziana turned and ran all the way to the reception building.

"Massimo! Massimo!" she called out before she reached the desk. Tiziana saw that Massimo was visibly startled to see her barging in, almost slipping on the marble floor, her clothes soaked and her wet hair plastered to her head. He came from around the desk and took her by the shoulders, leading her to sit down on one of the lounge chairs.

"What is it? Are you all right?"

Tiziana was shaking. "Some … someone … broke into my room. My … my things are all over the place … and they … left a message telling me to … to go home," she stammered as she wiped the dripping rain from her face.

Massimo bolted into action. He picked up the phone and made several calls. A few minutes later a woman appeared. She was dressed in the hotel's employee uniform, and Tiziana recognized her from the bar and lounge area.

"Stay with her and have something hot to drink brought over," he ordered just before grabbing his umbrella and heading out into the downpour.

Massimo hurried toward Tiziana's assigned room, and even before he entered it, he could see the mess through the open door. He checked the door itself and noted no forced entry. Whoever did this had picked the lock. He carefully glanced around the room without touching anything. Tiziana's jewellery was still on her bedside table, probably where she'd left it. One of her rings had three small ruby gems set on it and looked valuable. Clearly, whoever had come was not interested in stealing. The intruder must have been looking for something specific.

He then stared at the mirror. The writing on it was large and uneven, making it look ominous. He let out a long breath. There was no mistaking the meaning of the message.

He had a big problem on his hands.

CHAPTER 34

Massimo called one of his friends, a retired *carabiniere* and law enforcement officer, to investigate the break-in. He did not want the police scouring the hotel and its grounds. The Villa Irlanda had its reputation to uphold. Many respected and important people used its facilities and accommodations for their business and leisure, among them the De Medici family. The hotel staff was known for its impeccable service and discretion. In the past, when Massimo's father had served as head waiter, a few famous visitors had graced the hotel with their presence. Marilyn Monroe and Gene Kelly were the most memorable, including their very own Emmanuela Del Verde.

In addition, he surmised that Tiziana was connected to the De Medicis because she was seen often with Gian-Carlo. As to the nature of their relationship, he could only guess, but it was a protective one since Gian-Carlo had instructed Massimo that he was to provide anything to make Tiziana's stay comfortable. If a certain Giacomino came looking for her, they were not to allow him to pester her.

"It looks like whoever was here came to look for something in particular and to scare your guest away," said the retired officer. "Is she from around this area?"

"No. She's a Canadian tourist. A young woman." Massimo did not want to say too much. For some reason he felt the less he said, the better.

"I can see that," said the officer, looking in the direction of the lace bra and panties that were strewn on the floor along with camisoles and skirts. "Have her gather her belongings and change her room, or better still, she might have friends or relatives that would be willing to take her in. Suggest it to her. This case could be minor, or it could turn ugly, and that would be bad for her *and* for you, know what I mean? Especially if you don't want to involve the law."

"*Per la miseria!* We have surveillance cameras, and Franco regularly walks the grounds to verify that everything is fine. I can see who comes and goes. It's not even in the middle of the night, for crying out loud!" Massimo shook his head in frustration.

"Something like this could happen in broad daylight. Sometimes, it's easier that way. Someone walks into the grounds along with a group of guests and goes unnoticed, or it could even be one of the guests, a familiar face that doesn't signal any warning. One thing is for certain; whoever it was knew exactly what he or she was doing. Watch your staff carefully and question them discreetly. They may have seen or allowed someone in without realizing their intentions, or worst-case scenario, assisted with the break-in."

Massimo sighed heavily. "Enough said. I need to get back to my guest before she develops a chill. Things are bad enough as it is."

Massimo returned to the reception, where Tiziana was sitting lost in thought and shivering despite the warm sweater she'd been provided. Before speaking with her, he dismissed Lina, the employee who had stayed with her.

"Tiziana, I will have someone accompany you to your room so that you can gather your things. I don't think anything was stolen. We will change your room location. However, if you would prefer staying with a friend, I could assist you with the required transportation. There's no need to worry about the cancellation of your present accommodations with us, and I have decided to charge you only for a four-night stay. It's the least we can do for the inconvenience you've experienced within our premises."

Tiziana did not move. He could see she was cold. Her face was pale against her dark, wet hair. He hoped she was not one of those fickle females who fainted easily. The last thing he wanted to do was to have an ambulance here. He needed to resolve this problem immediately.

Tiziana looked at Massimo, whose face remained impassive. Why did she get the feeling that he preferred she didn't stick around? Ever since she came to Italy, she got subtly kicked out of establishments. First the orphanage, then the juvenile court, and now here. She wanted to snort with laughter, a hysterical laughter at this hilarious and ridiculous thought. Maybe she should call Giacomino. She pictured him running to her rescue and chastising Massimo as to how such a thing could happen to one of their guests.

"Tiziana. Are you alright?" Massimo was looking at her with concern.

"Uh … yes. Can I use your telephone?"

"But of course!" Massimo went behind his desk and pushed the telephone toward her.

Tiziana called Gian-Carlo's cell number. She was suddenly grateful he had given it to her. There was no answer. She replaced the receiver and stared at the phone. She couldn't go to her grandmother's home in Abruzzo. It was too far and too late in the evening. Perhaps tomorrow. She wondered if the person who had left her that warning message was out there watching her. If she stayed at the hotel, would he break in later tonight when she was alone in her room? She shuddered at the thought. Who would take the trouble to break into her room because he or she wanted her to leave? Did it have anything to do with why she had problems at the juvenile court today?

The telephone beeped and Tiziana jumped.

"*Pronto! Si, un momento per favore.*" Massimo handed the phone to Tiziana. "Gian-Carlo for you."

Tiziana took the phone. "Gian-Carlo?" Her voice squeaked.

"*Si, cara.* Is everything all right?"

Tiziana took a deep breath. "Someone broke into my room, messed up my things, and left me with the message to go home. Massimo offered me another room or the option of providing transportation if I wanted to stay at a friend's house. I was wondering ..."

Suddenly, Tiziana felt strange asking Gian-Carlo for assistance again. He was in Rome and so was Stefania, the other person she had thought of. What could they possibly do to help her but go out of their way once again? What must he think of her, always needing to be rescued?

"Tiziana, are you hurt in any way? Were you in the room when this happened?"

"No, no. I'd just arrived back from Naples when I discovered the break-in. Massimo investigated."

"Give me a few minutes. I will call you back, but stay with Massimo."

True to his word, Gian-Carlo called back less than five minutes later. "Tiziana, I have an aunt who owns a villa there in Gaeta. She will have a room available for you tomorrow when one of her guests leaves. If you are comfortable with the idea of staying at the hotel just this night, then I will make arrangements for someone to take you to the villa in the morning, say around eleven."

"That's fine. Thank you, Gian-Carlo. I'm indebted to you, twice."

"Not at all. I'm the one who's indebted to you. Don't worry too much about tonight. There won't be another break-in. I will speak again with you tomorrow. Now, let me speak to Massimo."

Tiziana handed the telephone to Massimo. What had Gian-Carlo meant by saying he was indebted to her? And what made him so certain there would be no other break-in tonight?

She could see Massimo nodding and glancing her way as he listened. "I will see to it myself."

Massimo ordered Franco to accompany Tiziana to her room and to remain with her until she had packed all her belongings. Once she finished, Franco took her luggage and several other bags, and Tiziana followed him to one of their finest rooms situated in the *Villa* building. After she settled her things in the room, she thanked Franco and closed the door behind him. She sat on the bed, shivering in her wet clothes.

It was going to be a long night.

Franco stood outside the door for a second, his eyes scanning the hallway. When he spotted what he was searching for, he walked toward it. He took hold of the heavy armchair at the far end of the hall and dragged it on the inlaid marbled floor until he reached Tiziana's door. He positioned the armchair in front of it and sat down. He let out a long breath. He wished he had brought the newspaper. Maybe he could sneak down to get it later. He could hear the shower running in Tiziana's room. A door opened across the hallway a few doors down, and a man came out. Franco could see the curiosity in the man's face as he passed by on his way out.

Franco's cell phone rang. It was Massimo. "*Tutto bene*? Everything all right?"

"So far so good. How long do I need to be here? All night?"

"I will have someone replace you at four."

"Who is this girl anyway?"

"Don't ask questions. Just do as you're told. It's always better that way."

CHAPTER 35

Chloe sat in the living room and waited. He was bound to come home sooner or later, and she would wait as long as she had to. It was time to put an end to this charade. Nothing had changed since that afternoon when he had come home and helped her put her tools away. They both went through their days like nothing was the matter, when in fact, there was an old issue to resolve once and for all.

She heard the click of the front door as it unlocked, and involuntarily her heart began to beat faster. She curled her legs underneath her summer skirt with only her pink painted toes peeking out. She placed the book she had barely read beside her. She smoothed the strands of soft curls from her strawberry blond hair that had escaped the low ponytail she wore. Even at fifty-two, she took care of her appearance and was pleased when her husband complimented her.

She watched as Steve entered the hallway, dropped his keys on the table, and sat his briefcase next to it. He started toward the kitchen and stopped when he saw her there on the sofa.

"Tiziana called," she said.

"How is she?" he asked, picking up the mail on the hallway table and skimming through it.

"A little shaken. She had two bad experiences today."

Steve looked up and stopped flipping the envelopes. Chloe could see that she now had his full attention. He threw the mail back on the table, came forward, and sat on the couch next to her armchair. He folded his arms.

"What happened?"

"Tiziana went to the juvenile court in Naples. They informed her that her documents were false. She was detained and interrogated because they thought there was a possibility her adoptive parents smuggled her out of the country. They only let her go without explanation when she called a friend by the name of Gian-Carlo De Medici."

Steve bolted out of his seat. "*Per la miseria*! What kind of *cafoni* are these men to mistreat a young woman who shows up on their doorstep? I knew she shouldn't have gone. I knew it!"

Chloe watched him closely, then in a steely, calm voice said, "Sit down, Steve, there's more."

Steve looked at her. She stared at him hard, determined to finish what she had started. He sat down reluctantly.

"When she returned to Gaeta, she discovered that someone had broken into her hotel room, messed through all her personal things, and left her a message that said 'Go home Tiziana.'"

Steve's face drained of color and his jaws tightened. After a few seconds he said, "She needs to come home. It's not safe there. I'm going to call her this very instant and tell her to take the next flight out."

"No. Tomorrow she will go stay with Gian-Carlo's aunt who has a villa in Gaeta."

"What? No! She will come home!"

This time it was Chloe who bolted from her armchair. "Why? So that she doesn't discover the true circumstances regarding her birth? So that she will never know who her birth parents are? So that she doesn't learn the reason you've kept her adoption a secret all these years?" Chloe's voice kept rising as she released the years of pent-up anger she had buried for the sake of becoming a mother.

"What are you saying, Chloe? Spill it!" Steve stood and faced her squarely.

"Why don't *you* spill it? It's about time you told me the truth! You owe it to me!" Chloe screamed in anger, her petite body brimming with tension as she looked up at the towering man before her. Suddenly, she swayed to the right and clutched the armchair to prevent herself from falling.

Steve lunged to catch her, but instead lost his balance with her. Together they toppled to the right, with Steve pulling Chloe so that she fell on top of him away from the glass coffee table. His strong arms went protectively around her, and his body cushioned her fall. Chloe cried out as the fall jolted her. She buried her head in the crook of his arm and clutched his chest as she released the onslaught of tears that couldn't be stopped.

"Chloe! Did you get hurt?" He turned her over, desperately searching for an injury. "Chloe, please talk to me! Where are you hurt?"

Chloe shook her head wildly from side to side. "My heart," she wept. "You broke my heart." She pounded her clenched fists on his chest.

Chloe felt Steve's body stiffen. Then he buried his face in her neck and said, "Oh, Chloe, I'm sorry. I'm sorry." He held her close.

The tears finally subsided and Chloe stopped moving, laying motionless for a while, listening to her husband's shallow, raspy breathing and the wild beating of his heart against her chest. A ray of hope was lifting her spirit. She wanted to save her marriage. She knew it was possible. He had suffered for his mistake, a mistake of long ago.

"Please, Chloe, don't turn away from me. Don't leave me ... Please forgive me," he whispered hoarsely in her ear.

They had both suffered enough, and it was now time to mend their relationship. Through his words, his touch, and his evident grief, she knew he was truly sorry. She knew he loved her. She had spent some of the best years of her life with him, and despite everything, she loved him fiercely. Slowly she lifted her arms and put them around his shoulders, holding him tight.

"I forgive you, Stefano."

Steve raised his head and looked at her. She saw the intensity of his gaze as he searched her face, his grey eyes filled with sorrow and regret. She gazed back at him steadily. His eyes began caressing her face, and then he placed his forehead heavily upon her chest.

"Oh, Chloe, Chloe, my life is nothing without you," he whispered. He looked up at her again and gently wiped the tears still lingering on her flushed cheeks. "Never again will I push you away. I've acted badly, and I'm truly sorry I hurt you. Don't give up on me."

"I never have."

"*Ti amo per sempre*," he said softly. Then he dipped his head and kissed her passionately, like a desperate man in need of quenching his thirst.

CHAPTER 36

Tiziana woke up in the middle of the night, lying very still under the sheets of the bed.

Something was wrong.

She realized with a start that she did not recognize her surroundings, but then remembered she was in a different room. With that thought, all of yesterday's events, from the juvenile court accusation and interrogation to the break-in and ominous message, came crashing in like a huge wave, engulfing her with a terrible sense of foreboding.

Something had pulled her from the deepness of sleep.

Tingles of fear crawled up her spine as she lay motionless, inexplicably afraid to move.

All of a sudden, she heard it again. It was the same noise that had woken her. Her heart leaped and began beating rapidly against her chest. She lifted her head slightly to peer into the darkness ahead of her. A shaft of light from the hallway stretched under the door into the room. She could detect no movement outside her room. A peek at the alarm clock told her it was 4:36 AM.

A short rumbling sound suddenly disturbed the silence, making Tiziana freeze. Her ears perked up, much like a dog's, and she listened attentively. It came from the direction of the hallway outside her door. Was someone out there?

Silently and stealthily, Tiziana slipped from the bed and began moving toward the door. She couldn't stay lying there waiting. If she was to outwit whoever was out there, it was essential the element of surprise be on her side. She crouched toward the left and groped the floor, relieved to find the umbrella Franco had given her last night. She curled her hand firmly around it, determined to use it as a weapon. She transferred it to her right hand and tiptoed to the left side of the door, so that if someone were to try to open it, she could hide behind it and catch the intruder off guard.

Tiziana took a deep breath and peered through the peephole of the door. No one was there. She peered closer, moving from the right to the left to get a better side view of the hallway.

It came again, a louder rumbling, growling noise that thundered through the silence, propelling Tiziana against the wall. She slammed her hand against her mouth to stifle the outcry of fear.

The terrible sound came from right outside her door!

And it sounded just like … *snoring*?

Tiziana stood unmoving, the pounding of her heart loud in her ears. She waited what seemed like minutes but in reality was a few seconds. The snorting sound came again, beginning low and increasing to a loud growling that suddenly stopped, followed by a whistling rush, a groan, and finally a singsong yawn.

What in the world?

Tiziana mustered up courage and put her left hand on the knob, holding tightly to her umbrella with her right hand. She slowly unlocked the door and gradually opened it. Just below her nose she spied a balding, silvery head that lolled to one side of the solid armchair parked in front of her door. The older man was wearing a hotel uniform, and she recognized him as the gardener.

Relief swept through her so swiftly that it left her weak in the knees. She closed the door gently, relocked it, and padded back to bed, placing the umbrella on the bedside table. So, she had a bodyguard. Gian-Carlo's idea, no doubt.

Tiziana snuggled once again under the covers, but sleep had fled and she was wide awake. The adrenaline still pumped through her system. Her mind played back all the emotional scenes from the previous day. She was convinced her parents had left out an important detail about her adoption. When she had called home and spoken with her mother regarding the strange turn of events at the juvenile court, her mother had listened quietly but reassured her that she hadn't been smuggled out of the country.

"Mom, isn't it bizarre that my legal adoption papers were signed and documented, and yet no record of my birth is found anywhere? How did you and Dad end up with falsified documents? You said you came to Italy to sign them, right? Was it at the juvenile court?"

"It was in an official building, of that I'm certain. I went with your father, who translated everything to me. I trusted I was signing papers to adopt a little baby girl whose birth mother gave her up, and that's what happened. We had no difficulties leaving the country. Our papers were never declared false. As a matter of fact, the same official who dealt with us for the final procedures was kind enough to escort us at the airport."

"Is that standard procedure when adopting in Italy?"

"Tiziana, sweetie, I was so ecstatic to finally become your mother. What difference did it make if it was standard procedure or not? We were initially nervous, as most adoptive parents, to be sure, but it turned out to be a smooth procedure and a happy time for both your father and me."

Tiziana had been more perplexed than ever. She wanted to talk to her father, who had made the preliminary steps. Since the woman had given up her baby, had they gone through a different method of adopting? What had been involved, exactly?

"Can I speak to Dad?" Tiziana asked.

"He's not home yet. I'll let him know you called as soon as he gets in."

"Mom, there's more." Tiziana went on to relate the state of her room when she returned to the hotel. "Nothing was stolen, except for my peace of mind when I read that message on the mirror."

"Oh, Tiziana, now I'm worried. You're there alone, in another country altogether, and I'd feel better knowing you're with family. I'll have your father contact his brother Silvio, in Abruzzo—"

"No need, Mom. Gian-Carlo arranged for me to stay with his aunt right here in Gaeta. I'll be fine there."

"Tizzy, you haven't quite explained to me who this Gian-Carlo is. For all I know, he could be behind all this."

"Mom, you need to trust me regarding Gian-Carlo. But just to put your mind at ease, the hotel staff knows him well. He owns a reputable photography studio, and his father is a senator in the Italian government in Rome. His family is also well known here in Gaeta, and his mother was the famous movie star Emmanuela Del Verde. I think Dad even has some of her movies in his collection."

"Oh … and are you two involved?" her mother asked cautiously.

"No, we're just friends." Tiziana thought she could hear her mother sigh in relief. "Hey, Mom, have you seen or spoken to Chris lately?"

"Uh, I saw him earlier in the week when he ran over here to find out who Gian-Carlo was. He was concerned about what kind of relationship you had with him. He seemed flustered and very jealous. I have never seen him like that. Have you spoken to him since?" There was hope in her mother's voice.

"Yes." Tiziana hadn't wanted to elaborate. "But he's spending an awful lot of time with Tracy."

"Tracy? Oh, no, they're just friends like you and Gian-Carlo are friends, I suppose."

This was food for thought. When Chris had asked her for an explanation regarding her time spent with Gian-Carlo, she adamantly defended herself. She realized she hadn't given Chris the opportunity to do the same. Had he tried calling her back? If he had dialed her old room number, he wouldn't have found her there.

When Tiziana finished speaking with her mother, she had tried to call Christopher both at home, where there was no answer, and on his cell phone, which had been turned off. Next, she informed Massimo at the front desk to transfer her calls to her new room.

As Tiziana lay tossing and turning, trying to fall back asleep, with the occasional muffled snore penetrating the silence of the early morning hours, she thought once more of Suor Annunziata. Before heading off to stay at the villa today, she wanted to go back to the orphanage.

She wanted to speak with the only person who had given her some indication she knew who her mother was.

CHAPTER 37

Tiziana drifted back into sleep and woke up slowly to bright sunny rays peeking through the curtains. The clouds had cleared and, although she wished she could sleep for a while longer, she decided to get up. It wasn't quite eight o'clock yet, but she was starving and wanted to head out early. After a quick shower in the marbled bathroom, Tiziana hurriedly dressed in cream-colored denim capri pants, an aquamarine cotton top that complemented her eyes, low sandals, a pair of long sea-green Murano earrings she had treated herself to yesterday while in Naples, and her new Nuovedive handbag.

Opening the door, she almost walked right into the armchair still placed in front of her door. The gardener was sipping coffee and reading the newspaper. A tray with empty plates on the floor next to him indicated he had already eaten breakfast.

He turned and smiled at her. "*Buon giorno, signorina. Dormito bene?*"

She smiled back. "Yes, I slept very well, thank you. And I heard you did too."

She left him with a puzzled look on his face as she locked her door, wished him a good day, and walked toward the dining room. She ordered a large breakfast of *frittata con funghi, macedonia di frutta*, and a glass of freshly squeezed orange juice. After ending her delicious meal with a double espresso, Tiziana refreshed her lipstick, put on her Dolce & Gabbana sunglasses, and headed to the front desk to ask for a taxi.

Julia spotted her even before she reached the front desk and motioned her over. "You have a message from Mr. Christopher Pierson." She handed Tiziana a small sealed envelope.

"Thank you, Julia. Please call me a taxi while I read this." Tiziana moved to a lounge chair and sat down, eager to read the message. She tore open the envelope. The short note read:

Dearest Tiziana,

I have tried to contact you several times and, to my relief, was notified you had changed rooms when I finally contacted the front desk. It is now too late to call you again, so we will speak another time. I apologize I was unable to take your call earlier today. I promise the next time we speak I will more than make it up to you.

Love, Chris.

Tiziana could see that the note had been printed from the hotel's contact e-mail address with the time reading after 2:00 AM local time. She reread it several times, pleased that Christopher had tried to contact her. She was disappointed he hadn't tried calling after he'd been notified of her new room number, no matter that he would have found her sleeping. She also wondered exactly how he was planning to make it up to her.

"*Ciao, bella*."

Tiziana looked up to see a young man staring at her. His dimpled cheeks broke into a wide smile, and his blue eyes sparkled as he quickly and expertly scanned her from head to toe.

"*Ciao*. Do we know each other?" she asked in Italian.

"I'll be around this weekend, so maybe we'll get to know each other, no?" As if on cue, he turned and placed himself in front of the reception desk just as a beautiful girl walked toward him from the direction of the washrooms.

"Oh, Fabiano," she gushed, "even the washrooms are gorgeous! We're going to have fun this weekend, huh?" She sauntered up to him and put her arms around him. He hugged the girl and simultaneously winked at Tiziana.

Tiziana rolled her eyes. Italian men!

The taxi arrived ten minutes later and, for the second time that week, Tiziana visited the orphanage. A nun she did not recognize answered the door this time. Tiziana asked for Suor Annunziata in her sweetest tone, smiling brightly at the nun. The nun informed her that Suor Annunziata was teaching class at the moment.

"Oh, I understand perfectly. But, I have traveled far to come see her, and I'm leaving today, so it may be the only time I get a chance to say a quick hello. I won't stay long, I promise."

The nun vacillated. "Who shall I say is calling?"

"An old friend," replied Tiziana with another brilliant smile.

"Your name?"

"Oh, I want it to be a surprise. Please, just tell her it's an old friend."

"Very well. Follow me, please."

Tiziana entered the cool, dark hallway and was led into the orphanage to an alcove that was situated on the left side at the entrance of the school section. She had missed it the first time she had visited. The small alcove had rounded walls with three wooden chairs, a wooden cross on one side of the wall, and a framed picture of Santa Maria Della Fede on the other. She was told to wait there. The nun disappeared quietly.

A few minutes later, Tiziana heard the swish of fabric and turned to find Suor Annunziata standing before her. Recognition registered on the nun's kind face the moment she looked at Tiziana.

"Oh, child, you should not have come back here. It would be best if you left immediately," whispered Suor Annunziata, as she looked nervously over her shoulder.

"Because you know something you cannot tell me? I've discovered there is a lot of mystery surrounding my birth and adoption. But you were here when I was born, weren't you? Probably held me in your arms and assisted the woman who gave birth to me—"

Suor Annunziata's face appeared so stricken that Tiziana stopped talking.

"Tell me her name," whispered Tiziana, hoarsely.

"I cannot ... my lips have been sealed for a long time."

"No one will ever know that you told me. I'm returning home next week. Please." Tiziana could hear the desperation in her own voice and was ready to keep supplicating when she saw the nun closing her eyes.

"Please forgive me," said the nun, shaking her head. Before Tiziana could utter another word, Suor Annunziata turned and walked briskly back down the hallway.

Tiziana began to follow her, but then stopped. What was she going to do anyway? Disturb Suor Annunziata during her teaching lesson? It would only attract undue attention and cause the Mother Superior to come marching over and order Tiziana to leave a second time.

With a cry of frustration, Tiziana whirled around and ran back to the entrance. She pulled on the heavy front doors but closed them quietly behind her. No use causing a commotion. She had caused quite a few already.

Suor Annunziata sat in the empty library. She needed to compose herself before getting back to the children. She had put the ugly memory behind her, but ever since Tiziana Manoretti's visit last Sunday, it had resurfaced—and the guilty feelings with it. Now the memory would never go away because she had seen the face of the daughter whose expressions resembled so much that of her mother's.

Twenty-seven years ago, she had assisted a private birth, knowing that the baby was to be given up for adoption afterwards. She remembered clearly the ecstatic look on the beautiful mother's face when she looked upon her baby girl for the first time. In her heart, Suor Annunziata secretly hoped the mother would have a change of heart and decide to keep the child. However, late the next night, a man in a black trench coat and hat pulled low over his face came with a nurse to fetch the baby. Madre Maria had ordered Suor Annunziata to quietly take the baby, wrap it warmly, and bring it to her.

Suor Annunziata reluctantly obeyed and took the baby, who had been sleeping in a crib next to its mother. However, the baby began to cry, and the mother awoke in alarm. To this day, the expression on the woman's face when she realized what was happening still haunted her. Suor Annunziata had clutched the baby to her, frozen in place and torn by what she was doing. The mother, still weak from giving birth, sprang from the bed but fell to the floor from pain. The Mother Superior barged into the room just then and quickly ran to assist the woman, who was desperately trying to get up to get her baby. The woman's eyes never left Suor Annunziata, who stood rooted as she held the shrieking, frightened baby.

"Go, now!" commanded the Mother Superior.

"I can't," whispered Suor Annunziata.

"You must! It is by her own wish that she is giving the baby away. Now go!"

"Not yet! I beg you, no!" said the mother.

"It is easier this way." The Mother Superior was holding the crying mother. "You must not get too attached. Now shush, let's get you back to bed. You are bleeding," she said gently but firmly.

Turning to Suor Annunziata, the Mother Superior repeated, "Close the door and leave immediately."

Suor Annunziata fled then, running with the baby through the dark hallways, praying to God to forgive her as tears poured down her face. She was followed by the unforgettable and lingering screams of a mother frantically calling by name the child she would never see again.

From that night on, the name "Tiziana" would forever be imprinted in Suor Annunziata's memory.

CHAPTER 38

Tiziana walked dejectedly down the road onto the street that would take her to the bus stop. She was oblivious to everything around her: the azure sky, the wind that fluttered her long hair against her face, the warmth of the sun's rays on her back, and the birds chirping happily as they scrounged for food and sang to each other in the verdant trees.

Tiziana thought of Suor Annunziata. She had sensed her deep sorrow, had been surprised by her stricken look. What exactly did she know about the circumstances surrounding her birth? Why were her lips sealed? Was it best for Tiziana not to know? Should she forget the whole search and move on?

"*Buongiorno, signorina.*" Tiziana was startled to find that the woman and child who were walking on the sidewalk toward her had stopped to greet her.

The woman continued, "I wanted to share a promise from the Bible with you this morning." She opened her leather-bound Bible. "It is found in Revelation 21:4, where it says that God 'will wipe out every tear from their eyes, and death will be no more, neither will mourning nor outcry nor pain be anymore. The former things have passed away.' Do you personally think that this promise will come true?"

Tiziana stared at the woman. She was caught off guard. "Uh … well … yes, I think so, if it's written in the Bible." The words recorded in the scripture, although hopeful and comforting, were slow to register in her mind.

The woman discerned this. "You're right. But I see that you are concerned with something else that's on your mind. Are you feeling well? Can I help in any way?" The woman's gentle manner and genuine expression of concern moved Tiziana. She leaned against the low stone wall along the sidewalk and took a deep breath.

"Are you one of Jehovah's Witnesses?" she asked.

"Yes. I am Gilda, and this is my granddaughter, Tina," replied the older woman with a smile. She had coiffed silver-white hair, intelligent eyes, and a presence that commanded respect. Her granddaughter looked like a preteen, about ten or eleven. Tina sported a cute bob cut and had doe brown eyes and a shy smile. She looked neat and fresh in her floral skirt with a white shirt and white sandals.

Tiziana was familiar with Jehovah's Witnesses. Her mother accepted their literature, and she occasionally read the articles in the *Awake!* and *Watchtower* magazines.

"My name is Tiziana. I'm a tourist from Canada, but I was born and adopted right here in Gaeta. I came primarily to search for my birth parents, and I'm not having any success." Tiziana paused, looking off into the distance. "What does God think of adoption?"

"Well, Tiziana," Gilda began slowly, "the Bible does speak of adoption. The most well known case is that of Jesus Christ. Jesus was not the biological son of Joseph, the carpenter, but Joseph adopted and cared for him as his own. I think it's interesting that God entrusted someone else, in this case an imperfect human, to raise his son. As a parent I know this is not an easy thing to do. And Joseph wasn't a rich man, but he was a spiritual man who loved his wife and his family. This is an indication of what God considers as qualifications for good parents."

"There's also Moses," Tina added. "Pharaoh's daughter adopted him and raised him as her own son even though she knew he was a Hebrew."

"That's right, Tina," her grandmother said. "And although it must have been the most heart-wrenching thing his mother did to put her baby in that basket to float along the Nile, it was ultimately to save his life from the decreed genocide against Israelite baby boys. Moses grew up and was instructed in all the wisdom of the Egyptians, the Bible says, and he was the one God chose to lead his people out of slavery."

Tiziana listened attentively. She continued to ask questions and to read along with Gilda and Tina the answers from the scriptures as they expertly flipped through its pages. Gilda's unassuming manner and knowledgeable comments spurred Tiziana to tell her about the day she learned about her adoption.

"I was angry with my parents for not telling me sooner, for keeping it a secret. My father, especially, did not understand my desire to search for my genealogical roots."

"Many adopted children feel as you do," Gilda sympathized. "It's a universal need to know one's roots. And it may be difficult for some parents to understand this for a reason you may be unaware of. But be patient, Tiziana, *cara*, your father will come around."

As they continued to talk, Tiziana lost track of time. Two buses came and went. At one point, Gilda said something that caught Tiziana's attention.

"Sometimes, a person may feel ashamed regarding the assumed circumstances surrounding his or her birth. For example, some may wonder if they were given away because their mother was raped or because her family did not allow her to keep a child out of wedlock. But is the child at fault? No, in God's eyes that child is innocent."

"My mom and dad have always told me that I'm a unique person in God's eyes, and it's how I live my life that matters to him," Tina said.

Tiziana couldn't help but admire this girl, whose intelligence, maturity, and emotional stability belied her young age. "I'm certain they're very proud of you."

Finally, Gilda turned to Ephesians 6:2, which said, "Honor your father and your mother, which is the first command with a promise."

"The term *father* and *mother* here applies to your parents whether they gave birth to you or not," Gilda said gently.

Tiziana nodded. "I'm thankful that I have good parents who love me and have raised me well. This adoption issue is still so new in my life, and I needed to explore it a little more. Talking about it with you has been helpful."

Tiziana's spirit was elevated. She no longer felt dejected, and the day no longer looked bleak.

Gilda and Tina packed their Bibles. "We have an appointment at eleven, so we must leave—"

"Eleven! Oh, my goodness! I'm late!" interrupted Tiziana, looking at her watch.

"Where are you headed?" Tina asked.

"The Hotel Villa Irlanda."

"*Nonna*, isn't that on our way to *Signora* Pepina's house?" Tina asked her grandmother.

"*Signora* Pepina. That wouldn't be the same *Signora* Pepina who has a son named Giacomino, would it?" Tiziana asked with raised eyebrows.

"Why, yes ... do you know her?" Gilda asked.

"Just enough to warn you to be careful she doesn't try to get cute Tina here to marry her desperate son."

Gilda and Tina burst into laughter. Tiziana proceeded to tell them of her adventures with *Signora* Pepina and her son, which brought on more fits of laughter.

Five minutes later they were still talking and laughing as Gilda drove them along Via Lungomare Caboto, her silk scarf around her neck flying behind her and the classical tune of *Arrivederci Roma* playing on the radio.

CHAPTER 39

An English gentleman was waiting at the reception building when Tiziana arrived.

"Tiziana Manoretti?" he asked politely with a pleasant British voice.

"Yes?"

"William Newton. Pleased to make your acquaintance." He extended his hand in greeting. "Gian-Carlo called last night and requested a room for you at our villa."

"Yes, of course!" exclaimed Tiziana, shaking his hand. She carefully observed the man before her. He was a little taller than she with silver streaks in his sandy hair and serious blue eyes set in a handsome face. He wore khaki cotton dress pants and a fawn-colored short-sleeved shirt.

"Thank you for taking me on such short notice, Mr. Newton."

"A pleasure, darling, a pleasure. Please call me William. May I help you with your luggage?"

Julia at the reception desk arranged for Marco, a bellboy Tiziana had never seen before, to transport her luggage from her room. It was done quickly since most of her belongings were packed yesterday. On their way back to the reception building, as Tiziana walked through the grounds for the last time, she suddenly felt sad she was leaving so soon. She loved being a guest at the Villa Irlanda Grand Hotel—the friendliness of the staff, the beautiful historic buildings and their luxuriant surroundings—all had served to make her short stay memorable. She remembered her first evening when she had met Gian-Carlo, and the day Christopher had spoken love words to her as she lay in her hotel room.

Tiziana waved to the gardener. "*Ciao, Signore!*"

"*Ciao, signorina.* Come back soon, *va bene!*"

"Yes, I will!" she promised.

The glistening blue water of the enormous pool looked as inviting as ever, and Tiziana regretted not having taken a dip in it. She spotted Fabiano, the young man she had met at the reception earlier this morning. He was splashing and frolicking with his girlfriend in the pool. He turned and noticed her walking with Marco, who was loaded down with her things.

"*Ciao, bella!*" he called to her. "Leaving so soon?"

"Ah, well, how unfortunate!" said Tiziana, feigning exaggerated sadness.

"Maybe we shall meet again?" He flashed his charming, dimpled smile and then threw her a kiss.

"Maybe," replied Tiziana, waving goodbye. She watched as his girlfriend tugged Fabiano's arm, pouting that he was still looking at Tiziana. But when he laughed and tickled her, she shrieked with delight and scrambled away, initiating a chasing game. All else was forgotten. Tiziana sighed as she moved along, wishing she was playing in the pool with Christopher.

William arranged her luggage in the trunk of his Renault, while Tiziana checked out of the hotel. He was waiting for her by the passenger's side, and he gallantly opened the door as she approached. Tiziana was quiet as they drove away, lost in thought. She wondered who had broken into her room last night and succeeded in his attempt to make her leave. Would she ever find out? Or would it be forever a mystery, just as Suor Annunziata's reason for keeping her lips sealed would be forever unknown? Could the two incidents be related?

Ten minutes later, William pulled up in front an impressive two-storey villa. It was of mustard-coloured stone with white shutters framing three small windows in the upper level and two larger windows in the lower level. The front double doors were painted a matching white. The villa was set amid a lush garden entrance. In the garden's center, a fountain with a statue of a lovely woman holding a water vessel trickled water, its sound both refreshing and soothing. The stone path that led to the villa split and wound around each side of the fountain and met at the portal, while to the right the path branched off, leading to the eastern side of the villa, where a secluded *terrazza* was located.

Tiziana followed William into the interior marbled hallway. It was cool and bright from the muted sunlight streaming in through the white translucent curtains, which billowed gently as the occasional sea breeze entered the open windows. He led her up the staircase to the second floor and set her luggage down in the third room on the east side. It was a large room whose open window allowed the sun's rays to infuse it with its warmth and light. And unlike the standard hotel room at the Villa Irlanda, this resembled a guest room prepared with love and attention.

The mahogany furniture, which included a dresser and two night tables on either side of the queen-sized bed, was shined to a burgundy lustre. Fresh-cut flowers in a crystal vase adorned the dresser. The bedspread was cream coloured with hand-embroidered roses on lace that ran along its border and center.

Matching pillows were piled on the bed, inviting one to sink into their softness. At the foot of the bed was a heavy trunk and on it, a pretty square basket of essential toiletries. Neatly placed in the cotton-lined basket was a toothbrush, toothpaste, a facecloth folded in the form of a fan, cotton swabs tied with a ribbon, a scented soap bar, and miniature bottles of shampoo and conditioner. In the trunk were extra pillows and blankets, kept fresh-smelling with cedar wood chips.

Against the left wall was a low book shelf containing books in various languages. Next to it stood a small round table and an armchair upholstered in a champagne-and-burgundy-coloured brocade. The olive green walls were tastefully decorated with paintings of the Gaeta landscape.

William allowed Tiziana to take in the details of the room before he discreetly said, "I shall take my leave so you can get yourself settled. We usually serve two meals, breakfast and supper, which begins at seven this evening. However, if you are hungry, I can have Giuseppe prepare you a quick lunch. The rest of the information regarding the villa will be found in the top drawer of your dresser. If you have any questions whatsoever, please do not hesitate to ask."

"Thank you, William. This is all so … so very accommodating. I'm very much obliged."

William smiled. "Not at all, darling. Any friend of Gian-Carlo is more than welcome. And lunch?"

"Yes, I will accept lunch a little later if it's not too much trouble." Tiziana wanted to settle in and plan for the next week. She also wanted to call her parents before they left for work.

"No trouble at all. My wife, Caterina, will be returning from Formia later this evening, so you shall meet her then. In the meantime, feel free to roam around and make yourself at home."

He left, closing the door quietly behind him.

CHAPTER 40

Flavia Amato walked through her spa facility to the reception area, keenly but discreetly observing the way her newest aesthetician was greeting her client. She had hired her two months prior and was pleased the girl was dedicated and professional. She would do well. She glanced over at the display case of her complete line of exclusive European products, noticing that the newest addition of anti-aging cream was selling well. She made a mental note to remind Clara to stock the shelf and—were those fingerprint smudges on the glass?—to wipe the glass clean.

Flavia took pride in her business. It had taken years of hard work to achieve this prestigious level in her commerce. The competition was fierce, especially in a country where fashion and beauty reigned. She owed part of her success to her mother, a woman who encouraged Flavia to pursue high goals without being pushy or greedily ambitious. Her mother had taught her how to deal with people, with utmost respect and interest, no matter what their station in life. When introduced to someone, Flavia memorized the person's name and listened carefully. She paid particular attention to detail, and this served her well as she served her customers. She knew their needs and provided excellent service based on what the clientele desired and her extensive knowledge of the field. And she meticulously followed up, gaining a loyal clientele throughout the years.

Flavia stopped at the reception area, adjusted one of the leather couches so it was perfectly aligned to the one directly in front of it, and straightened the magazines on the rack. She glanced down on the low table and noticed an article in the open *Gente* magazine that caught her interest. Picking it up, she saw it was a piece that compared swimsuits worn by actresses in the past with those today that were known to set fashion trends. The article focused more on the psychological reason why these women were trendsetters than on the fashion of the swimwear itself. It was a fascinating read. Once Flavia started she was reluctant to stop, and so she sat down on the couch to continue.

The photograph that interested her the most was that of Emmanuela Del Verde. She was wearing a fiery-coloured swimsuit that emphasized her curvaceous body. Photographed in a half-lying, half-sitting position, with her head thrown back in laughter, the caption read how Emmanuela's vibrant personality made fiery red a popular color that year. Flavia looked over the picture and noticed something about Emmanuela she had never seen before. She scrutinized the photo further and suddenly sat up straighter. Could it mean anything?

"Clara," she said to the girl sitting behind the reception desk, "I'm going to the photo studio. Call me if you need me."

Flavia walked the few steps to the photo studio next door and went in with the *Gente* magazine in her hands. "Is he shooting?" she said, addressing Alessio. He nodded promptly and continued speaking on the telephone.

Flavia went into the back and spotted Gian-Carlo talking to a model. He readjusted her position and snapped a few more pictures. He scanned the computer screen and nodded to the model. It was late afternoon, and Flavia could see he was wrapping up the shoot. After the team dispersed, Flavia approached Gian-Carlo.

"Gianni, I need to show you something."

Gian-Carlo looked at her and then wordlessly moved toward his office. Flavia discerned he was tired or unhappy about something. She noted the way he closed the door of his office, leaned against his desk, and folded his arms, waiting for her to speak. She sensed he was in a pensive, dark mood again.

She opened the magazine to the photo of Emmanuela and showed it to Gian-Carlo. "Did your mother have a pink birthmark on her left upper thigh in the form of a triangle?"

Gian-Carlo slowly took the magazine from Flavia and zeroed in on the photo of his late mother. "I don't remember. Why?"

"Do you have a magnifying glass? I need to look at this closer."

Flavia watched as he studied her face momentarily, and then went around his desk to open the top center drawer to retrieve the magnifying glass she'd seen him use occasionally when his eyes suspected a flaw on a photograph. Flavia felt his penetrating gaze as she took it from him, sat at his desk, and pulled the halogen light closer to her. She scrutinized the birthmark, which was barely perceptible.

"Gianni, look here and tell me what you see."

Gian-Carlo came closer to the desk, stooped down next to Flavia, and looked through the magnifying glass. "I see a rosy birthmark in the shape of a crooked triangle. And so?"

"And so, would it be reasonable to think that this birthmark might be hereditary?"

"I doubt it," he said with a shrug, "but it would be a remarkable coincidence.

"I saw this same-looking birthmark in the same place on someone's left upper thigh."

Gian-Carlo's face was inches away from Flavia's. "Whose thigh?"

Flavia did not speak. She was gazing into his green eyes, observing the fine lines that were now perceptible around them, the stubble beginning to show after a long day at work, the hard line of his jaw, the well-defined lips.

"Whose thigh, Flavia?"

She answered his question indirectly. "I think your search may be over, Gianni."

He frowned at her, and Flavia watched as comprehension of what her statement meant dawned on him. He looked once more at the photograph and then back at her.

"You think it's possible."

"More so than all the other ones." Flavia remembered how in the beginning they had searched together, but as the years passed and his quest became an obsession, it was harder to keep up with him. She had represented his voice of reason many times throughout the years; nevertheless, the past pained him and had driven him to venture in faraway lands. She had been patient, knowing his motive. Her love was strong; still, her self-respect screamed for acknowledgement. She was loyal because, throughout their lifetime, he had looked out for her, sometimes more so than her brothers. He had taken a personal interest in her business, assisting in its birth and growth when it was fragile and new. He was her best friend, the only man she would ever marry.

The biggest blow had been Mara, the supermodel he had dated and who had tried to convince him to marry her. A glimmer of hope had resurfaced only when he had chosen not to pursue that relationship any longer, showing up at Flavia's doorstep to announce this turn of events and then driving away with little explanation. That had been the deciding factor in her refusal of Roberto's marriage proposal.

Gian-Carlo went to his filing cabinet and retrieved a heavy folder, which he handed to Flavia. She opened it slowly and began to look through the photographs that were in it. She browsed and peered and inspected for a long time. Finally, she looked up at him, and he raised both eyebrows in response.

"Okay," she began, getting down to business, "has anyone else seen these?"

He nodded. "My father."

"And?"

Gian-Carlo pulled a chair next to Flavia and started to share with her what he knew and suspected. They spoke for half an hour, going through possible ways to get more information. Flavia felt his excitement build as they talked. At one point, Gian-Carlo stopped talking and gazed at her. His look was so intense, so penetrating, she felt he could see right into her mind. He stood and pulled her up out of the chair. Holding her by the shoulders, he stared into her blue eyes and said, "Flavia …" before he drew her to himself, holding her tightly.

He didn't even give her a chance to catch her breath before he pulled away and said, "Flavia, will you have dinner with me? Tonight? I want to take you someplace I've been planning to for … a while."

Flavia stared back at him. "Yes."

Later that evening, Gian-Carlo and Flavia were zooming in his Mercedes along the autoroute toward Ostia. There was a little restaurant by the beach they used to frequent together as teenagers, where Flavia recalled Gianni telling her she was the most beautiful girl he knew. When he parked his car in front of it, she laughed gaily. Their dinner was simple and authentic, tasting of their childhood. She saw the old Gianni sitting before her, smiling and relaxed. They reminisced, bringing to mind the fun days of their youth. After dinner, they strolled along to *La Gelateria* for some gelato. She chose the flavours she used to get whenever they came here—hazelnut, amaretto, and chocolate—while Gianni chose his favourite: apple, pineapple, and lemon. They walked away with their cones piled and topped with *panna*, whipped cream. They sat on the beach, savouring the yummy dessert, licking their lips and listening to the waves lapping gently on the shore. It was an exceptionally warm evening with a clear sky and twinkling stars.

Gian-Carlo finished his ice cream in no time, but Flavia tasted hers slowly. When she munched on the last of her cone and turned to look at him, she saw that he was smiling.

"You haven't changed. You still get gelato dripping down your chin." He leaned forward and kissed the gelato away until he found her mouth and kissed her. He pulled her to him and kissed her more deeply.

"Flavia, marry me," he whispered as he let go of her mouth.

She pulled away to look at him. "What did you say?"

He put his forehead against hers and said again, "Marry me, Flavia. I want you to be my wife."

Flavia looked into his eyes, serious green orbs that conveyed everything he felt about her. He had taken her back to their humble beginnings, to a place where their happiness had begun, where they had run wild and free without any cares, a place where they had first pledged their love for one another.

"Yes!" said Flavia, as he pulled her up and swept her in his arms and swung her around and around, their laughter carried away by the rhythmic sounds of the ocean on a hot summer night.

CHAPTER 41

Tiziana paid the taxi driver, opened the door, and nearly stumbled out as she juggled the shopping bags in her hands. It was late evening, almost ten o'clock, and she was returning from sightseeing and shopping in Gaeta.

She had eaten a delicious lunch at the villa earlier, prepared by the friendly Pasquale, a man who clucked his tongue and commented on her being too thin. "*Mangia, mangia*," he had insisted as he placed a variety of sliced cold meats before her, including mortatella, capicollo, prosciutto, cheeses, crusty bread, marinated eggplants, sun-dried tomatoes, olives, fruit, and red wine. He had served her at the table on the large *terrazza* overlooking the gulf. A canopy of grapevines already loaded with small clusters of unripe grapes had served as shade from the hot midday sun.

Tiziana had made several attempts to call both her parents and Christopher. Neither had responded. With the whole afternoon stretched out before her unplanned, Tiziana had decided to go into town. She wasn't certain how much longer she would be in Gaeta, so she wanted to take advantage of her time to continue exploring the beautiful town. Gian-Carlo had called just after lunch to confirm that she was now settled at the villa and had promised to visit the next day. She looked forward to his visit.

The taxi drove away. Although the villa was shrouded in darkness except for the two outdoor lights by the entrance, Tiziana could hear voices coming from the *terrazza*. It sounded like the other guests were still at dinner. Opening the heavy front door, Tiziana made her way to her room and freed herself from her shopping bags. She had fun buying gifts for her parents and Christopher, but all the walking and sightseeing had exhausted her. She hadn't foreseen being out so late. All she wanted to do now was to get into her lounge pants and tank top, wash her face, put her hair into a ponytail, and relax. She could pack the gifts tomorrow. The voices outside carried all the way up to her window—the laughter and merriment accompanying Tiziana as she prepared for bed. She had yet to meet Caterina, Gian-Carlo's aunt.

The smell of coffee mixed with the scents of the flowers wafted into her room, and Tiziana smiled in contentment as she hugged her pillow and thought about her day. Fatigue soon took over, and within a few minutes she was fast asleep.

She woke up thirsty and bothered by the light from the bedside lamp, which was still lit. She squinted as she read 12:14 AM on her watch. She got up groggily and looked into her purse for her water bottle. It was nearly empty. She craved fresh water. The cold cuts from lunch and her dinner of seafood linguini had left her parched.

Opening the door quietly, lest she wake any of the other guests, Tiziana made her way to the kitchen. The light was on above the sink, making it easy for her to find a glass and fill it with water. She gulped the refreshing liquid and was going to refill it when she heard a sound coming from the *terrazza*. The French doors were being locked, and Tiziana could see the form of a woman approaching. She stood rooted by the sink, biting her lower lip, unsure of what to do because of her scare at the hotel last night.

The woman came into the kitchen and stopped abruptly when she saw Tiziana. She was wearing a green sleeveless dress that complimented her figure. Although in her fifties, she looked younger, with layered dark hair that fell in waves to her shoulders. Her emerald green eyes were remarkable, and they stared openly at Tiziana without a word. Tiziana stared back, trying to discern the woman's expression. *This must be Gian-Carlo's aunt.* The woman continued to search Tiziana's face, staring hard. Tiziana began to feel uncomfortable, wondering if she had somehow offended the woman by trespassing into her kitchen.

When the woman finally spoke it was but a whisper. "Are you the young woman William picked up this morning?" Her English was heavily accented.

"Yes."

"What is your name?"

"Tiziana Manoretti."

"Ooohh!" The woman exclaimed so loudly that Tiziana nearly jumped out of her skin. The woman clasped her hands together, shut her eyes tight, and with her face to the heavens said, "*O, Dio mio! Non è possibile, non è possibile.*"

"What's wrong?" asked Tiziana. The woman did not answer. "Is something wrong?" She was afraid to approach the woman.

The woman opened her eyes, which were now filled with tears. She shook her head and with a trembling smile walked toward Tiziana.

"Is your father's name Stefano Antonio Manoretti?"

How does she know that?

"Yes." The woman was now so close Tiziana could see the darker green ring around her pupils.

"Were you born on March 12, 1980?"

Tiziana's heart slammed against her chest. "Yes ..."

"Are you ... an adopted child?"

"How do you know that?" She looked deeply into the woman's hopeful eyes.

The woman began to cry. She took hold of Tiziana's hand and led her to the kitchen table. "Please sit down. There's a story I need to tell you. I've been waiting twenty-seven years to tell it." A sob escaped her. She searched her pocket and retrieved a handkerchief, composing herself as she wiped the tears.

"My name is Caterina Ariosto. I am Gianni's aunt. Yesterday when he called, he spoke with William, who later told me of your plight. Gianni also mentioned to him that you were a friend visiting from Canada in search of your birth parents. Is that correct?"

"Yes," replied Tiziana, whose heart was now racing.

"Has your father given you any information regarding your birth parents?" Caterina asked cautiously.

"No." Then Tiziana clutched Caterina's arm. "If you know anything, please tell me. I want to know."

Caterina put her hand over Tiziana's. "Is your father in approval of your search? Does he know this is what you're doing?"

"He knows, although initially he didn't want me to come to Italy."

Caterina nodded. She sighed and caressed Tiziana's cheek. "You have her expression, you know. The same intense look. I've always wondered what you would look like." Fresh tears rolled down her cheeks.

Tiziana could not contain herself anymore. "You know my birth mother?"

Caterina paused, and then seemed to come to a decision. "You are the daughter of my late sister, Emmanuela Del Verde."

Tiziana was speechless. The daughter of Emmanuela Del Verde! Gian-Carlo's own mother! But that meant ...

"Gian-Carlo is my brother?" she asked, not quite believing what she was hearing.

"Your half brother. Eduardo De Medici is not your father."

Tiziana sat back in her chair, absorbing all this information. She wondered if Gian-Carlo knew he had a sister. How could he possibly know? And how had she come to be adopted?

"Caterina, there is something I don't understand. How did my parents—my adoptive parents—adopt me from Emmanuela Del Verde?"

"This is the story I wish to tell you, but first, I need to show you something. Come with me." Caterina led Tiziana upstairs, where she told her to wait in her room. "I will return."

Tiziana walked into her room, and not a minute later Caterina knocked and let herself in. She was carrying a large round box with printed roses, a gold cord handle, and a black ribbon that sealed it. Caterina sat in front of Tiziana on the bed and handed it to her.

"This belongs to you. I have waited many years, always hoping that one day, somehow, you would find me, and I could pass it to you. In it are some of Emmanuela's personal, private things that no one in our family has seen but her and me. I know she would have wanted you to have them." Caterina took Tiziana's hand in hers. "Perhaps, this will help you to understand the decision she made regarding you. I will leave you alone to discover what is in it. Once you are ready, I will further explain."

Caterina kissed Tiziana on the forehead and got up to leave. Before she reached the door, Tiziana said on impulse, "Caterina, did you ever search for me, knowing you had this to give me?"

"No, I couldn't."

Caterina had made the same promise to two men that she would never go looking for Emmanuela Del Verde's adopted daughter—to Eduardo De Medici and to Stefano Antonio, otherwise known as Steve Manoretti.

CHAPTER 42

Tiziana sat on her bed with her arms around her legs, chin on her knees, staring at the box in front of her. Was she dreaming or truly awake? She touched the box. It felt real and solid.

She took the box into her hands and pulled on the black ribbon to loosen it, but it was tied fast. With trembling fingers she tugged at the knot and eventually removed the ribbon. Slowly, she lifted the lid and put it aside. Inside was yellowed tissue paper that wrapped the contents in the box. She opened the paper and looked inside. The first thing she saw was a knitted baby's garment. It was a soft pink pyjama with a matching cap and blanket. It looked like it had never been worn. Had this belonged to her as a baby? Tiziana fingered the miniature clothing gently and wondered if Emmanuela had made it. She took a ragged breath as she held the garment in her hands and then put the clothing aside.

Underneath this she found a photograph, a key attached to a key holder with the Grand Villa Irlanda Hotel insignia on it, a silk scarf with a red and white motif, and a pack of letters tied with a red ribbon. Tiziana picked up the photograph. It was a group photo taken, it seemed, while the subjects were sitting at a table on the very *terrazza* of this villa, only the tiles and surrounding greenery were different. She recognized the smiling Emmanuela instantly and saw next to her a young man whose face was turned partly toward her. Tiziana looked closely and then jerked back suddenly.

No! It couldn't be. That man looked exactly like a young version of ... *her father*!

Tiziana looked again. Yes, it was him! Or maybe it wasn't. Could he have known Emmanuela personally? She noticed that next to the man that looked like her father was Caterina with a young boy on her lap. He looked about five and resembled ... Gian-Carlo. He had the same brooding look as the day when Tiziana had seen him for the first time by the pool. It took Tiziana a little longer to recognize the other couple as being her Uncle Maurizio with a young woman who looked like Aunt Maria. The third man in the photo she did not know at all.

Tiziana frowned and scrutinized the photograph once more, beginning to believe that the man could be her father if her Uncle Maurizio was present. Was this how her father had come to know of Emmanuela's wish to give up her baby, perhaps through her sister, Caterina? Tiziana flipped the photo and saw a date—April 1978. A quick calculation showed that Emmanuela wasn't even pregnant then since Tiziana was born in March 1980. She was puzzled.

She took the pack of letters and untied the red ribbon. The envelopes were all light blue with the red-and-blue-chequered border indicating a long-distance correspondence. Scanning through the dozen letters or so, Tiziana noticed that the return address was always the same. It was an address in Montreal without name of sender. They were all addressed to Emmanuela Ariosto, with the address in Gaeta that Tiziana recognized as being the one of this villa that belonged to Caterina.

Tiziana took out the first letter, which was handwritten in Italian. It began with *Cara Nella.* The writer stated how surprised he'd been with the news of her pregnancy, so surprised in fact that he still couldn't believe the words of her last letter.

With her heart beating faster with every word she read, Tiziana continued to read the neat but sometimes undecipherable scrawl on the thin onion paper.

> ... I have been waiting for nearly five years for my wife to tell me those very words that you have stated so simply on paper. To think that you are carrying my child makes me want to shout for joy, and yet, how will this all come to be? You said you've told no one, and at the moment, I cannot encourage you to tell your husband unless you want to make him believe that the child is his. This very thought brings me anguish. The more I dwell on the matter, the more I want this child.
>
> Nella, what are we to do? This secret, how long can we keep it and with what consequences? I am torn as to what we should do. You have not spoken of your feelings regarding this pregnancy, only that you wish it had never happened. It was not my intention to leave you with child, but now that you are expecting, I cannot say that I feel the same as you. Please write me to tell me what you will do regarding the baby because whether you like it or not, I am

involved. I will not leave you stranded. I will take the necessary steps, no matter the consequences, to assume my responsibility as father.

With love,

It was signed Stefano M., a signature Tiziana would have recognized anywhere.

CHAPTER 43

Tiziana sprang up from the bed, dropping the letter as if it had burned her fingers. She clasped a hand over her open mouth and began to pace back and forth in the room.

Oh, my goodness! What in the world did I just read in that letter? Oh, it can't be! No, no, no!

That letter was signed by her own father! She glanced at the letter, which had fallen on the bed. There was no doubt that was her father's signature. Tiziana took a few deep breaths. *My father cheated on my mother! My father had an affair with another woman! My father slept with Emmanuela Del Verde! My father is really my birth father!*

Tiziana paced the room in agitation for a while as her mind reeled with the discovery of this long-held secret. Her mind staggered with the revelation that her father had betrayed her mother and had a love affair with Emmanuela Del Verde, resulting in *her birth*. She was at once ecstatic to learn that her father was also her birth father, but mortified to be privy of this fact through letters to his lover. Her mind and heart were in turmoil as she contemplated the words she had read, tangible proof that she was indeed the daughter of Emmanuela and her father, Steve. No wonder he had been so adamant about not telling her she was adopted.

She moved a little slower until her heartbeat returned to a more normal pace, although she could still feel the adrenaline flowing through her, making her feel flushed and warm. Tiziana looked at the rest of the letters lying on the bed next to the pink baby pyjama. Should she read them? Could she stand reading her father's love letters to another woman who was not her mother, but was her birth mother? Did she have the right to read them?

Tiziana stood a long time, looking at the letters, contemplating what to do. Part of her did not want to look at another letter, but another part of her wanted to know what had happened between Emmanuela and her father that resulted in her being adopted—an adoption that was strange, to say the least, since her father adopted his own daughter. Did her mother, Chloe, know about her father's betrayal and that she was Steve's daughter—a direct consequence from his affair with another woman?

A mixture of emotions flooded Tiziana as all these questions ran through her mind. She was angry, sad, happy, confused, shocked, and flabbergasted all at once.

Tiziana approached the bed and sat on it once again. She pulled off the elastic that tied her hair, letting it tumble down around her face. She massaged her scalp with her fingers to sooth the area where her hair had been pulled upwards. Through the open window, she could hear the waves washing ashore and the crickets singing their nightly song. Tiziana remembered that she was in Italy, the place of her birth, in a villa that carried the history of the beginnings of her life. She had come here in search of her birth parents, in search of the truth. In these letters that lay before her, she could find some of that truth.

She picked up the next letter that followed the first one she read, assuming they were in chronological order. A quick look at the dates confirmed this. The date on the first letter was August 14, 1979. Tiziana looked at the letter in her hands, dated September 30, 1979, and began to read. She skimmed over it, feeling somewhat guilty for reading it, and then a phrase caught her attention.

> I beg you please to reconsider. I know that having this baby will be difficult in your circumstances, but an abortion is not the answer. You would be taking away from me the child I have so desperately desired. Please, Nella, I beg you again not to go through with it no matter what Eduardo thinks. He cannot force you to do it if you really don't want to, and I know that is not what you want.

Tiziana took a deep breath and continued to read her father's words. He went on to explain he would take care of any expenses related to the baby, and he would do anything she asked to make her go through with the pregnancy.

Tiziana opened the next letter and could tell right away that the tone was different. In the previous letter he had been pleading, whereas in this letter, he sounded angry and upset.

> I'm not asking you to give up your career, Nella. I never did. You made it clear from the very beginning that our love affair was not going to get in the way of your acting, and now I am making it clear to you that this will not get in the way of my marriage. My wife is not at fault. I am the one who turned away from her because of our

problems. I will not leave her, Nella. Despite what I did, I still love my wife …

… although our affair was passionate, it was brief and we both knew it was temporary. We found each other in a time of need, but we lead different lives in different countries. You know full well I did not intentionally want to get you pregnant. It was the last thing on my mind, considering it never happened in my own marriage. I am only asking you to keep our baby. If Eduardo will not allow you to keep it, you must make a decision. I know you don't love him, but he has a strong hold on you, which I don't understand. You need to find the courage to leave him and keep the baby with my assistance, or allow me to raise the child as my own if you choose to stay with him. You cannot put an end to the life of our child, Nella. You cannot …

Tiziana returned the letter to its envelope and lay back on the bed. Tears filled her eyes as the words rang in her head, *you cannot put an end to the life of our child*. Had Emmanuela not wanted her? Would she have chosen abortion had her father not insisted she keep the baby?

Tiziana wiped furiously at her tears and sat up again. She picked up the next letter. In it, Steve informed Emmanuela that he would be at the Hotel Villa Irlanda for Maurizio's wedding. He wanted to see her again so they could discuss the future plans for their child. It was a short letter; however, through his words Tiziana could hear her father's excitement to see Emmanuela again.

The following letter was written in November, when Tiziana guessed Emmanuela was five months pregnant. Tiziana's heart beat a little faster when she read the opening words.

Carissima Nella,

Seeing you carrying my child, looking beautiful and radiant, has made me a happy man again. Your decision to allow me to raise our child is the best one, considering the threats from Eduardo. I do not trust him or his "friends." He is a dangerous man, and I want you to stay with your sister at the villa until I come again. Whatever you may need, I want you to ask me. You can also call me at the following number …

The next three letters were slightly different because her father now wrote about the legal adoption procedures that would be necessary once the baby was born. Then a section in yet another letter made Tiziana stop. She read it over and over again to make sure she had truly understood the words.

> Nella, I am so frustrated with the lack of functionality with Italy's legal system that I am ready to take you back with me and risk everything rather than deal with them again. I am flying yet again to try to shorten the procedure, but it's becoming harder to do without giving away your identity and revealing too much to Chloe. There has to be another way ... I know Eduardo wants to be rid of me, but I have yet to trust his schemes. His offer is tempting because no one will know about your giving birth to the baby, and my wife will never suspect the child is really mine, thinking it to be an adoption established from the courts.
>
> I will see you shortly, but I am bringing Chloe with me this time, so we will need to be careful. I assure you she is a good and kind woman who will love the child as much as I ...

Tiziana grabbed the next letter dated early March of 1979 and began reading.

> Cara Nella,
>
> I spoke to your sister today while you slept, and she reassured me that you and the baby were doing well. She tells me you miss your son and that Eduardo forbids the boy from visiting you. I'm sorry it has come to this. Secrecy can be a cruel mistress when it controls your life as it does mine. Eduardo has his own selfish motives, but in retrospect, it will be worse if Gian-Carlo sees your pregnancy come to full term.
>
> I don't know what you said to Eduardo, but after I contacted him, he took care of all the details like the smooth politician he is. He made certain that I understood the bargain well. We are never to see or contact each other again, and the child must never know who its mother or father truly is. After my meeting with him, I was convinced we made the right choice. He wants my "bastard child" out of his sight as soon as possible. I swear if he lays one hand on you or that child, I will kill him with my bare hands. I don't care who he is.
>
> Nella, since this may be one of the last times I write you, I want to tell you that I love you for giving me our child. It is the best gift I will ever receive. You are an exceptional woman.

I want us to have no regrets, Nella. We've both made the best decision for this child, who will soon come into the world. I want you to name the child for me so that every time I will say its name, I will remember the gift you gave me. Take care of yourself. I will only look upon your beautiful face again, my love, when I see it on the movie screen.

Forever indebted to you,

Stefano M

Tiziana crumpled in a tired heap on the bed and bawled like a baby.

CHAPTER 44

Tiziana cried until she had no more tears. She was exhausted and numb. She cried for herself, her father, her mother, and for Emmanuela, whom she had never met—the woman who had given birth to her. Finally, she fell into a deep sleep and awoke the next morning past 8:30. The curtains were billowing softly with the morning breeze from the open window, and the birds were chirping loudly. The smell of coffee wafted through the window again, this time from the breakfast being served below on the *terrazza*.

Tiziana rubbed her swollen eyes and rolled to the edge of the bed. She heard the crinkling of paper and looked down. Letters were strewn all over the bed, crumpled and misshapen from the tossing she must have done in her sleep.

The letters!

Tiziana began to pick them up one by one, smoothing and sorting them out as she looked for their envelopes. Fresh tears sprang to her eyes, as her father's words came tumbling back into her memory. Words of pain and words of betrayal. Words of love and words of hope. Tiziana put the letters in the same order she found them and placed them back into the round box next to the hotel key, the scarf, and the photograph. She understood what the other items were—mementos of the time Emmanuela spent with her father. Lastly, Tiziana placed the little pyjama in the box and replaced the cover.

Leaving the box on the bed, Tiziana went to the bathroom. The shower was refreshing, washing away the swirling thoughts from her mind and the dried salt on her face from the tears she had shed. She dressed in a floral skirt with a matching halter top, leaving her hair full and loose down to her shoulders.

As Tiziana descended the stairs, she met a couple who were returning from their breakfast. They greeted her and struck up a conversation with her. They were from Germany.

"You just arrive, yah?" asked the woman whose smile crinkled her whole face.

"Yesterday."

"Ah, you will love it here. Such a beautiful place. It has, how do you say, a magical quality."

Yes, my father had a love affair here.

"Come, *liebe*, we need to start our packing," the husband said. Turning to Tiziana he added, "Enjoy your stay."

"Thank you."

Tiziana found Caterina, whom she now realized was also her aunt, outside on the *terrazza* clearing the breakfast dishes. When Caterina saw her, she immediately stopped what she was doing and looked at her. Tiziana watched as Caterina searched her face. Then she came forward and embraced her. Tiziana responded by wrapping her arms tightly around Caterina.

"I read the letters," Tiziana stated in Italian.

"It wasn't easy, was it?" replied Caterina, compassion marking her lovely face.

"No, it wasn't. I would never have imagined that my father ... that he ... that he was actually with someone else ..." Tiziana faltered. Voicing what she now knew of her father was more difficult than she had thought.

Caterina nodded. "Come here." She guided Tiziana to a chair and sat next to her. "It was a long time ago, but I remember it as if it were yesterday."

"Caterina, you must tell me why Emmanuela chose to give me away rather than raise me herself."

Her aunt looked away toward the gulf waters and took a deep breath of the fresh morning air. "Ah, Tiziana, you must know that it was the most torturous decision my sister ever made. How she cried for you! To this day, I do not know how she endured the separation." She turned toward Tiziana, pain etched on her face. "She did love you, dear girl. I can vouch for that." Caterina took Tiziana's hand in hers, caressing it gently.

"Tell me what happened."

"I will tell you what I know. It's all I can do. What really happens between two people, only God truly knows." Caterina looked out over the sea again for a moment, gathering her thoughts.

"The first time I met your father, Stefano, was at a friend's party in the winter of 1978. He was with Maurizio, who was dating Maria, a close friend of my sister Nella. That was our nickname for Emmanuela. He was alone, unaccompanied by a woman, that is. I wasn't aware he was married at the time. He was different from the young men we knew and handsome, of course. We girls called him the Italian-American." Caterina paused and smiled at Tiziana. "You remind me of him. Anyhow, he didn't seem to notice the girls who were vying for his attention but stayed close to his brother and said little. It was only after Nella walked into the room that I noticed a change in him. They were like magnets. The attraction between them was so evident you could feel the vibes." Caterina paused again and then she said softly, "They were two lonely people who gravitated to each other, and I could already see where it would lead right from that very night."

"What do you mean?" asked Tiziana, knowing what she meant but wanting to hear it from Caterina anyway.

"Let me tell you a little more about my sister, and I think this will help you understand. Nella was a beautiful soul, but she struggled with her image, her self-esteem, even her confidence—"

"But she was a successful actress!"

"Yes, and part of her success as an actress was her ability to portray vulnerability on the screen. She craved the attention she received, and she thrived on it. When she first met Eduardo, she was a struggling young actress, and he was from a wealthy family of nobility and already engaged in the world of politics. He introduced her to the right people, which helped her career take off. He courted her for a few years before she finally consented to marry him. He was an extremely jealous and possessive man, obsessed with Nella to the point where she was stifled by him and yet dependent on him in a way I cannot understand, even to this day. My sister and I are very different in that way. She must have loved Eduardo in her own way, I suppose."

Caterina stopped talking, apparently dwelling on her last thought.

"And Gian-Carlo? When was he born?" Tiziana probed gently.

"In … 1972, I think. Yes, that's about right, he's now thirty-five. Well, it was a bittersweet time for Nella, who adored her boy and took him along with her on the set whenever she could. But she and Eduardo fought often, especially regarding the upbringing of the boy. Nella had taken on a role in a comedy that didn't go well—she was very much the drama queen, you know, with the talent to make even a blind man cry when watching her films. So when Stefano, whose own marriage was suffering because he couldn't have children, came into Nella's life, they instantly bonded. I had just bought this villa, and I would commute from Formia while I was renovating it. So for a time it became their rendezvous place. I tried to talk Nella out of seeing Stefano because I was worried what Eduardo might do in his jealous rage if he found out. I could also see Stefano was torn between his life in America and his relationship with Nella." Caterina stopped and took a deep breath.

"Did Eduardo find out about the two of them, or did Emmanuela end up telling him because of the pregnancy?"

"Oh, he found out all right," said Caterina, shaking her head with the memory. "And it was ugly. Stefano had just left town to fly back home, and Nella was getting ready to leave when he stormed in here. I think if Stefano had been here Eduardo would surely have killed him. I happened to be here because I was waiting for a shipment that was to arrive on that particular day. I tried to calm him, afraid of leaving him alone with my sister. Although Nella stood up to him, there were many threats. It was only when he threatened to take Gian-Carlo away from her that she consented to stop seeing Stefano. Eduardo is a powerful man with connections in high places, and that was one threat she could not risk ignoring. She told me she saw Stefano one last time at the Hotel Irlanda, where under Eduardo's nose, she snuck away for an hour while attending a political conference with him in that hotel. By then she knew she was pregnant, but she decided not to tell Stefano because he told her he wasn't leaving his wife."

Tiziana got up from her chair and walked to the edge of the *terrazza*. She looked out over the blue expanse of the gulf waters. She had never suspected her parents had once been on the brink of separating. As a child she had happy memories growing up in the security of their love for her and each other. This almost felt like someone else's story. She wondered if her mother knew. If she did, then she was an amazing person. She had forgiven and moved on. Could she do the same? It was ironic that her father's act of betrayal had caused her birth, making her oddly angry and grateful at the same time.

She turned back to Caterina. "And then what happened?"

"For Eduardo, this news came at a time when he was climbing up the political ladder, and a scandal would have squelched his ambitious pursuits. Emmanuela was well liked and respected as his wife, and he avidly used her notoriety to his advantage; but this could have easily backfired if the community found out she was pregnant with another man's baby. It was imperative for Eduardo to keep the entire situation top secret and to deal with it quickly and with the least amount of repercussions. Once more, he threatened to take Gian-Carlo away if she left him. The way he saw it, Nella belonged to him, and he would not let her go. Nella knew it would be difficult if she decided to keep the baby because Stefano was already married with a life across the other side of the ocean. She was contemplating abortion, which Eduardo was pushing for, when I convinced her to write Stefano to let him know that she was carrying his child. He needed to know, and I was convinced he would help her."

"I read in the letters that Eduardo struck some sort of deal with my father."

"Stefano really wanted you, his child, especially since he and your mother were childless. But this situation with Nella was very complicated. Had he left his life in America to be with Nella, Eduardo would have made their lives miserable. He was not a man to be crossed, and the situation was already precarious. Not only had Nella cheated on him, but she had become pregnant with another man's child when Eduardo had made it clear *he* would have liked another child. His portrayal of a family man was important. Gian-Carlo was already six at the time, almost seven. It was time for another child."

Caterina paused for a moment, lost in thought. "Anyhow, Stefano begged Nella to reconsider and to allow him to raise the child. I don't know how Nella finally convinced Eduardo, but it was decided that she take some time off from her acting career to have the child in secret and for Stefano and your mother to adopt the baby. Because no one was to know about the baby, Eduardo somehow obtained papers to allow your parents to bring you home without an actual legal adoption having taken place in the courts. I was sworn to secrecy, and I promised never to go looking for you, especially after Nella died."

"So my adoption papers *are* false, just like the courts informed me!" Everything made sense now—the behaviour of the Mother Superior and Suor Annunziata at the orphanage and the court officials who had scrutinized her documents. "I was detained at the juvenile court in Naples and interrogated until Gian-Carlo rescued me."

"You walked into the courts with those documents? You must have had an astute officer to recognize the counterfeit papers because they were drawn up by an officer from the courts and passed inspection at the airport without a hitch."

"My mother told me they were escorted through the airport by an official from the courts."

"Of course, Eduardo would have thought of that."

There was something else Tiziana desired to know. "Caterina, did Gian-Carlo know his mother was pregnant?"

"Yes, he did. No one told him, but he was a discerning boy, even at that age, and he figured it out in no time. He was happy thinking he would have a brother or sister. It broke my heart seeing him with his mother, touching her belly even though she was still not showing much. When Nella could no longer hide her pregnancy, she came here in seclusion and then spent the last few weeks at the orphanage. Gian-Carlo was forbidden to see her, and he hated his father for this. They told him his mother miscarried."

"But I believe he thinks he has a sister somewhere in this world named Tiziana."

That explains his behaviour toward me.

Caterina stared at Tiziana for a long time. "I don't know exactly how he knew this, but I suspect he overheard enough to put the pieces together. He came to me several times asking me questions, but I had to remain silent."

"Then why have you chosen to tell me?"

"Because *you* came to me. I couldn't look you in the face, knowing full well you are my niece, the daughter of my late sister, and not say a word. Too many years have passed. My sister is no longer alive, and I made a promise to myself that if you ever came here searching, then I would feel free to talk. I have prayed about it, and God has answered my prayers."

Caterina clasped Tiziana's hands in hers. "Finally, I have found you, and you've turned out to be better than I dreamed. From Gian-Carlo, William, and my own impressions of you, I could see you are a fine young woman. It was this that helped me decide I could trust you with this information."

Tiziana smiled at Caterina, but her joy was muted. "My father cheated on my mother," she said, looking away.

"Tiziana, do not judge him so harshly." Caterina spoke gently. "It was an emotionally trying period in your father's life. Nella knew he still loved your mother, which is why in the end she consented to give you away to them after your birth. It was the best thing for you, isn't that so, *cara*?"

Tiziana nodded. "I had a very good childhood."

"It's what Nella wanted the most for you," replied Caterina, sighing deeply. "Many nights I have lain in bed, wondering what kind of life you had, if you were happy, if your parents had told you about the adoption ... if I would ever see you again."

Tiziana looked at her aunt, still marveling that this woman had known her as a baby and had suffered with her sister on account of her.

"Caterina, what about Eduardo? Won't he be upset you divulged this information to me?"

"I really couldn't care less what Eduardo thinks. I kept my end of the bargain not to come looking for you and not to tell anyone of your existence, but that doesn't apply to you now, does it?" Caterina raised her eyebrows, and a sly smile crossed her lovely face.

Voices from inside the villa became louder, until the guest couple Tiziana had met earlier came out onto the *terrazza* and stood by the French doors.

"We're sorry to interrupt your conversation, dear Caterina. We just wanted to say goodbye before we left, yah?" said the woman, affectionately.

"Oh, yes, Margaret and Herbert, I will be right with you!"

Caterina turned to Tiziana and whispered, "Now enough about the past. We will rejoice in our reunion because the last time I saw you, you were but a tiny baby in my arms. Now, I want to know everything about you!"

"Okay!" Tiziana whispered back. Her aunt's excitement was contagious. A beautiful smile spread on Tiziana's face. She realized her aunt had waited half her lifetime to finally meet her late sister's only daughter.

CHAPTER 45

Tiziana sat on the *terrazza* under the grapevine canopy in a villa between the Neapolitan mountains and the Mediterranean Sea, contemplating all that Caterina had disclosed to her. Suddenly she was ravenous. The emotional upheaval of the last twelve hours had left her hungry and with waning energy. She turned toward the table and saw that some of the breakfast meal was still there. Picking up a croissant, Tiziana cut a slice of the now cold mozzarella and mushroom frittata and made herself a sandwich. She wolfed it down in no time. She helped herself to the two last slices of juicy cantaloupe, feeling better with every bite.

When finished with her breakfast, Tiziana stretched and got up from her seat. The morning breeze caressed her face as she lifted it to the sun with her eyes closed. It felt so good. She opened her eyes and stopped short when she saw Gian-Carlo standing by the French doors. He was staring at her, one of his hawk-like stares that made her feel caught, just like on the first day they met. His penetrating eyes were searching her face, and at once Tiziana knew that he knew who she was. She approached him and he did the same, coming to stand right in front of her, never once letting go of her with his eyes.

"Gian-Carlo ..." she began, but stopped when her voice faltered.

"Tiziana," he said gently. Then he smiled down at her—a smile that transformed and brightened his face with hope and expectation. Her heart soared.

"How did you know I was your sister?" she managed to ask with a lopsided, teary smile before she broke down again. He embraced her, holding her tight without saying a word. Tiziana could hear his thundering heartbeat against her ear. His cotton shirt felt smooth under her cheek as her tears began to wet it. He smelled manly and exotic, and she revelled in the knowledge that this person was her brother, the brother she never knew she had until yesterday.

When he finally spoke it was a hoarse whisper. "Just before she died, on the night of her accident, my mother told me I had a sister named Tiziana, the baby she gave up for adoption. She asked me to find you and to give you this." Gian-Carlo released Tiziana and removed a gold chain from his neck and transferred it to hers. The necklace was warm from his body heat, and it felt solid and heavy on her chest. Tiziana could see it had a pendant with the letter *T* on it.

"It belonged first to my grandmother, whose name was also Tiziana, and then to my mother, who wanted to pass it on to her daughter if she had one." Gian-Carlo's nose flared as he looked at Tiziana with suppressed emotions. "I'm sorry it took so long to give it to you, but my moth—our mother—died before she could give me more details regarding you. I only had your first name and my instincts to guide me."

"Thank you, thank you so much." Tiziana was holding the pendant. "If I hadn't come to this villa, I may have never known. Your au—*our* aunt," Tiziana laughed quietly, "she gave me a box with some of our mother's things. I found love letters written from my father to her that made me understand who she was—"

"Your father?" Gian-Carlo frowned. When she didn't say anything, she could see his eyes scrutinizing her face, but she could not hide the truth in her expression.

"Of course ..." he began as the truth dawned on him. "You are not Eduardo's daughter." He kept observing her face. "There is nothing of his character in you, no resemblance whatsoever. I always suspected another man, but I couldn't be certain." He looked away for a moment when he said, "I wondered how a father could give away his own daughter. On the night my mother died, I overheard her accusing him of being a monster for taking her baby away. After she died, I saw him only as that monster. I hated him."

"When I read the letters, I was shocked to learn my father had betrayed my mother. For a moment, I hated him too. But hate is destructive. My mother taught me that. Forgiveness is healing and upbuilding and the only way to be at peace with yourself, with others, and with God," said Tiziana, thinking of her discussion yesterday with Gilda and Tina.

Gian-Carlo turned back to look at Tiziana. "Do you know," he said with a smile "that I liked you so much after we met that I would have made up a reason, any reason, to claim you as my sister?"

"Mmm, a crazy brother ..." Tiziana giggled as she looked up into his face.

"Are you making fun of your brother already?" Gian-Carlo pulled Tiziana into a bear hug and kissed her affectionately on the forehead. He held her and said, "She would be happy to know I have finally found you."

Something must have caught his attention, for Tiziana felt Gian-Carlo turn to look toward the French doors. He stiffened at once, and Tiziana followed his gaze. She took a quick breath and froze in his arms.

Standing at the threshold of the French doors was the last person Tiziana expected to see. The disbelief on his handsome face and the hurt in his chocolate brown eyes as he stared at them made Tiziana's heart slam against her chest. His eyes took in the loving embrace, the closeness between her and Gian-Carlo, and that was when the wounded and pained expression changed. His jaws locked and he swallowed hard.

Christopher turned away from the doors without saying a word.

CHAPTER 46

Christopher whipped through the villa back to the front door. He heard Tiziana calling to him, but he was too upset to listen. He stepped on the stone path and marched to the rented Alfa Romeo parked in front of the villa. What a fool he was! He had made the impulsive move, flying to Italy to surprise Tiziana. Instead, he'd been the one to receive the surprise. He would never forget the look of adoration and happiness on her face when embracing that man. He felt sick to his stomach. At least with Victoria, his former wife, he hadn't had the displeasure of catching her in the arms of another man.

As Christopher reached the car, he made the mistake of turning around. Tiziana was moving quickly toward him while holding hands with the man he now assumed was Gian-Carlo. The moment Christopher spotted them, Gian-Carlo let go of Tiziana's hand. She ran breathlessly up to him. Christopher turned his face away and opened the car door. He wanted to leave, but he waited.

"Christopher, didn't you hear me? Gian-Carlo is my brother!" she exclaimed.

Christopher stood very still. What had she just said? Slowly, he turned to look at Tiziana. Her eyebrows were furrowed and she was breathing hard. He opened his mouth and let out an astonished breath.

"That's what I've been trying to tell you, but … but you took off so fast you didn't give me a chance."

Christopher's eyes zoomed in to look more closely at Gian-Carlo, who now had a small smile on his face. Christopher's gaze shifted back to Tiziana. She nodded, and suddenly a big smile spread across her face.

"That's your brother?" Chris lifted his right eyebrow.

"Yes, I have a half-brother, Chris. His name is Gian-Carlo De Medici. We have the same mother, but she died a long time ago in a car accident. He's been searching for me, too, so that he could give me this chain she left me." Tiziana looked down and fingered the pendant gently.

Christopher's mind began to absorb all that she had said as his eyes took in the scene before him. His anger had deflated fast, replaced by such intense relief that he nearly felt weak in the knees. He was now very aware of her closeness, after having long anticipated and desired this moment when she would be standing before him. She looked more stunning than he remembered. Her hair was shiny and full, her skin glowing from the sun, and her figure feminine and curvy in her floral outfit.

"Oh, Tizzy ..." Chris now stood directly in front of her. He ran a hand through his hair and down his face. "I'm sorry."

"It's alright. It just makes me see you're ... crazy about me," she teased.

Christopher grinned. "Crazy enough to almost kill that guy."

He glanced toward Gian-Carlo, who gave him a thumbs-up. A few minutes ago, just looking at that man leaning by the front door, watching Tiziana like a hawk, made him want to drive a fist into his square jaw. Now, Christopher turned to Tiziana and gazed at her happy face. "Wow, Tizzy! You've got a brother. That's great news."

"Yes! Isn't it amazing?" Her shimmering grey-green eyes searched his face. "And now you're here. I feel like I'm dreaming ..." She stopped talking. They stood staring at each other, both fully aware of the other's vibrant presence.

Then, Christopher noticed that about two dozen feet behind Tiziana stood the woman who had greeted him earlier when he arrived at the villa looking for Tiziana. She had been busy escorting her departing guests and had indicated to him how to get to the *terrazza*, where she'd left Tiziana. Now she, another man, and the two guests, with their luggage still on the sidewalk, were all standing watching the interchange between him and Tiziana. By the looks of it, they had witnessed the whole scene and seemed to be waiting for the final outcome.

Christopher looked back at Tiziana. He had waited for this moment, dreamed about it for the last few days. It had almost been destroyed by a simple misunderstanding. But now Tiziana stood before him, under a gorgeous azure sky in sun-drenched Italy, and it was enough to make his heart start pounding like African drums. It was all he needed. The unexpected audience didn't really matter.

"Tiziana, I have loved you for a long time, first as a friend and now as a man. My problem was that I was afraid, afraid of committing." He caressed her face with his eyes, stopping to gaze longingly at her half-open lips. "But I am not afraid anymore. I wanted to tell you in person that I love you ... that I'm crazy about you, and I want to be with you forever ..." Before he even finished speaking, he swept her into his arms and kissed her passionately.

They stood on the sidewalk in front of the open door of the Alfa Romeo, holding each other tightly, as cheers erupted from the group of eager onlookers, who smiled and rejoiced over the beauty of young love.

CHAPTER 47

Tiziana, Christopher, and Gian-Carlo sat around the wrought iron table on the *terrazza*, along with Caterina and William, sipping espresso and talking about the eventful morning. Tiziana kept looking at Christopher. She could see he was travel weary with a shadow of stubble on his face. His blond hair was bleached from the sun and had grown past the nape of his neck. His shirt complemented his broad shoulders, and he wore his trademark Levis. He looked bigger than life, but his face was home to her.

"Christopher, how did you know I was here at the villa?" she asked.

"I didn't. I only found out once I got to the Villa Irlanda Grand Hotel. The guy at the reception refused to tell me where you had gone, but for some reason I suspected he knew. I waited around until a woman named Julia was at the reception. Well, that changed everything," he said with a boyish smile.

Gian-Carlo started laughing. Tiziana gave him a pretend scathing look, and then she turned back to Christopher. "When did you leave? I tried to reach you to tell you I was changing hotels, but I couldn't get a hold of you."

"I took a plane with Tracy to Toronto very early Friday morning so that I could catch the earliest flight out from there. I swore everyone to secrecy so that you wouldn't guess what I was up to if you called."

"Everyone but Meredith, that is. She answered the phone and told me about you traveling with Tracy, until your sister, Kathy, intercepted the conversation. She was acting strange on the phone, and I thought she was covering up for you because of your interest in Tracy."

"Tracy? No way. I made it clear from the beginning that I had no interest in pursuing a relationship with her, Tiziana. She didn't stand a chance." He smiled at her with his warm chocolate eyes. "Anyhow, I drove in from Rome early this morning. I got lost a few times, but I finally found the place."

"I apologize for not escorting you to Tiziana myself," Caterina said. "It may have avoided the whole misunderstanding. William and I were wondering what in the world had gone wrong when a few minutes later you came barging outside with Tiziana running after you."

"You were quite the surprise, Christopher," Gian-Carlo said.

"So were you," replied Christopher. The group started laughing, especially when William recounted the reaction of the guest couple who were wondering what was going on.

"By the way, there's another surprise for you, Tiziana," said Christopher. "I went to see your parents just before I left early Friday morning, and I couldn't believe the transformation between them. I don't remember the last time I saw them so happy and … so in tune with each other."

"In tune with each other?" Tiziana asked.

"They were like two lovebirds."

"Really?"

"*And*," Christopher stressed, "if they were able to get those last-minute seats like they said they would, they're going to join us in Abruzzo by Monday."

"What?"

"Your father was going to make all the arrangements yesterday. I'm supposed to call today to see which of your relatives will be accommodating us. I think it might be your Uncle Silvio because your grandmother lives with him. She wants to meet me."

"Oh, Chris, that's wonderful!"

"What's wonderful?" said a familiar voice from the entrance of the *terrazza*.

All heads turned to see Flavia approaching them. Her sleek chestnut hair was loose from its usual chignon, and her hyacinth-blue eyes sparkled. She greeted Gian-Carlo first, and immediately Tiziana noticed the deeper intimacy between them. Flavia then kissed Caterina and William, and finally turned to Christopher, whose arm was around Tiziana's shoulder.

"So this is Christopher!" she said, smiling. "Tiziana's *ragazzo.*"

"Yes," Christopher replied proudly, "pleased to meet you." They kissed each other on the cheek.

"Good morning, Flavia," said Tiziana, kissing her. She turned to Christopher and said, "And Flavia is Gian-Carlo's *ragazza.*"

Flavia paused and then smiled in surprise. "She's razor-sharp, Gianni, just like you. But I shouldn't be surprised since …" She stopped and raised an eyebrow in Gian-Carlo's direction.

Gian-Carlo nodded. "She's the one, Fla. Tiziana is my sister."

Flavia turned back to Tiziana, who said, "Caterina gave me a box with Emmanuela's personal letters. That's how I learned the truth."

Flavia hugged Tiziana tightly. "Oh, Tiziana, I'm so happy Gianni has finally found you! We suspected, you know, but we weren't quite certain. It was so highly coincidental. You have her mannerisms, to be sure, and then we discovered the birthmark, but besides—"

"What birthmark?" Caterina asked.

"I noticed a birthmark on Tiziana's left upper thigh during her massage treatment, and it's exactly the same shape and in the same place as the one Emmanuela had."

Tiziana's eyes widened.

"Show it to me," Caterina said.

Tiziana lifted her skirt cautiously so that Caterina could see the birthmark on her thigh. "I hate this birthmark."

"So did Emmanuela." Caterina looked at Tiziana, and they both let out a small laugh.

Gian-Carlo turned to Caterina. "I did well to send her here, didn't I?"

"Yes, Gianni, I'm very grateful you did."

"And speaking of surprises, I have something I want to show you," he said, addressing his aunt once more. Gian-Carlo went inside and returned shortly with a large envelope. As the group settled itself once again around the table, he removed a heavy folder from the envelope and spread out the photographs he had taken of Tiziana three days ago in his studio. Caterina's inhaling was audible as she picked up one of the photos and stared at it. Tiziana could feel the intensity of her gaze as she kept looking first at her and then at the photos. The others began doing the same, and Tiziana blushed profusely as they all began to scrutinize her. Christopher was the first to verbalize his reaction.

"Tiziana, you look absolutely gorgeous! Look at you, absolutely amazing …" he trailed off before turning to Gian-Carlo. "Did you take these?"

Gian-Carlo nodded but didn't say a word.

"She looks like her mother," Caterina whispered.

Tiziana caught Christopher looking at Gian-Carlo and nodding in understanding. The two men smiled at each other. It pleased Tiziana immensely.

The high sun signaled the end of morning, and Caterina summoned Pasquale to prepare a meal. They enjoyed spicy mussels cooked with fresh chopped tomatoes and crushed garlic; roasted zucchini and peppers marinated in an olive oil, balsamic vinegar, and oregano dressing; and fennel salad. The bottle of white wine clinked against the goblets as Pasquale refilled them and graciously accepted their words of praise. Initially, Christopher stared at the fare before him. Tiziana, knowing he disliked mussels, coaxed him to try them. He shrugged and dug in. Soon after, he was smacking his lips and imitating the others as they scooped up the sauce with their mussel shells and sipped the savoury, hot liquid. He winked at her, and she winked right back.

The sun dipped lower in the sky as the lazy afternoon wore on. The cheerful sound of mixed voices and laughter, together with the tinkling of plates and cutlery as the meal progressed, surrounded Tiziana like a comforting memory. She took pleasure in every moment. She had found family members she didn't even know existed a few months ago.

Around three o'clock Tiziana and Christopher prepared to drive to Pescara in Abruzzo, where they would be staying with Tiziana's grandmother and uncle. A call to Tiziana's parents had confirmed they were indeed making the trip to Italy and meeting them in Abruzzo. Tiziana could hear happiness in her father's voice. She didn't mention her discovery of his relationship with Emmanuela, deciding to wait until she saw her father in person again.

She made Gian-Carlo promise to visit her in Canada.

"It depends. You might visit me again soon before you know it," he said, looking at Flavia, who was standing close to him.

"Ah ... and it's about time, too." Tiziana smiled. "I recall you once telling me that men and women can't be best friends."

Gian-Carlo chuckled as he embraced and kissed her.

"I will return again to see you, *Zia* Caterina, in this villa where we first met," Tiziana promised her aunt, who hugged her for a long time.

When the last of Tiziana's things were packed in the trunk of the Alfa Romeo, they said their reluctant farewells, promising to meet again before Tiziana and Christopher left to return home.

The car left the curb slowly as Tiziana stuck her head out and waved until she could no longer see all of them standing on the sidewalk, blowing kisses to her. She blew a last kiss as the car turned a corner. Then suddenly she spotted a short man across the street at the corner bar who was watching her. He raised his arm as if to catch that last kiss she had blown. Then a look of utter delight lit up his face.

"Tiziana, is that really you?" he called in surprise. He began to run toward the car. "*Mamma mia*, I knew we had chemistry. Where are you going? Come back to me," he panted in his strong Neapolitan dialect.

Tiziana watched open-mouthed as he attempted to close the widening distance between himself and the departing car. She couldn't help the laughter that spilled out. "Giacomino! I'm leaving Naples! My *ragazzo* came to get meeee!" she called out as the car picked up speed and left him behind. She vigorously waved goodbye.

Christopher looked out from the rearview mirror. "No way! Is that the same Giacomino you told me about?"

"The one and only!"

"Tizianaaaa, come back! I want to marry yoooouuu!" Giacomino hollered.

"He certainly doesn't give up, but then again, I don't blame him."

"*Ciao*, Giacomì!" Tiziana kept waving until he disappeared.

She turned to Christopher. "I think I'm going to miss him, actually. He made me laugh the whole time I was here."

She settled back in her seat as the car made its way down the twisting streets to the waterfront and onto Via Lungomare Caboto. Tiziana laid her head on the seat rest, content to watch the sea as they drove alongside it, heading west toward Abruzzo. Turning, she saw Christopher looking at her with soulful eyes.

A slow smile stretched across her face. "I feel like I'm in a dream somehow. Are you really here with me in Naples, driving along the Mediterranean Sea with love in your eyes?" she asked.

Christopher took her hand and kissed it. "Is that real enough?"

Tiziana smiled. "Yes."

"I wrote you a song, but it's not quite finished."

"Can I hear it?"

"Not yet. This will do for now." He pressed the CD button and chose a song on the disc he had inserted. The music started with the guitar strings of Nickelback's *Far Away*. The beautiful lyrics began as the melody enveloped them through the surround sound system in the rental car. Christopher sang the words to Tiziana as the chorus rose high and strong.

I love you
I have loved you all along
And I miss you
Been far away for far too long ...

So far away
Been far away for far too long ...
But you know, you know, you know
I wanted
I wanted you to stay
'Cause I needed
I need to hear you say
That I love you
I have loved you all along ...

Tiziana's heart soared with the music as she listened to Christopher's emotions pour out through the words. The wind whistled in her ears through the open windows as the car rolled smoothly on the hot pavement, bringing her to new beginnings.

Tiziana was moved to say a small prayer of thanks for the blessing of being loved as a friend and now a woman. And as the car closed the distance to their final destination, Tiziana thought of her waiting family and was grateful for the blessing of being loved first and foremost as a daughter.

As she had always been.

EPILOGUE

Eduardo De Medici returned to his office from lunch with his wife, Sofia, an outing he endured for publicity's sake. Both he and Sofia were masters at putting on an excellent front for the paparazzi—the senator and his cool, beautiful wife, eldest daughter of *Judice* Berdinelli.

They had a convenient marriage. She helped to embellish his role in politics, and his presence added clout to her ambitious pursuits in the world of jewellery and fashion. Nothing fazed Sofia. She knew exactly what she wanted and could be ruthless in her determination to get it. They understood each other well. She was unlike his first wife, Emmanuela, who had been passionate and warm and emotionally unstable. Emmanuela—the only woman he had ever loved and wanted. But his love had been distorted with jealousy, a jealousy so strong it had driven him to do things he somewhat regretted.

Eduardo dropped his leather case on the armchair in the corner of his luxurious office, forcing his mind to return to the day's agenda. He still needed to prepare for the parliamentary meeting next week.

There was a knock on the door and Angela, his secretary, entered. "Excuse me, Signor De Medici, you have a visitor who has asked to see—"

"I wasn't expecting anyone, Angela. You know my schedule. We have a busy day ahead."

"I'm aware of that, sir. However, she insisted you would see her."

Eduardo picked up a document from his desk and lifted his eyebrows, waiting to hear who would be audacious enough.

"Her name is Caterina Ariosto, sir."

Eduardo froze. After a moment he said, "Very well, tell her I will see her." He adjusted his tie, smoothed his hair back, and took a deep breath.

A few seconds later, the door opened and Angela escorted Caterina into the office. She quietly closed the door as she took her leave.

"Caterina, what a pleasant surprise," Eduardo said with a charming smile as he approached her with open arms to kiss her on both cheeks. She offered her cheeks but did not kiss him back.

"Thank you for seeing me on such short notice. I realize you're a busy man," she replied, as he pulled out a chair for her.

He leaned against his desk next to her, looking down at her with piercing eyes. "You're looking beautiful, as usual. The years have agreed with you." The last time he had seen her had been more than twenty years ago at the funeral. Caterina had barely spoken to him since then. He wondered why she was here today, and his instincts warned him he was not going to like the reason. As he expected, she ignored the compliment and got right to the point of her visit.

"A young woman named Tiziana Manoretti came to my villa two weeks ago," Caterina said, looking Eduardo straight in the eyes. "After confirming that she was the adopted daughter of Stefano Antonio Manoretti, I knew that she was, in fact, the child who my sister Emmanuela gave birth to, in March of 1980."

Caterina paused. Eduardo said nothing. He could see Caterina was closely observing his reaction to her announcement.

"A few weeks after she was born, I promised you that I would never go searching for her nor speak to anyone of what I knew, and I have kept that promise. However, Tiziana came to me, Eduardo. She came to Italy with the intention of looking for her birth parents. I couldn't very well look the girl in the face and remain silent. It's been twenty-seven long years."

Eduardo's nose flared as he stared down at Caterina, who stared right back up at him. Abruptly, he pushed himself off the desk and walked over to the window. With his back to her, he asked, "What exactly did you tell her?"

"In summary, that she is the daughter of Emmanuela and Stefano, that Emmanuela gave her up because she was already married, but that Stefano wanted to raise her because he was childless. I ... I endeavoured to explain to her that the issue of secrecy was essential because of the very public lives you and Emmanuela led. She's a smart woman, and she understood the situation."

"What about Gian-Carlo? Did you tell him, too?"

"No. Emmanuela did."

Eduardo turned around, his eyebrows furrowed in a frown.

"She told him the night she died. She asked Gianni to look for his sister but to tell no one, especially not you, for fear you would stop him. He came to me twice, but I played stupid."

Eduardo turned to face the window again. His son had known all these years! The night Emmanuela died they had fought, and the boy had witnessed their feud. No wonder his son hated him. That night he had lost both of them. His heart constricted, and his breathing became shallow.

Eduardo thought of how he had known who the girl was that day he had watched her by the pool. A quick verification with reception had confirmed her name. He had taken the necessary precautions with the Mother Superior at the orphanage, but when Tiziana was seen about town with Gian-Carlo, he knew he had to keep a close watch on her. It was by chance that Gian-Carlo had come to see him at the office the day she had gone investigating at the courthouse. After that, Eduardo was determined to send the girl home.

"When did the girl come to you at the villa?" he asked, suddenly understanding where his actions had brought her instead.

"On a Friday morning, after an incident happened at the hotel that scared—oh, my goodness …"

Eduardo stood there for a long time, thinking how he had ultimately led the girl back to her roots. The very place where he knew Emmanuela had met Stefano in hiding, possibly where Tiziana had been conceived. His heart was still in a vice.

Finally, Caterina spoke again. "I wouldn't worry about exposure now that Tiziana knows. Her father's name is implicated as well, and she loves her parents. She and Gianni have formed a bond already, and she wouldn't do anything to hurt him. Before she left to return to Canada, she told me that she is happy and that she will honor her birth mother's decision by leading a life that would've made her proud."

Caterina stood slowly and cleared her throat. Eduardo did not turn around. His shoulders slouched and he suddenly felt tired. He heard Caterina moving toward the door.

"Caterina, why did you come here to tell me this?" His back was still to her.

She took a deep breath. "Because I don't want to live in the past, and I don't want any regrets."

Eduardo turned around. "I loved her, you know. I only did what I thought was best for us."

Caterina stared back at him. Even from across the room, he could see sorrow in her expression. She was the only one who had witnessed and knew of the dark period in his life with Emmanuela. Finally, she nodded in response. He nodded back at her.

"*Addio*, Eduardo."

"*Addio*, Caterina, and … thank you."

She smiled briefly, opened the door, and left.

Eduardo stared at the closed door for a while before he finally sat down heavily on his chair. He sat there, oblivious to all the documents waiting for his perusal. He looked at the telephone instead. His hand itched to dial the number. He glanced toward his credenza, where a small photo of himself, Emmanuela, and a very young Gian-Carlo smiled into the camera. He straightened his already very straight tie, smoothed his hair back, and took a deep breath. He picked up the phone and dialed the number.

"*Pronto!*"

"Gianni, it's me." He used the nickname he had stopped using years before.

There was a pause on the other line. "Yes."

"Your aunt Caterina was just here. We spoke. She told me about … Tiziana."

A moment of silence. "She told *you* about the sister I finally found?"

"Yes."

"So why are you calling? To relay more of your threats? Scaring Tiziana out of her hotel room wasn't enough?"

"No, Gianni, I just wanted to say I'm glad you found her."

"Why are you telling me this?"

Eduardo could still hear Caterina's words. "Because I don't want to live my life with the regrets of the past."

"Isn't it too late for that?"

"Is it too late to establish a relationship with your sister?"

"No, but I would have liked to have known her sooner."

"I cannot change the past, Gianni. I could only go forward. What about you?"

"What do you want from me?" asked Gian-Carlo.

"Whatever you want to give me. I won't ask for more."

There was a long silence, with only Gian-Carlo's breathing audible. "I'm hosting an exhibition next month of all my best photographs. It will serve as the launch of my new book. You're welcome to come."

"Give me the time and place, and I'll be there."

It was the promise of a father, not of a politician.

Printed in the United States
205271BV00002B/148-309/P